Praise for *Awakening of Spies*

'A richly detailed, and deeply engrossing espionage thriller. Brian Landers is the real deal'
Andrew Raymond, author of the Novak and Mitchell thrillers

'This book is authentic and gripping. It is written with great authenticity and terrific sense of pace. It is the first in what I believe will be an unmissable series of novels'
Peter Oborne

'Very impressive... I look forward to the next'
James Hamilton-Paterson

Also by Brian Landers

Empires Apart: The Story of the American and Russian Empires

The Dylan Series:

Awakening of Spies
Coincidence of Spies
Exodus of Spies

FAMILIES OF SPIES

BRIAN LANDERS

Red Door

Published by RedDoor

www.reddoorpress.co.uk

ISBN 978-1-913062-34-7

A CIP catalogue record for this book is available
from the British Library

Cover design: Rawshock Design

Typesetting: Tutis Innovative E-Solutions Pte Ltd

Printed and bound in Denmark by Nørhaven

Joseph, Alexandra and Catherine

PROLOGUE
7 July 1977

Eveline 'Bunny' Sadeghi was smiling happily as she sailed to her death.

The sun had been rising behind them as they left the harbour at Sami yesterday. Now a glorious sunset was welcoming them to Syracuse, only an hour away. The winds had held steady and they had the sea to themselves. As they sailed westwards across the Ionian Sea there seemed to be more planes going their way than ships. Her brother-in-law's yacht, *Mahsheed*, was not as sturdy as her own beloved *Bunny Hopper*, which she had left safely moored at home on the Solent, but it was a lot more comfortable. As they approached their destination, her husband Davoud was down below fixing a welcome gin and tonic.

Bunny had enjoyed their few days in Kefalonia although Davoud's brother, Behzad, was not an easy man. His villa, some miles inland from Sami, enjoyed spectacular views but she was never able to completely relax there. The isolation was total. Despite the heat of the sun the villa always seemed cold, the accommodation, while spacious, was rough and masculine.

Behzad seemed to have no need for female company, he shared the villa only with his driver, and Shahryar, whose role never seemed clear. Two women from the village came in to cook and clean but Bunny had never seen Behzad talk to them, hardly surprising as he seemed to have made no effort to learn Greek and they could certainly not speak Farsi.

On Sundays, which the two women had off, Shahryar would disappear somewhere and return with a parcel of books and letters and a mountain of kebabs and rice he had presumably picked up in the village taverna. Behzad certainly read voraciously and Bunny enjoyed their conversations about opera or Russian literature, but sooner or later Behzad always turned to politics and her heart would sink. It was not a subject that gripped her at the best of times and it brought out the worst in her brother-in-law. Behzad's paranoia would be comical if it were not so overpowering. Everyone was out to get him. Usually it was the Shah's secret police, the SAVAK. He insisted that when he was at home in Paris they kept him under constant surveillance. Here on the island SAVAK apparently had paid informants everywhere. And if it wasn't SAVAK it was the Israelis, and if not them the American CIA or even, heaven forbid, the British.

She had asked her brother, who was now something high up in Intelligence, whether there could be any truth in any of it. It had been just ten days ago at their niece's wedding. Gordon had just laughed and said that he could imagine all sorts of conspiracies in the feuding world of Iranian exiles but one thing he could guarantee was that the Shah did not maintain a nest of spies on an inconsequential Greek island in the Ionian Sea.

Bunny's thought drifted in a different direction. It had been a lovely wedding. Julia was her favourite niece and the last to marry. Her new husband was not at all what Bunny would have expected, a minor civil servant of undistinguished pedigree.

'Thomas has a First from Durham and is fluent in four languages,' Julia had indignantly proclaimed after deciding that Bunny was insufficiently welcoming.

Certainly his wedding speech had been surprisingly impressive and genuinely amusing. Whether he took after his pugnaciously argumentative father or rather dreary West Country mother time would tell.

Julia had looked enchanted and enchanting. Bunny smiled broadly at the memory, tightening the mainsail as the wind had dropped.

Right ahead she spotted a small fishing boat seemingly becalmed. As she drew closer Bunny could see two men standing by the tiny wheelhouse, looking in her direction, and another man inside. She waved but there was no cheery response. As the boats came closer, perhaps eight or ten yards apart, the fishing boat's engine sprang into life. Bunny was startled and instinctively steered away. She looked up to see one of the men point his hand at her, but it was not just his hand. She saw the gun just as it fired and registered the thought 'Pirates' in the instant before the bullet struck her thigh.

The force of the bullet knocked her back against the tiller and the yacht slewed around directly towards the other boat. Davoud, emerging with two gin and tonics, was thrown on to his side. His first thought was that they had crashed into something. Then someone seemed to have thrown a cricket ball at him. He didn't have time to register that it was not a cricket ball: the grenade exploded with such force that yacht, crew and very nearly their attackers disappeared in a storm of splintered wood, metal and shredded sail.

1

Trying to look back over my life in the secret, and sometimes not-so-secret, world of British Intelligence I find that many of my oldest memories are starting to fade.

I joined what was then called the Defence Intelligence Staff in 1974 as a civilian analyst, a civil servant hired to sit behind a desk in Whitehall and write reports, but I have no idea now what most of the reports were about. In any case they were only ever read by a handful of people in the Ministry of Defence before being locked away in the enormous array of filing cabinets we referred to as our library. It was a very different world in those days and not just in terms of technology. The thinking was different. The Intelligence community was slowly emerging from an age that had already disappeared everywhere else. I remember one old-timer questioning me about military developments in 'Bantu Africa'. Was there anywhere else in British society where such a term would even be understood?

'Our bosses are obsessed with colonies and Communists,' one of my younger colleagues told me. 'They still feel betrayed by the politicians who gave our empire to the natives and by so many of their university chums who gave our secrets to Stalin.'

By the summer of 1977 I had decided that I needed to take time out to think seriously about my future. I was not convinced that Whitehall was my natural habitat. Fortunately, I would not be pondering the future on my own. I had met Julia in

Chicago, fallen in love with her in Brazil and eventually shared an apartment in Hammersmith.

Just a few months after I was recruited I had unexpectedly found myself working with Julia in Brazil. When that operation moved to its successful, but violent, conclusion in Tobago I discovered that I had found a soulmate. It had taken Julia much longer to reach the same conclusion.

That operation changed both our lives and not only because it had brought us together. For me seeing violent death at first hand had been a profound shock. Producing endless reports, which is all I did when the operation was over, seemed so inconsequential in comparison. Now, three years later, Julia and I were to marry and we were both determined that, with the wedding ceremonials out of the way, there would be plenty of unhurried time on our honeymoon to sort out just how we wanted to spend the rest of our lives; quite possibly new careers for both of us.

I don't remember having had much to do with the wedding plans but I do remember endless discussions about the honeymoon. It was to be two weeks of pure joy without a cloud in the sky or a spy in sight. How wrong we were.

I had wanted to return to the Caribbean for our honeymoon but Julia insisted that trying to recapture the past was never a good idea. After much debate she conceded that sometimes it made sense to travel back in time and we would start our new life with a dose of antiquity, a week in Rome followed by a week in Athens. As always Julia was right, just as she had been about the wedding.

I would have been happy to settle for a civil ceremony, certainly that is what my militantly atheist father would have wanted now that he had flung off the non-conformist traditions still clung to by my mother. But Julia would have none of that.

Her family's traditions were very different and nothing less than Worcester Cathedral, morning suits, elaborate hats and a glittering reception in a marquee would be enough for a grandchild of the first Lord Grimspound.

When I first introduced Julia to my parents my father had rushed off to the local library and came back gleefully to report that Julia's grandfather had been a Birmingham industrialist who had bought his peerage from Lloyd George. The Grimspounds were no more aristocratic than we were.

Julia had laughingly acknowledged the fact before pointing out that on her mother's side she could trace her line directly back to the Norman Conquest and on that side her family tree was speckled with barons, earls and even the odd duke. Some of the apparently limitless number of her late mother's relations who, it transpired, had to be invited to the wedding certainly managed to convey an effortless sense of superiority. Unfortunately that was not matched by the munificence of their gifts.

'Fag-end aristocracy' was my father's dismissive description.

'*Nouveaux pauvres*' was the present Lady Grimspound's kinder explanation – or excuse.

In the event, however, the wedding was everything Julia had hoped for and nothing that I had feared.

My father discovered that debating the relative merits of football and rugby could be just as entertaining as debating transubstantiation. Any reservations he had about my marriage disappeared when to his astonishment he discovered that Julia's uncle, like him, followed the fluctuating fortunes of the Plymouth Argyle football team. My mother was completely won over by the Grimspounds when they invited her to help organise the wedding flowers, an operation on a scale she had never seen before.

Julia's family were not as frightening as I had first imagined them to be. Her uncle, the present Lord Grimspound, I already knew. He was my boss. He had been appointed Director General of Defence Intelligence a year or two before I joined and was now approaching the end of his time in the role. I found it difficult to imagine what the Defence Intelligence Staff would be like without him as DG and equally difficult to imagine him sinking into gentle retirement. Time proved me right. His successor was a disaster and his retirement was anything but quiet.

It had taken me some time to get used to Admiral Lord Grimspound's somewhat circular approach to problems and I had initially put his conversational rambles down to approaching senility. That was far from the truth. Behind his rigid naval manners and ruthless determination was a butterfly mind that floated off in the most surprising directions – and produced ingenious lateral thinking. There was also a genuine humanity. Julia's parents had been killed in a Swiss avalanche more than twenty years ago and Lord and Lady Grimspound had immediately taken Julia under their wing. It was perfectly natural that he would be the one walking her down the aisle.

Gordon and Anne, as I was to call the DG and his wife away from work, had what seemed to be the perfect marriage.

'That's because,' I told Julia in jest, 'Gordon makes all the decisions.'

'Yes he does,' she had replied, 'because he knows Anne so well that he doesn't need to ask what she wants him to do.'

There was a lot of truth in that. Anne Grimspound was quietly forceful. She had spent much of her adult life moving two of her own children, Julia, various dogs and a collection of fragile-looking furniture from one naval base to another. Invariably, Julia told me, she had done so without the help of her husband:

Gordon was always away at sea when most needed at home. At each new posting Lady Grimspound rapidly established that she was not there just to attend tea parties and look after the children when they came home from boarding school. She threw herself into work with the Girl Guides and with SSAFA, the charity providing support to service families. When in the UK she was also an active member of her local Conservative Association – not something that initially endeared her to my father. But within an hour or two of meeting her even he was captivated not just by her practised charm but by the essential decency that so plainly informed everything she said, did or thought.

Julia's aunt Bunny was an altogether more intimidating figure. The first time I met her she had described at some length the gale she had recently encountered in the Bay of Biscay when sailing back from the south of France in her boat *Bunny Hopper*. Searching around for something to say I asked if she and her brother ever sailed together; being an admiral I assumed that he was also a keen sailor.

She looked at me for a moment before responding dismissively, 'Young man, in my experience the Navy can't sail.'

As I was to discover it was a typical Bunny remark, both cryptic and categoric.

Trailing in her wake came her charming and slightly exotic husband, a distinguished Harley Street surgeon. My father mistakenly referred to him as an Arab and then, when corrected, insisted on using the term 'Persian' rather than what he considered the newfangled 'Iranian'.

'If Xerxes and Darius were happy to be called Persian I don't see why it isn't good enough for the posturing nincompoop on the throne today,' he proclaimed. As so often with my father the fact that his reasoning was mangled and his facts simply wrong did not stop him holding firmly to his opinions.

My oldest friend and best man, Bob, just setting out on a career that would see him become one of the country's leading electrical engineers, had commented that Julia and I made the perfect couple until you saw us in the context of our families. He might have said in the context of our families and friends. Julia tried to like Bob but found it impossible to comprehend that anyone could have absolutely no interest in any sport whatsoever while I felt some of her friends had arrived from a different world. Her old boyfriend Rupert was one I would have been happy not to invite to our wedding.

Rupert was a member of the hunting, shooting and, as it proved, philandering brigade. Trying to be as objective as possible I concluded he was average, affable and irredeemably boring. As I told Julia, I simply could not understand how she had fallen for a six-foot, well-muscled, blonde ski champion who had just inherited a small estate in Shropshire. He had been Julia's love interest at Oxford and they had split up just before finals. I sometimes wondered if that had influenced Julia's unusual choice of career. Shortly before Julia came down from Somerville the RAF College at Cranwell announced that for the first time it would allow women to enrol and that is exactly what she did.

Knowing Julia as I do now the RAF does seem a very odd choice, despite the illustrious service careers of some of her family. At that time none of the forces were really welcoming to women: the RAF still expected female officers to resign if they married and pregnancy meant automatic discharge. Nor could they expect to become pilots. Julia certainly had some second thoughts during her two years at Cranwell. When she finished the course strings were pulled for her so that she avoided the usual postings and, uniquely, managed to move directly into her uncle's office in the Whitehall headquarters of the Defence Intelligence Staff.

Julia insisted that she still loved everything about the RAF, except the uniform. Nowadays a woman officer's dress uniform is not dissimilar to a man's but in the 1970s it was a drab blue empire line dress apparently specially designed to hide Julia's curves. Worst of all was the material: an artificial fabric called crimplene manufactured by Imperial Chemical Industries and considered the height of fashion for a brief period in the previous decade. On it had to be worn a small enamel brooch indicating rank.

I thought I was being witty in suggesting that the uniform might be more appropriate for our wedding ceremony than virginal white; Julia made plain that any more juvenile cracks like that and the wedding was off. I took the hint and, with Anne Grimspound unequivocally in charge, the ceremony and reception met every expectation until we reached the hotel where we were to spend our first night as Mr and Mrs Dylan. After unpacking Julia sent me down to the bar to fetch two much needed whiskies.

When I returned I found her lying suggestively on the bed wearing nothing but her blue crimplene uniform and a specially made enamel brooch reading 'Commanding Officer'.

II

The sun had shone for the whole of our wedding day and had been shining almost continuously since we arrived in Rome for our honeymoon. I had spent time there studying Italian and knew the city well. For Julia it was all new. We spent a week wandering around the city ticking off the Colosseum and St Peter's Basilica, the Trevi Fountain and the Pantheon, before returning wearily each evening to our hotel near the Spanish Steps. On the last day we arrived back at the hotel particularly well fed and even better watered; we had taken full advantage of Italy's vineyards before setting off for the land of retsina and ouzo. Julia had insisted on Prosecco for our last night in Rome which I had then followed up by splashing out on a bottle of Amarone, the powerful red wine from the Veneto made with dried grapes.

I was looking forward to collapsing into bed but there were three messages waiting for us at reception, all three from the man who was both Julia's uncle and our employer.

In today's world of instant global communication it seems odd that in 1977 the only way that the Director General of Defence Intelligence in London could contact two of his team in another European capital was by leaving potentially garbled messages in a hotel pigeonhole. That was the way it was then.

The first message had been left at ten o'clock in the morning. It simply said 'Hope you are enjoying yourselves in the Eternal City. Please contact me before leaving Rome.' The second, left at 7.30, was even less chatty. 'Please phone me this evening.' The first two messages had been simply signed Gordon. The third, received just a few minutes earlier, ended 'Lord Grimspound' and brusquely read: 'Phone me as soon as possible have changed your flight.'

'Is very important message, very, very important,' explained the elderly receptionist, 'comes from a *marchese*. He checks every word I write.'

Clearly the DG was becoming anxious and was determined that whoever was writing down his messages would appreciate their importance.

'What does he mean "changed your flight"?' I asked.

'Only one way to find out,' replied Julia.

We had already discovered that the phone in our room did not work and so we waited in the hotel lobby while the receptionist endeavoured to reach Julia's uncle. When he had finally got through Julia almost snatched the phone from his hand and I was left to guess at the conversation going on. Obviously whatever news the DG was imparting was not good. Equally obviously it concerned Julia's Aunt Eveline, or Bunny as I had learned to call her. It was a long conversation.

'Bunny's disappeared,' said Julia when the call was over. 'She and Davoud were sailing to Sicily and they never arrived.'

'Storms?'

'No, perfect sailing weather apparently.'

'And your uncle wants us to go home?'

'No, he wants us to go to Greece, somewhere called Sami in Kefalonia. That's where Bunny set off from.'

'And what does he want us to do when we get there?'

Julia looked around at the receptionist who was standing attentively a few yards away. Picking up our room key she headed for the stairs murmuring quietly to me.

'Well for one thing he wants us to convince Davoud's brother that Davoud has not been kidnapped by British Intelligence.'

She said nothing more until we had reached our room. Only then did she fill me in on the details of the call. Bunny and Davoud had borrowed his brother's yacht to sail to Syracuse in Sicily. They never arrived. It seems they had promised to call as soon as they reached their destination but did not do so. There was no radio on the boat. Davoud's brother Behzad had then contacted the DG demanding to know what had happened to his brother. There had been a heated conversation made more difficult by the fact that Behzad seemed to be calling from a local taverna.

'But why would Behzad think his brother had been kidnapped and why on earth would he think we had been involved?'

'Behzad has always been a bit odd. The only time that I ever met him was at Bunny's wedding more than twenty years ago. I was a schoolgirl then and didn't really pay much attention to Davoud's relations. I know Behzad lived for a long time in Paris but it seems he now has a villa in Greece as well. His family used to be wealthy in Iran but fell out of favour when the Shah's supporters seized power in the early fifties. Bunny said Behzad was lucky to get out alive. Davoud had wanted him to come to London but Behzad insisted that the Shah would soon fall and he and his friends would be returning to Tehran. Paris was the best place to prepare for the coming revolution.

'Of course the revolution did not come despite the plotting of Behzad and his friends. Behzad Sadeghi seems to have become quite paranoid and believes that the Shah is after him. And of course because the British helped put the Shah into power he thinks the British are also after him.'

10

'That still doesn't explain why Behzad thought Davoud had been kidnapped.'

'No it doesn't. Uncle Gordon was obviously rattled.'

'He would be,' I agreed, 'his sister has disappeared.'

'Yes but there's more to it than that. Apparently Behzad was really insistent, saying he knew British Intelligence was involved. And, strangely, he knew what my uncle does, he called him on his official line. How on earth did he get hold of that number?'

'Your Aunt Bunny must have told him.'

'She would never have done that. I doubt that she even had that number and if she did have it, she wouldn't have given it to Davoud let alone Behzad. And she surely wouldn't have mentioned her brother's job to Behzad, knowing how neurotic he was.'

Julia sat silently for a minute. 'Bunny and Davoud are good sailors. They have their own yacht on the Solent. I've been out on the *Bunny Hopper* with them. There is no way they could just vanish on a flat sea. Something must have happened.'

We took our scheduled flight to Athens early next morning and had to collect our luggage before we could fly on to Kefalonia. During the three-hour stopover Julia phoned her uncle again but there was no real news. The DG had obviously used all his considerable influence. Not only were aircraft and ships from Greece and Italy retracing the route Bunny and Davoud should have taken but every NATO vessel within a very wide area had been alerted. A US navy destroyer reported hearing an explosion well out to sea but that was far to the north of Bunny and Davoud's planned route. Nevertheless the search area had been extended but without success. There was simply no sign of Behzad's yacht or of any wreckage.

11

'I've never known Uncle Gordon to be like this,' Julia reported, an anxious frown crossing her brow, when she had finished the call. 'He is usually so certain of everything but not now. He just wants to do something - anything - although I'm not sure we will gain much by going to see Behzad. He's just going to rave on about Davoud being kidnapped; apparently he's totally paranoid and sees little green men round every corner. We are not to tell him that we're anything to do with Intelligence. We're supposed to find out as much as we can about the boat itself and whatever Bunny and Davoud may have said about their plans. Then, if there's no news, fly back to London.'

'So the honeymoon's over,' I said a little sadly, taking her hand.

'Postponed at least,' she agreed, gently kissing my forehead. 'But at least we shall be together.' Which we were, more or less.

III

We landed in Kefalonia to discover that the DG had arranged for a hire car to be waiting. Unfortunately he had not arranged for a driver so we tossed a coin and I lost. The drive over the mountains took us along roads still not fully repaired after the earthquake which had devastated the island more than twenty years before. The setting sun enhanced the beauty of the countryside but would have made finding our destination even more difficult had the DG not arranged for detailed instructions to be left in the hire car.

We arrived in Sami and then turned inland just as the skies opened and a torrential downpour seemed to obliterate the road in front of us. Fortunately there appeared to be no other cars on the road. I gave silent thanks for the DG's attention to detail, with no signposts that we could understand we would have been completely lost without his map. I still remember the rain beating on the roof of the little hire car with Julia calmly telling me to turn left, turn right, carry straight on like a modern-day satnav. It took us nearly an hour to arrive at Behzad's villa with the rain gods having a last laugh as the storm then passed as quickly as it came.

We had not warned Behzad Sadeghi of our arrival but fortunately lights were on inside the villa. Julia got out of the car and approached the heavy metal gate that blocked the short drive up to the villa. As she did so a figure appeared inside the gate, almost as if he had been waiting for us. It was clearly not Behzad.

The man looked at us suspiciously and I heard him bark questions in what seemed to be pidgin Greek. Julia replied in English which the man clearly understood although his suspicions only seemed to deepen. I joined her and Julia explained who she was and that she was here to talk to her aunt's brother-in-law, Behzad Sadeghi. The man disappeared, leaving us standing outside the locked gate.

I looked up at the villa and saw a tall figure in suit and tie looking out. For four or five minutes nothing happened and then the first man reappeared.

'Mr Sadeghi is unwell,' he said in heavily accented English. 'He apologises but you will return tomorrow. He will receive you at eleven o'clock.'

With that he turned away and there was nothing for us to do but drive back to Sami.

'What was that about?' I asked.

'Status,' answered Julia. 'He just wants to put us in our place, show us we can't just drop in without warning. He will be insufferable tomorrow.'

She returned to her side of the car and opened the door. I had been about to suggest she might like to drive but it seemed I was now the one being put in my place. I started the car and retraced our steps.

About five minutes down the road another car came towards us, his lights startling me as he rounded a corner. A huge Mercedes swung on to the verge and passed us without slowing down. Julia clicked on the interior light.

'What's that for?' I asked.

'I just want to jot down that chap's number.'

We had known each other for nearly three years but Julia still managed to surprise me. 'And why would you want to do that? Did you recognise him?'

'No, not at all. If I had recognised him I wouldn't need to write down his number. I didn't really see him at all, just his cap. But don't you think it odd that the gorilla on the gate back there seemed to be expecting someone. Behzad's lost his brother, is angry enough to phone London but when we turn up he neither sees us nor refuses to see us, we are just told to come back later.'

'I thought you said that was just putting us in our place.'

'Perhaps, or perhaps he was expecting someone more important, someone he didn't want us to meet.'

'Could be,' I agreed. 'If Behzad was the man I saw at the window he looked as if he was dressed up for something, certainly not about to go to bed with some mysterious ailment.'

We continued in silence. The DG's organisational skills had extended to finding us a room at a hotel on the beach a short walk along the shore from Sami. Eleni, the formidable looking woman who greeted us, turned out be the soul of hospitality, apologising profusely that the hotel did not serve food in the evening and directing us to a nearby restaurant. The menu proved to be rather basic but the food when it came was remarkably good. We ordered fish with *agliada*, which the restaurant owner proudly explained when he took the order was the local version of the *skordalia* served on the mainland. That information told me nothing and when it arrived I didn't recognise the fish at all but it was grilled perfectly and *agliada* proved to be potato mashed with olive oil, salt cod broth and an enormous quantity of garlic. Fabulous but not ideal honeymoon food.

We returned to the hotel where a small covered bar beside the swimming pool would have looked more inviting had there

15

been anyone serving drinks. As we approached Eleni appeared and immediately summoned her husband, Giorgos; they were, it seemed, the hotel's proud owners and nothing was too much trouble for them.

After discussing the merits of Greek brandies with Giorgos the three us settled down to sample his favourite. It was smoother than I expected but I suspect French brandy makers had little to fear.

'You only stay for one night,' Giorgos said with evident disappointment. Before he could extol the virtues of a longer visit, Julia explained why we were on the island.

Bunny and Davoud's disappearance was clearly the main topic of conversation in Sami. There was nothing wrong with the boat, asserted Giorgos. He himself had seen it and, as a fisherman from a family of fishermen, he could tell me 'the Persian' kept the yacht in perfect condition. And there was nothing wrong with the weather, the winds were light but steady, the sea calm and the sky cloudless. No, the problem, said Giorgos glancing at Julia, must have been the crew. It was said that when they left harbour the woman was in charge. Perhaps they were not experienced sailors. The Persian who owned the boat always left the sailing to the two men who worked for him. Perhaps his brother should have sailed with one of them.

'Bunny is a marvellous sailor,' Julia insisted. 'She's sailed all her life. And her husband too. They have their own yacht which they've sailed across the Atlantic.'

Giorgos looked unconvinced. 'The Ionian Sea between here and Italy is busy. Lots of big vessels. Perhaps at night, if they fall asleep, a tanker might not see a little boat like that until too late, perhaps not see it at all.' He paused and finished his brandy.

'Whatever happened it was not near here, the conditions here were perfect. And we would have found something by now. I don't know why they are still searching off Kefalonia.' He seemed to take the mere idea that Bunny and Davoud might have suffered some misadventure in Greek waters as a personal insult so we decided it was time to bid Giorgos goodnight and head for bed.

The next morning we visited the port where Bunny's voyage had started but learned nothing new. At eleven o'clock we were back at Behzad's villa and were greeted by the same man as the night before. This time he introduced himself. 'I am Shahryar,' he said without smiling. That seemed to be all his small talk. A second man unlocked the gate, signalled for us to drive in and then locked the gate again behind us. With our two new companions squeezed into the back seat we drove up the drive and then round to the back of the villa. As we all emerged from the car I noticed an automatic pistol stuffed into Shahryar's waistband.

I followed Julia into the villa where we were greeted by Behzad Sadeghi. I wasn't sure what to expect. Julia's family seemed to regard him as a paranoid fanatic but the man who advanced towards us was a picture of cultured elegance. He wore a dark grey linen suit with plain cotton shirt and red patterned tie. There were no rings on his fingers but large gold cufflinks sat above his wrists. Despite the fact that we were in the middle of nowhere, and had arrived without warning the previous evening, he now greeted us as if we were meeting for dinner at the Ritz. He was a tall man with a prominent hooked nose and dark brown eyes, his hair, greying at the temples, was overly long but beautifully cut. I wondered where he managed to find such a proficient stylist in the middle of a Greek island.

17

His handshake was warm and confident and he motioned us towards two comfortable easy chairs. Behzad said something to Shahryar in Farsi. The man left the room but returned immediately with soft drinks which were placed before us. He then disappeared.

'I'm afraid there is no alcohol in this house,' Behzad said. 'Your aunt brought a large bottle of gin but unfortunately she took what remained on the boat with her.'

He sat down and turned towards Julia. 'I don't think we've ever met,' he remarked.

'Only briefly. I was a child when your brother married my Aunt Bunny,' said Julia. 'All I remember is an enormous marquee full of flowers and very sticky, delicious cakes.'

'Yes,' remembered Behzad, smiling slightly in reminiscence, 'with a priest in a long purple cassock and my brother mouthing prayers to a God he didn't recognise. That was a very long time ago. And what do you do now?'

'I'm a secretary,' said Julia. It was an answer that he seemed to find entirely satisfactory while I tried hard not to let my mouth twitch with amusement: my wife would make a very unhappy secretary.

'And how about you?' he asked, turning to me.

'I'm a journalist,' I replied. His eyebrows arched faintly and I clarified: 'A sports journalist. I write about rugby, cricket, lacrosse – that sort of thing.'

'Not real journalism then,' he responded dismissively.

The pleasantries over Behzad turned away, looking out to the tree-covered hills. 'Why are you here?' he enquired in an altogether colder tone.

'We want to find Aunt Bunny and Uncle Davoud of course,' explained Julia, frowning in her obvious anxiety. 'Is there any news?'

Behzad turned to look directly at her. 'What news would I have? They sailed away in my boat and nobody has seen them since. You must have spoken to Eveline's brother, Lord Grimspound. He must be worried about his sister. What did he say? If anyone can help us it is surely him.'

Julia chose to misunderstand. 'If there are any Royal Navy ships in the area I'm sure Uncle Gordon has made contact with them. Lots of people are looking but nobody seems to have found anything. A boat can't just disappear. Was it really seaworthy, suitable for sailing all the way to Sicily?'

'*Mahsheed* is a beautiful boat. There are no problems there. Davoud and I were brought up on boats. Every summer my family used to sail on the Caspian.' He paused and again looked off into the distance. 'As you say boats do not just disappear. Someone must have taken it. But why would anyone do that? The boat is not particularly valuable. Davoud and you aunt are not valuable, nobody has been in touch to demand a ransom. No – I am fearing that Davoud and Eveline are in trouble but that they, whoever they are, were not after Davoud. It is me they want. I should have been on *Mahsheed*. Somebody wanted to kidnap me, or,' and Behzad's voice dropped, 'kill me.'

'But who could possibly want to do that?' I interrupted, allowing incredulity and apparent alarm to colour my question.

'You ask me that? It is your wife's uncle you should ask: milord Grimspound the Director General of Defence Intelligence in London.'

Julia and I tried to look bemused. 'Uncle Gordon is an admiral,' Julia corrected, but Behzad had moved on.

'The British have never wanted to see democracy return to my country. They fear they will lose control of our oil, but they

19

lost that years ago. Now the Americans have it all, perhaps one day the Saudis will pull the strings – or the Israelis.'

Behzad was looking outside again as if we were not there. It was a disconcerting habit and I wondered if the man was perhaps not entirely sane. Then suddenly his head swung around again and he looked directly at me.

'What do you know about the history of Iran?' he asked.

IV

'I know your nation's history goes back a very long way,' I said.

'Ah yes it does, but I'm talking about modern history, twentieth-century history. What do you know about that?' Behzad Sadeghi paused. 'I have a simple question for you. One man has had a greater impact on the modern history of my country than any other. Can you tell me the name of that man?'

I shook my head. 'I really don't know much about Iranian politics.'

'Ah but that man was not Iranian and you will know his name well.' He paused again for effect: 'Winston Churchill.'

'Iran is a colony. Not formally, not legally but in practice Iran has been a colony ever since an English geologist discovered oil at Masjid Sulaiman in 1908. We Iranians had no idea of the significance of that discovery but one man did, the First Lord of the British Admiralty, Winston Churchill. War with Germany was approaching and Churchill wanted to convert his coal-fired battleships to oil. The British took control of all the oil concessions in Iran and for the next forty years Britain made every important decision in my country. You know about the British invasion in 1941?'

I shook my head and Behzad seemed unsurprised by my ignorance. 'Iran wanted no part in your Western war. We were neutrals. Iranian Embassies handed out thousands of passports to Jews so they could escape from the Nazis but we also allowed

German businesses to continue to operate in Iran. The British could not accept that. They invaded along with the Russians, a surprise attack like the Japanese at Pearl Harbor.' He turned to Julia. 'Without warning the Iranian Imperial Navy was destroyed by your uncle's Royal Navy, our cities were bombed, our people killed. Of course the old Shah had to surrender. He was shipped off to South Africa and Churchill and Stalin divided Iran between them.'

It was clear that this was a speech Behzad had repeated often before. There was no point in trying to stop him.

'Do you know,' Behzad said, 'we were not even allowed to name our own country. The Shah had issued a proclamation that we should only be known as Iran but Churchill made him revert to the name he was happy with, Persia.

'Things had to change. In the Second World War the forces of dictatorship were destroyed. It was time for democracy in Iran. Time to take back our country. A new prime minister was elected. I say new – Mohammad Mossadegh was nearly seventy. He was no dangerous radical: he had been a government minister for years, before that his father had been a minister too. He understood what needed to be done but the British refused to negotiate. So Mossadegh was forced to nationalise the oil concessions. The British prime minister Clement Attlee was outraged and organised an economic boycott.

'Then fate intervened. Churchill replaced Attlee. He immediately started planning to oust the elected government in Tehran. The British called it "Operation Boot". But Churchill discovered he wasn't strong enough to organise a coup on his own so he turned to the Americans. The American president Truman refused to help but he was replaced by Eisenhower and everything changed again. Operation Boot became CIA Operation Ajax, led by a man named Kermit Roosevelt, a grandson of one American president and cousin of another.' Behzad sneered: 'That's the way things work in Western democracies.'

He paused for breath, as if inviting us to disagree, but when we said nothing he carried on.

'Roosevelt was given enormous sums of money by the CIA and the big oil companies and used it to bribe whoever needed bribing, especially in the Army and police. He organised a team of American and British agents, men like Harry Bastamente who set up death squads by bribing local gangsters and Jack Milwauk who bribed newspaper editors and journalists. When all was ready they pounced. Democratic leaders were rounded up, many were executed. Hundreds were killed, our father amongst them. He was on a CIA death list. The foreign minister who had been negotiating with the Americans was arrested and executed. Army generals who had refused to be bribed were all executed once the coup was complete. Mossadegh himself was imprisoned and then put under house arrest where he died. The young Shah was now in control but with his strings being pulled from Washington and London.

'And do you know what?' Behzad continued, 'Churchill lost the oil concessions anyway. The Americans made sure that most of them went to American companies and Kermit Roosevelt left the CIA to work for Gulf Oil.'

Behzad smiled disarmingly at me, a hint of self-satisfied superiority turning up the corners of his lips. As I really did know nothing about Iranian politics I decided to keep quiet. Julia showed no such restraint. 'What about the Russians?' she asked. 'Weren't they egging Mossadegh on, waiting just across the frontier to grab the concessions themselves?'

Behzad seemed startled by her intervention, as if debating such matters with a woman was a novelty. 'Nonsense,' he said, 'the Communists were no friends of Mossadegh. Stalin could have moved his troops but he didn't. The Americans had promised that he would get some of the oil after their coup, but of course they reneged on that promise too. The Communists suffered as much as anyone afterwards but at first they refused to believe what had happened. They would not join with the rest of the opposition in exile. Neither would the Islamists. It has taken twenty years to persuade people to cooperate but now the moment is coming when the Shah's regime is ready to fall. The only question is who will be there to pick up the pieces.'

'You think you will be.'

'Perhaps, now that Ali Shariati is dead.'

He stared at me as if expecting some sort of reaction but again I said nothing. I had never heard of Ali Shariati.

'You don't know who I'm talking about, do you?' he said. 'The ignorance of the English always astounds me. Ali Shariati was a philosopher imprisoned and tortured by the Shah. To many he was a hero. Just a month ago he was released from prison, sent into exile in your country and then last week he suddenly died. A healthy young man dies in England for no reason. Don't you think that is strange?'

'This isn't helping us find Bunny,' interjected Julia. 'You can't really expect us to believe that our government would try to kidnap or murder an exiled dissident however important he may think he is. I want to know what has happened to my aunt. I don't think you know and I don't have time to sit here listening to fairy tales. Why would anyone have thought you were on that boat? They would only have to watch the yacht leave Sami. Even if they had mistaken Uncle Davoud for you they would soon have seen that you were still on the island.'

'That's where you are wrong,' Behzad responded angrily. 'Perhaps they didn't see *Mahsheed* leave, perhaps they were waiting out at sea or even outside Syracuse at the other end of the voyage.'

'But why would anyone expect you to be on a yacht outside Syracuse? It's ridiculous.'

'Not so ridiculous – I had been planning to travel with them. Only at the last minute did circumstances change.'

There was a moment's silence. 'Why were Bunny and Davoud going to Syracuse?' I asked. 'Did they know anybody there?'

'I don't know,' Behzad replied. 'It was Bunny's idea. She didn't say why.'

He stood up. Our conversation was over.

We had arranged to fly back to Athens that afternoon and while we could have changed our flight there didn't seem much point in staying on.

Behzad Sadeghi shook our hands formally when we left. He seemed to have returned into his own private world. It was difficult to know what he was really thinking. There had been flashes of emotion when talking about the Shah or when Julia questioned the seaworthiness of his boat but there was no sense of real concern for his brother and Bunny. Behzad seemed to see the rest of the world only as it affected him personally.

'What did you think of that?' I asked as we drove away.

'Well, the idea of you as a sports reporter covering lacrosse is utterly ridiculous, what do you know about lacrosse?'

'I know you used to play for England. What else do I need to know? And as you know perfectly well, I meant what did you think about Behzad?'

'Something's not right there,' Julia said. 'All that paranoid stuff about British Intelligence we can ignore but there were a couple of oddities. Deciding just to say "I'm off to Sicily" is exactly the sort of thing Bunny would do. But not to have some objective in mind is totally out of character. If she had decided to see Syracuse there would have been a reason. It might have been to sample the food or admire the architecture or simply to enjoy the sailing. And she would have talked about it. What's more we are supposed to believe that Behzad himself had been planning to go with them to Syracuse but never asked why they wanted to go. That's just not credible.'

'I agree. And another thing which I found odd is that Behzad used the term Director General of Defence Intelligence.'

'Yes, you're right. It is absolutely who my uncle is, but it's far too precise. Bunny would never have used that term. It's conceivable she might have mentioned that Uncle Gordon is something to do with British Intelligence, although I don't believe it, but I would be astonished if she had ever heard of the Defence Intelligence Staff. It's not something like MI5 which everyone knows. The DIS has only been around for ten or twelve years. Uncle says he's never talked about his work to anyone in the family.'

'Except you.'

'Of course, except me. And you too my love, you're part of the family now.' That made me smile as I remembered how utterly beautiful Julia had looked coming down the aisle towards me, just a few days ago.

We drove back to the airport deep in thought. It really was an odd way to spend a honeymoon.

'Do you think any of that political stuff is true?' I asked eventually. 'Winston Churchill and Operation Ajax and all that.'

'Oh that part is true,' Julia replied. 'Bunny and Davoud have talked about that. They were different times. Remember the British Empire really meant something to Churchill's generation. British geologists had found the oil fields, British engineers developed them, British companies paid for them. To Churchill it was British oil. He wasn't going to let a load of natives take it. Unfortunately he didn't have the wherewithal to keep it, which is why he had to invite the Americans in. And one thing the Americans are not is subtle. They take no prisoners. Davoud and Behzad's father was one of the generals who stood by the elected president and that is why his name was on the death list. After the coup he was tortured to death along with hundreds of others. Bunny was always scathing about the Shah. When he had that ridiculous coronation ten years ago she told us all about the ordeal Davoud's family went through. Davoud and Behzad were lucky to get out alive, but of course that was years ago. Things have changed. I can't imagine the DIS or even MI6 getting involved in toppling elected governments today.'

'No, but the Americans might.'

'Perhaps.'

'There's no perhaps about it. Look at the colonels' coup right here in Greece. The CIA may not have organised it but there's no doubt the local CIA station was very close to the action.'

When we pulled into the airport car park I spotted something decidedly odd. I nudged Julia. 'Look over there,' I said pointing.

'I can't see anything special.'

'That car,' I said.

Suddenly Julia was scrabbling at her handbag. She retrieved a piece of paper and then exclaimed excitedly, 'You're right. That's the car we saw approaching Behzad's villa yesterday. Look where it's parked, it must be a hire car. You park the car here.'

'What are you going to do?'

'I want to find out who hired that car.'

'And how do you propose to do that?'

'Oh I'll think of something. I'll act like a damsel in distress and say that the driver of the car deserted me and I need to know his real name.'

Julia disappeared inside and a few minutes later came out smiling.

'So the damsel in distress routine worked,' I observed.

'Not at all,' she replied, 'but a handful of drachmas did the trick. The problem is that I'm not sure that we are any further forward. I have a name, Henry Ramone, but the address is in Toronto.'

'Toronto, Canada?'

'That's the only Toronto that I know. Come on, let's give our car back and catch our flight.'

V

When we arrived in Athens there was another message waiting at the airport from the DG. It seemed he had reverted to his normal character; the message, handed to me as we stepped off the plane, was in fact an order. We were to catch the Olympic Airways flight about to leave for Rome. The DG was considering what to do next. By the time we reached Rome he had made up his mind and yet another message was waiting for us at the airport there. The next morning I was to catch the first flight to London and would be met at the airport. Julia would be flying down to Sicily. No explanations, just an assurance that the Service had a man in Syracuse who knew the local area. He would look after Julia's arrangements.

We managed to check back into the hotel we had left the day before and tried to rekindle the carefree joy of our honeymoon. It was only as I was getting dressed next morning that I was struck by the last part of the DG's message. He had a man in Syracuse.

The DIS has fewer than 800 staff, most of them in London. The rest in major capitals or war zones. How could we possibly have someone stationed in a tiny little town on a militarily insignificant island in the Mediterranean? What was going on?

The DG had a curiously roundabout way to approach problems combined with a desire to keep things to himself that went beyond the needs of security.

29

I remember on one occasion being summoned to his office and spending the first five minutes listening to a story about a party he had once attended at Dhekelia, the British sovereign base in the east of Cyprus. Only after describing at length a marathon drinking competition he had witnessed between befuddled Army and RAF officers did he turn to the business in hand. He wanted me to produce a new report on the base the Russians had recently built at Tartus in Syria. I spent two days poring over the limited information we had on what the Russians insisted was a 'maintenance facility' before I realised that Tartus was located directly across the Eastern Mediterranean from Dhekelia where GCHQ, then still an organisation clothed in mystery, were plying their trade. Somehow our first report on the new Tartus base, written by one of our few remaining Arabists and focussed entirely on Russian objectives in the Middle East, had completely missed the significance of its proximity to Cyprus.

I was still puzzling over the fact that the DIS apparently had a man in Sicily's third city when I arrived back in London. To my astonishment the DG's personal assistant Janet, an intimidating Welsh dragon who had never before been known to leave her lair outside the DG's office, was waiting for me as I disembarked. Waving an official-looking pass she led me into the VIP area.

'The DG's meeting some of our more unpleasant friends,' she said, 'and you are to sit beside him and keep your mouth shut. Just take notes and say nothing.'

'Who's there?' I asked.

'Nobody you know. An American who insists on calling the DG Admiral and a couple of self-important Foreign Office types. They were late so the meeting may not have started.'

She knocked on a door and pushed me in. The DG and four strangers were standing at one end pouring themselves coffee.

It was easy to tell who each man was, no women of course in those days. The senior American was introduced to me as Harry Bastamente. Most of the CIA men I had met were analysts, cultured Ivy League types more at home in country clubs than in the field, men with whom meetings were quite likely to drift off into discussions of modern art or medieval history. Bastamente was quite different. Although his suit had an expensive Italian look about it his weather-beaten face had not been acquired behind a desk. Deep brown eyes sat below heavy eyelids and sparse dark hair. He advanced towards me and shook my hand in a grasp that was too strong to be considered merely firm. His younger colleague did the same.

'I've heard of you,' said Bastamente, 'I like to do my homework. You tangled with one of our teams in Brazil a couple of years ago. I thought you would be older.'

I simply replied, 'Pleased to meet you.' There was no point in mentioning that I had also heard of him, just the day before when Behzad Sadeghi mentioned the CIA agent who had organised death squads in the coup against Mossadegh in Iran twenty-four years earlier.

The DG introduced the two Britons as coming from our sister organisation, which I took to mean the Secret Intelligence Service, MI6. The senior man, George Ffortiscue, simply nodded in my direction as did his companion, a tall young man with severe acne and a black tie with turquoise stripes. In those days an Old Etonian tie still carried weight in MI6.

The two junior men said nothing in the entire meeting and today I can't remember either of their names.

I poured myself a coffee and sat between the DG and Ffortiscue. Bastamente started speaking and it was evident that this was his meeting.

31

'We have a couple of issues in Sicily and as I was passing through London I thought we might just compare notes. I don't see anything connecting the two issues but if you gentlemen disagree I would like to know.

'First we have a Russian agent or agents inside our naval air station at Sigonella. We know that information has been passed on about our joint manoeuvres in the Mediterranean. We don't know how much and for how long it's been going on. I have a small team there headed by Jack Romney. Jack's been with the Agency almost as long as I have, he's one of our best men in Europe. He knows the Russians and he knows Italy. And thanks to Admiral Grimspound here for seconding your man Morgan. We're getting support from the Italians but despite all that we're not getting very far. Security there is godawful. Nearly thirty people had access to that information, more than half of them locals. The SID are trying to help, they've sent a top guy down from Rome, but you know what the Italians are like, they've got more police forces and more intelligence agencies than I've had pizzas. The SID are in a mess, constantly reorganising themselves.

'And now we have the Admiral's sister disappearing. We don't know how and we don't know where. But last night an Italian fishing boat found some pieces of wood in the sea that may have come from their boat. We can't know for sure yet. The local police have passed them on to the SID and we'll see what they say. What we do know is that your sister was in a boat that belonged to an Iranian exile, named Behzad Sadeghi, who has been on our radar for a long time and we know that his brother was also on the boat. We also know that Behzad Sadeghi has a lot of Communist connections, we don't know if his brother swings the same way.'

The DG looked up. 'Davoud is completely apolitical.'

'Do you know that?' interrupted Ffortiscue. 'Or is that just what your sister believes?'

'I know that,' replied the DG, 'but I'm sure you could ask Five if you're on speaking terms with anyone there.' I smiled to myself, it was well known that MI5 and MI6 were in the midst of one of their periodic turf wars.

Bastamente resumed. 'Things are hotting up in Iran. Four years ago everyone was excited by all the new money pouring in when the oil prices went up but now the economy is dipping again. The Shah is coming under a lot of pressure, not least from the new man in the White House who probably thinks Tehran's some place in South America. Behzad Sadeghi is trying to pull all the opposition groups together – the Communists, the liberals, the ones they call the red Islamists, even Khomeini and his hard-line followers. It's Khomeini and the black Islamists who are the real danger. Now that the red Islamists have lost their leader, Shariati, they might peel away and join him. If Sadeghi and the Communists then ally with the Islamic nuts we could really have problems. Brezhnev will be creaming himself. The Russians have a lot of tanks sitting on the Iranian border.'

'Behzad Sadeghi isn't an Islamist,' said the DG.

'He is not an Islamist or a Communist,' responded Bastamente. 'He's an opportunist and that makes him really dangerous. We know he's taking money from the Communists, his family money is running out and the Russians have been channelling money to him through their Embassy in Rome. He wants to go home and he wants to go home in triumph. He'll do anything that might weaken the Shah.'

'Which is not good news,' put in Ffortiscue, 'for the United States or for the United Kingdom. Iran is currently the world's second biggest oil exporter. The Shah's making himself very unpopular and we don't think his prime minister, Hoveyda, can last more than a month or two. We're all agreed that it is essential that the position be stabilised and Her Majesty's Government will use all its endeavours to that end. However, having said that, I'm not sure that what's happening in Tehran has anything to do with Gordon's sister vanishing. The most likely explanation for her disappearance is either that the yacht collided with a tanker during the night or that its gas cooking canister exploded. An American destroyer heard an explosion at sea on the night Mrs Sadeghi disappeared.'

'That was way off to the north,' said the DG, 'we shouldn't have widened the search area that far.'

The conversation went on for another forty minutes but I learned nothing more. The revelation that there was a possible Russian spy ring in Sicily was exciting and explained why the DIS had a man in Syracuse but it seemed obvious to me that there was no connection with Bunny's disappearance. As the conversation wound down everyone seemed to reach the same conclusion.

Suddenly Bastamente turned to me. 'You've been remarkably silent, young man,' he said. 'Didn't you learn anything from your visit to Behzad Sadeghi yesterday?'

If he was trying to surprise me he certainly succeeded. Ffortiscue too swung round to look at me with a startled expression on his face.

'No,' I said, 'nothing new.'

Bastamente let it go. 'Just doing my homework,' he said as he rose from the table. 'Thank you for your time, gentlemen. Now, if you don't mind Admiral, George and I have a few little issues in South America to discuss. Please be assured the United States is doing everything possible to discover what's happened to your sister.'

It would seem the DG and I were dismissed.

Janet was hovering outside the door and led the way to an empty office she had managed to commandeer at the other end of the building. The DG was not in a good mood.

'That man's a dinosaur. It's surely only a matter of time before Turner puts him out to pasture.' Stansfield Turner was the man President Carter had recently appointed head of the CIA with a brief to shake the organisation into shape. 'I will not be patronised by a man like that.'

The DG sat down and his mood changed again. 'What did we learn?' He looked at me with the same intimidating stare my old university tutor used when asking me a question he was confident I would not be able to answer. 'What did you learn young man?'

'I learned a lot. First I learned there's a Russian spy ring in Sicily.'

'Apparently so. The CIA has a network in Italy, they call it Casarecce. It's been there for years and Bastamente is very proud of it, although this is the first time they've produced anything solid. He actually has a source inside the Russian Embassy in Rome. His source managed to get copies of a great stash of papers that seem to have been stolen from the US base at Sigonella, north of Syracuse, and somehow found their way into the Embassy. Nothing devastatingly secret but secret nevertheless. Details of NATO exercises in the Mediterranean, flight plans, code words, weapons shipments, troop movements. Nothing that politicians will lose any sleep over but alarming to us, things we don't want the other side to know. And the real worry is what else there may be that we don't know about. All hell broke loose two months ago when Bastamente turned up at a meeting in Washington with all this stuff and demanded that his people be allowed into

Sigonella to investigate. The US Navy was not best pleased to think they had a leak but the papers he had were genuine and must have come from someone on the base. Our Navy wasn't pleased, Sigonella is important for the whole of NATO.

'The base has been crawled over ever since but nothing's turned up. Bastamente's source in Rome tells us that the leak's still active but can't get hold of anything else that's been taken. The background of everyone there has been gone over but nothing discovered. Bastamente's right about one thing, our colleagues in the *Servizio Informazioni Difesa* are not perhaps as professional as we consider ourselves to be. They've had a few upsets lately and their minds are probably on other things.'

A smile crossed the DG's face. 'Having said that, Bastamente has no right to moan about the Italians reorganising themselves when you think about what's happening in the Company right now.' When he was first appointed, the DG had objected to people referring to the CIA by its nickname, the Company, but it seemed he was now more relaxed. His tutor face reappeared.

'What else did you learn?'

'I learned that Bastamente is thorough and the CIA keeps good records. When you told him I would be at the meeting he was able to find out about my little adventure in Brazil.'

'But I didn't tell him you were coming to the meeting. Nor did I tell him you had been to see Behzad in Greece.'

The DG paused to let that sink in. If Bastamente did not know I was going to be at the meeting why had he made an effort to check me out? It must have been because he heard that I had visited Behzad. That meant that either Behzad or someone else in the villa had spoken to him or he had the villa under observation. I couldn't believe that the Company would maintain a surveillance team in Kefalonia on the off-chance that Behzad would do something interesting. Nor did I believe that Behzad himself would have anything to do with Bastamente. The most likely explanation is that one of the two men I had seen at the villa working for Behzad Sadeghi was also working for the Americans. That still left a big question in my mind.

'Why did Bastamente ask me about yesterday's visit? What did he expect to learn?'

'He didn't want to learn anything. He just wanted to show us that he has eyes everywhere, he is in control. To remind us that we are just a little bunch of amateurs while he's got the massive resources of the Central Intelligence Agency behind him. It's a way of telling us to mind our own business. Anything to do with Iran is his territory. Bastamente is part of the old guard. He was with Allen Dulles in the OSS during the war. When Eisenhower made Dulles head of the CIA Bastamente was right there. Operation Ajax made his name. Anything else strike you?'

'Just one thing. I was sitting next to Ffortiscue, he had a folder in front of him which he referred to a couple of times when we were talking about Bunny's disappearance. I couldn't see any of the papers in it but it was a standard manila folder with the filing details on the front. There was a title, a code name, Tortellini.'

'I'll follow that up,' said the DG. 'It's a new one to me.'

'It wasn't just the code name that was interesting,' I continued. 'Just below that was printed a date which I assume was the date the file was opened. And that date was December last year.'

'And you say he referred to it when Bunny's disappearance came up?'

'Yes, and when Bastamente mentioned my visit to Behzad, Ffortiscue made a note in that file. He had another folder with his papers on the Russian spy business, I couldn't see the cover of that one.'

'Food for thought,' said the DG quietly.

It could mean nothing at all. Perhaps George Ffortiscue had just picked up his loose papers that morning and pushed them into an old manila file that happened to be lying around. On the other hand if, over the last seven or eight months, Six had been running a project with the code name Tortellini and somehow Bunny's disappearance was connected to it then there were a lot of questions to answer: the biggest being why hadn't Ffortiscue mentioned it? Perhaps he didn't want the Americans to know anything about it, more likely he didn't want us to know. It might even be an American operation and Six didn't want the Company to realise that Six knew anything about it.

Janet appeared with my luggage and led us to the DG's car. The three of us sped out of the airport without any of the formalities normally associated with arriving at Heathrow. On the way I mentioned Julia's discovery that Behzad had been visited by a Canadian named Ramone. Again the name meant nothing to the DG but like Tortellini he promised to follow it up.

When we reached Hammersmith the DG's driver turned off and we were soon parking in one of the nicer parts of Notting Hill. I recognised the town house belonging to Julia's missing aunt. The DG produced a set of house keys and let us in.

Leaving the driver outside we set about searching the house.

'What are we looking for?' asked Janet.

'I've no idea,' replied Lord Grimspound. 'Anything unusual, anything that might refer to Behzad or to Kefalonia or to Sicily.'

The house was furnished in an extraordinarily eclectic style. The gloom of heavy Victorian and marquetry furniture in the dining room and study, almost certainly Bunny's family heirlooms, was relieved by modern Scandinavian pieces elsewhere. Bright

Persian carpets introduced splashes of colour. There were books everywhere. I ran my eye along two rows of travel books and found a book on the Greek islands and a gloriously illustrated book on the art treasures of Florence but nothing particularly relevant. I couldn't find a single book that might be described as vaguely political and the only books on Iran seemed to be entirely concerned with art and architecture.

The DG found a letter lying on Davoud's desk. In the wastepaper basket below the desk he found the accompanying envelope bearing a Greek stamp. The letter itself was written in Farsi.

'We had better take this with us,' he said, 'but I doubt whether it will tell us anything new.'

Bunny and Davoud also had a weekend cottage in Bosham near Chichester. I was dispatched to search the cottage and the boat which they kept moored nearby. It was past six o'clock when I got back to London, having discovered nothing at all. The DG was still in his office and did not seem surprised by my lack of results.

'I've sent that name, Henry Ramone, off to our friends in Canada,' he said. 'Let's see what they turn up. I'm waiting for Behzad's letter to be translated. I thought it better to have it translated by someone I know rather than letting the Foreign Office pass it around all over the place.'

Just then Janet entered and passed him a couple of typed sheets along with the original letter. He read the sheets quickly and passed them to me. As we expected, the letter was from Behzad to his brother. Most of it was about the arrangements for Davoud and Bunny's forthcoming visit. Behzad apologised that he might not be there the whole of the time, explaining that events were moving quickly and he might have to go to Italy.

Later in the letter he hoped that they would all be able to do some sailing together, perhaps even combining it with his trip to Italy.

'It does suggest that Behzad was planning to be on that boat but for some reason decided not to go,' mused the DG. 'I wonder what events were moving quickly.'

There was nothing more to do and with no news from Julia I prepared to go home. 'Good idea,' said the DG. 'You have an early start tomorrow. I hope you are travelling light.'

'Where am I going?'

'The RAF have a flight down to Sigonella tomorrow. Wentworth has got you on to that. You fly out of RAF Northolt at 0745.'

I groaned inwardly. When the DG needed to travel Janet made all the arrangements and they worked like clockwork. I had no doubt she had organised the trip to Kefalonia. When anyone else needed to travel an RAF warrant officer named Wentworth, the DIS Travel Coordinator, took charge. He always seemed to find an uncomfortable but free RAF flight which he insisted would be the quickest possible way to get anywhere 'when you allow for all that time you have to waste at civilian airfields checking passports'. He was always wrong.

VI

Next morning, when I arrived at RAF Northolt, I discovered there was no flight to Sigonella. I was flying to RAF Laarbruch in Germany from where Air Support Command had, at some unspecified point in the day, a flight planned to Sigonella. As it was, I wasted most of the day in Laarbruch waiting for an air vice-marshal to join us for the flight to Sicily. It gave me time to read all the latest London newspapers which had been brought out on the Northolt flight and sat unread on a table. In the *Telegraph* I found a small item in an inside page confirming that a London knee surgeon and his wife were still missing in the Mediterranean.

The previous evening I had managed to find my copy of Lampedusa's *The Leopard* which I had struggled through in my first year at university. Reading the book back then the Sicily Lampedusa described had seemed remote and the values to which he tried to cling impossibly old-fashioned. Now I would see for myself how much had changed. It was well into the evening, and I had just finished the novel's wistful conclusion, when we came in to land at what the US Navy called its 'Air Facility' at Sigonella.

I had naïvely assumed that a US Navy facility would be on the sea but in fact the base at Sigonella was some miles inland, to the west of the road from Catania to Syracuse and about twenty-five miles from Mount Etna. We flew in from the east over the sea and then above a wide flat valley. The countryside was completely unspoilt until the radar masts of the US base came in to view. The only buildings I could see on the road that led towards the base belonged to what seemed to be some sort of disused military barracks now crumbling into decay. Beyond the radar masts low, dark green buildings appeared inside what I later discovered was a simple barbed wire fence. Then as we touched down a mass of more modern brick buildings hid the fence and the road from view. As the aircraft started to taxi back to its stand I noticed accommodation blocks at the far end of the base, not far from the main entrance. A great deal of construction work seemed to be underway which must have made security especially difficult.

US Naval Air Facility Sigonella had been there for twenty years and was now one of the largest US bases on the Mediterranean, perhaps even the largest. Italian, British and other NATO forces used the base but it was very much US territory. I was greeted not only by our own man, Morgan, but also by Jack Romney, the man Bastamente had told me headed the CIA team on the base.

The two men could not have been more different. Charles Morgan was typical DIS, a young army captain on secondment: smart blazer, Parachute Regiment tie and brightly polished shoes. I discovered later that until a few weeks earlier he had been attached to the Embassy in Rome, his first DIS posting. Romney was very different. A huge broad-shouldered man now somewhat past his prime, a man I thought in the Bastamente mould. Nondescript suit, white buttoned-down shirt and plain brown tie. He looked like someone who had enjoyed more than a few beers in his life. It was Romney who advanced towards me as I left the plane and took upon himself the role of official welcoming party. Captain Morgan held back, looking faintly embarrassed.

'Welcome to Italy,' Romney boomed as if addressing a planeload of arrivals. It struck me that Jack Romney, even at this hour, had more than one beer inside him.

Romney, it seemed, had personally been leading the search operation for Bunny and Davoud. 'Our whole Navy has been out there,' he assured me, 'and we have had search planes up ever since day one. And of course we've had the Italians and Greeks searching as well and your people. If that boat's still floating we'll find it. But we've got to be realistic. Chances are that boat hit a rock and went down.'

It was a relief when Romney decided his duties had been done and disappeared into one of the buildings near the main gate. Morgan led the way to a new Lancia Beta Montecarlo parked nearby. That car was not bought on a DIS salary I thought, Charles Morgan was clearly a man of private means.

'Let's get out of here,' he said, 'and go and find your wife. I'll fill you in on some background.'

Most of the background seemed to concern the various battles going on between the host of agencies involved. Beyond that there was very little that was new. As Bastamente had mentioned in London the previous evening, a fishing boat had discovered what looked like the remains of a wooden vessel some way out to sea. It seemed likely that there had been some sort of explosion on board although the alternative possibility of a collision at sea had still not been ruled out. From where the wreckage had been found and a knowledge of the prevailing currents, it would seem that Bunny had been only an hour or two from Syracuse. If that was true it meant that whatever had happened had happened in daylight and so the collision theory looked less and less likely.

The investigations into the Russian spy ring at the airbase were getting absolutely nowhere. Morgan explained that there are in fact two American bases at Sigonella. Naval Air Facility One was built on the site of an old Luftwaffe airfield and now housed medical facilities, admin support and some accommodation, mainly for officers. Everything else was at Naval Air Facility Two, referred to as NAF II, which had just been green fields and orange groves when the Americans arrived in 1959. It was now the actual airbase at which I had landed and that's where Morgan had been given a temporary office. The two bases were about twenty minutes apart and it was from NAF II that the papers discovered by the CIA mole in the Russian Embassy had been stolen.

The Americans were convinced the spy or spies must be Italian. The Italians were equally convinced the spy must have been an Allied serviceman; they pointed out that none of the papers found in the Russian Embassy related to the Italian military. Morgan was appalled that so many people seemed to have access to the stolen papers. 'It looks like a random selection of papers were filched from a central archive of temporary files to which nobody paid much attention. The really secret stuff the Americans keep to themselves and there was only one small report in that category, although I'd love to know how that got leaked. We don't know when the papers reached the Embassy but most of them would be quickly out of date.

'The Italians have sent down a team from Rome under a man called Di Benedetto and they've been working closely with Romney. Together they have interviewed absolutely everybody who could have had access to those papers and gone over their backgrounds in minute detail. They've found a couple of the locals with family connections to the Communist Party but in both cases haven't been able to turn up anything concrete. They're running surveillance, tapping phones and generally chasing around all over the place but they have found absolutely nothing. The Agency's source in the Russian Embassy has reported that another batch of papers has arrived and been sent to Moscow but we are no closer to finding out how they got out of Sigonella.

'You'll have seen all the construction work going on. None of the construction workers should have been able to get anywhere near the files that were stolen, but who knows. My bet is that it's far more likely that the papers were filched by a Communist building worker who just grabbed what he could find rather than by an undercover Russian mole. We're getting so desperate that the Italian intelligence guy, Di Benedetto, is treating anyone who's ever come within a mile of the base as a suspect.

'All Romney and Di Benedetto seem to have done is pissed off everyone else. I'd better tell you something about both of them because if you're going to be here for long you can't avoid them.

'Romney's an old Company man, helped set up the Casarecce network and doesn't want anything queering his pitch before he retires. The Office of Naval Intelligence already had people here before he arrived and started throwing his weight around. The ONI play by the book, Romney prides himself on not having a book. He's not an easy man. Definite opinions and he obviously sees himself as a hard, no-nonsense sort of guy but something's missing. There's a bit of a loser about him.

'You remember all the stuff about the American supercars entering the Le Mans 24 Hours race last year and how they would change the world of motor racing?'

'I have a vague recollection. They were awful weren't they?'

'They certainly were. One of them, a Dodge Charger, had to retire after just two laps. Well Romney bought into all the pre-race publicity and had a Dodge Charger shipped over here. Not only that, he had his car painted up in the same colour scheme as the race car, white and gold. He must have felt a complete idiot when the race took place and it came in last. But somehow the whole episode seems to sum him up.

'And on the Italian side we have Di Benedetto from the SID, a man who tries hard to look elegant and only ends up looking effete. A bit like our friends in MI6. Nobody here seems to have any respect for the SID since the Borghese fiasco. You know about that?'

I nodded. In 1970 a group of well-placed unreformed fascists tried to organise a coup to overthrow the Italian government. The attempt didn't get off the ground but the following year the press got hold of the details of what they called the Borghese Coup and numerous high-ranking generals and politicians were arrested. One of those arrested was the head of the SID, General Vito Miceli.

'When I arrived,' Morgan continued, 'there was a *Carabinieri* officer conducting investigations but he fell out with the SID. That's a pity because he seemed pretty professional. As well as the *Carabinieri* the financial police, the *Guardia di Finanza*, are involved as well, which is not as strange as it seems. The *Guardia di Finanza*, like the *Carabinieri*, are a military police force, they're responsible for patrolling Italy's territorial waters. They've been leading the Italian search for our missing yacht along with the Italian Navy and the Coast Guard.'

'Sounds like a bureaucratic nightmare.'

'It is, the police forces in this country are Byzantine. And I haven't even started on the police proper yet, the civil police. Your wife was going to meet the municipal police today. They are at the bottom of the pile, enforcing local bylaws – parking, that sort of thing. I don't think she will get anything useful out of them.

They're the guys who first heard about the supposed wreckage when it was brought in. Julia wants to know if anything more has turned up. Then she was hoping to see the real police, the *Polizia di Stato*, who were the first ones to examine the wreckage in any detail before the SID took it away for proper forensics. I've given her contact details from the files back at the base.

'We haven't told anyone outside the base that you and Julia have any connection with British Intelligence. You are just relations of the missing woman who were on honeymoon in Rome and have decided to come down here to see if you can help find out what has happened.'

'I might need to be a bit flexible about that,' I said. 'The Americans know I'm DIS. I met a couple of them in London yesterday.'

'OK,' said Morgan. 'I spoke to the DG an hour or so ago and he seems to think we should keep our cards very close to our chest; the problem is that right now we don't have any cards. He mentioned Project Tortellini but I've never heard of it. The only tortellini I've come across are the little stuffed pastas the Italians sometimes put in their soup.'

I smiled. Just a few days ago I had taken Julia to one of my old haunts in Rome and shown her the plates of tortellini with prosciutto in cream sauce, or simply with melted butter and sage, that had been the staple food of my student days, filling and cheap. But not, as Julia had pointed out, particularly healthy, especially as it had always been accompanied by cheap red wine. I told her that one of my Italian friends used to refer to the little round pastas as bellybuttons because of their shape but Julia insisted they looked more like baby sun hats.

'I'll drop Tortellini into a conversation with Romney tomorrow,' promised Morgan. 'The DG also asked about the name Ramone but it means nothing to me. Apparently the Canadians haven't come up with anything.'

I mulled over what Morgan had told me as we headed south. Today the A18 autostrada races through a series of magnificent tunnels down to Syracuse and beyond but back then the roads were patchy at best. Morgan was a car enthusiast and had driven from Rome down to Sicily but, even with him gunning the Lancia, the sun had long gone when we reached the hotel.

The Grand Hotel Villa Politi proved to be majestic and expensive. In the middle of the nineteenth century a wandering Austrian noblewoman named Maria Teresa Laudien found romance in the arms of a young Syracuse painter, Salvatore Politi. With her money and his flair, in 1862 they built the Villa Politi on a hillside looking down on the city and the sea beyond. I wondered whether it had been the DG or Morgan who had decided this was the most suitable hotel for two newlyweds.

Morgan swept up the drive to drop me at the base of one of the two marble staircases that curled up to the low, white Grand Hotel Villa Politi which stretched out on either side. A uniformed attendant took my bag and led me inside where the heavy wooden furnishings, heavily padded seats and red plush walls seemed more redolent of Countess Laudien's home country than the baking heat of Sicily in July. The one truly Sicilian feature was the elaborately patterned flooring in red, black, grey and white marble. On the left were the bar, restaurant and ballroom and on the right behind the reception desk two discrete lifts ready to take me up to my room on the second floor.

Julia, however, had seen my arrival and emerged from the bar. We embraced lingeringly and waited for Morgan to appear after parking his car. Then Julia led us to a table where she had clearly been chatting happily to an impeccably dressed Italian about the same age as me. I immediately recognised him as the playboy type: deep suntan, boyish figure, long delicate fingers and dark flashing eyes.

'This is Giuseppe,' said Julia, 'he's been so helpful I was sure you would want to meet him.'

Giuseppe rose and held out his hand. 'You are the lucky husband,' he said, in near-perfect English.

I didn't need him to tell me how lucky I was but I nodded in agreement. His handshake was strong and confident and I realised that first impressions could be misleading. Giuseppe had not acquired those muscles raising martinis.

A waiter appeared and he ordered a second bottle of the local frizzante and two more glasses. Morgan insisted he would stay for just one quick drink, explaining that he had to drive back to Catania.

'You are in the military,' said Giuseppe to Morgan more as a statement of fact than as a question.

Morgan looked startled. 'Why would you say that? I am a businessman.'

'You hold yourself like a military man,' came the reply, 'and of course the tie. I was a parachutist too, *il 9º Reggimento d'Assalto Paracadutisti.*'

Morgan looked impressed. '*Il Nono*, the Italian equivalent of the SAS.'

'Just for five months,' said Giuseppe, 'part of my national service.'

I was beginning to feel uncomfortable. Julia happily sipping frizzante with an effete Italian playboy was one thing, palling up to an all-action hero was another.

'And what do you do now?' I asked, perhaps a little sharply.

'Giuseppe's a policeman,' Julia responded admiringly. Fortunately I knew Julia well enough not to feel jealous. At least not very jealous. Her next words brought me up sharply. 'I went to see Giuseppe this morning about Bunny and Davoud's disappearance but something else has happened. Giuseppe's been investigating the murder of a tourist and he thinks it may be related.'

'The murder of a tourist? What can that have to do with Bunny?'

'Not with Mrs Sadeghi,' the Italian policeman put in, 'with Mr Sadeghi. We believe the man who was murdered last week was Iranian and I can tell you, Iranian tourists in Sicily are exceedingly rare. When another Iranian disappears out at sea at the same time, don't you think I'm right to consider that just possibly the two cases could be connected?'

VII

Morgan and I sat back expectantly to hear what Inspector Giuseppe Falzone had to say. It appeared that five days earlier the body of a middle-aged man had been discovered on wasteland here in Syracuse, in the west of the city. He had been shot once in the back of the head. As there was no indication that the body had been moved it appeared that the man had been killed where he was found, probably around midnight on the night before. There were no signs of any struggle. There were no documents on the body. The man was well dressed. All his clothing was French with the one exception of his underpants, which were Russian.

On the basis of the foreign clothing the police had started checking hotels in Syracuse and the surrounds. They eventually discovered that a guest was missing from a hotel very close to the Villa Politi where we were sitting. The guest's name was Farhad Jahandar and it was soon established that this was the dead man. He had checked in for a week two days before he died but on the day of his murder had announced that he would be leaving the next day.

The hotel staff could say very little about the man. He had given his nationality as French. The receptionist on duty when he checked in confirmed that he had been accompanied by another foreigner but the description of that man was annoyingly vague: well built, thirties or forties, dark hair. None of the hotel staff noticed Jahandar on the day he was killed and they could not

51

say what time he had left the hotel or whether he was with anyone. A double room had been booked for him three weeks before he arrived but the maid confirmed that he appeared to have slept alone. When asked if they remembered anything unusual, most of the staff on duty on the night Jahandar had been killed had been unhelpful. The night manager, however, seemed to be unusually observant, although it was not clear that what he observed meant anything. He recalled a guest he had never seen before coming into the hotel shortly after midnight. The same man had gone out again half an hour or so later. The manager gave another vague description: well built, late thirties or early forties, but this time with short light brown hair starting to thin out. 'Not an Italian,' insisted the manager who, it then transpired, had not only not seen the man before but had not seen him since.

'How do you know he was a guest?' he had been asked.

'Because he had a room key. He came in taking the key from his pocket and walked straight to the lift.'

Inspector Falzone had concluded that the killer had quite possibly removed the hotel key from the body and then used it to let himself into Jahandar's room. Certainly when the police searched the room they found nothing of interest: no papers of any kind. They discovered more French clothing but it was immediately obvious, Falzone insisted, that the man was not French. 'His clothes were ugly. He even had trousers in that awful stuff I think you English call crimplene.'

Julia tried to suppress a grin. Falzone must have noticed but I was not about to explain why the mention of crimplene caused a conspiratorial smile to pass between us.

Since discovering the name of their corpse the police seemed to have made very little progress. They had received confirmation from Paris that the dead man was born in Iran and had become a French citizen just two years earlier. He had no criminal record of any kind and his occupation was given as journalist. Other than that Julia's new friend Giuseppe had been able to discover virtually nothing. The French police had promised a further report but nothing had yet been received. His credit card details had been taken when he checked in and this was something else the French police had promised to follow up. The Italian security service, the SID, confirmed that Jahandar was unknown to them. Inspector Falzone had established that Jahandar had flown into Palermo from Paris eight hours before he checked into the hotel in Syracuse. How he had made the 150-mile journey across Sicily was still unknown. He had not hired a car so it was assumed someone had collected him from the airport, quite possibly the man who arrived at the hotel with him.

Nobody reported hearing a shot near the place where Jahandar's body had been found. A couple passing nearby shortly after midnight reported seeing a man walking away from the area. They had noticed him because, although not running, he seemed to be in a definite hurry, striding along quickly in the general direction of Jahandar's hotel. The description they gave was yet again so vague as to be practically useless. Tall, well built, perhaps in his forties, short hair of indeterminate colour. It had after all, they explained, been a very dark night.

Falzone had arranged for Jahandar's photo to appear in the local newspaper and be shown on the television news. As a result there had been a number of possible sightings reported but none led anywhere. One sighting the inspector considered definite was at lunchtime on the day he died. Jahandar had a leisurely lunch at a well-known and expensive fish restaurant but as he dined alone the sighting took the police no further forward.

'It is all most unsatisfactory,' Falzone concluded. 'Nobody has come forward to say that they knew this man even though we know that there is at least one man on this island who was well enough acquainted with our victim to have brought him to the hotel. It seems unlikely that he was here as a tourist, he had just cut short his stay at the hotel and booked himself on a flight back to Paris. If he was a journalist what was he investigating? Until we receive something more from Paris there is very little that my team can do.'

It did seem an incredible coincidence that misadventure should befall two Iranians in a tiny ancient city like Syracuse but we could see no way the two cases were linked. Falzone gave us copies of the dead man's photo but neither Morgan nor I recognised him. Morgan pocketed his copy and I hoped he would be sending it to the DG as soon as possible. Our conversation turned to Bunny and Davoud's disappearance.

'I'm going to be in the papers,' said Julia. 'Giuseppe arranged for me to meet a journalist from the local paper.'

'From *La Sicilia*,' put in Falzone. 'It's published in Catania and everyone reads it. It's a good story for them, beautiful woman desperate for news breaks off honeymoon in Rome to search for her missing aunt.'

It seemed to me the emphasis on 'beautiful' woman was unnecessary but he was right, it made a good headline and a photo of Julia would grab attention.

Morgan finished his drink and left and I was hoping Giuseppe Falzone might do the same but he had other ideas. After finishing the frizzante and making a quick phone call he insisted on showing us real Sicilian food and we found ourselves in a restaurant he obviously knew well. There was much backslapping and hugging before we could sit down. I was not surprised when our new friend ordered for us and was not at all disappointed when the food arrived.

By the time we had finished the main course, two bottles of Nero d'Avola red wine had disappeared and we had learned a lot about Sicily and Giuseppe, as he insisted we call him, had learned a lot about us. At times it felt like we were being interrogated. Where did we work, how had we met, why had we fallen in love, how had we met Morgan? He wanted to know all about Bunny and Davoud, asking Julia to recount her childhood memories of her aunt.

In return Giuseppe talked not about himself but about the island. His ability to redirect the conversation was disconcerting but at the same time the picture he gave of Sicilian life was every bit as colourful as Lampedusa's. When I asked if he was born in Syracuse he explained that he was from Ragusa about two hours away and launched into a description of the difference between the two places. People from Ragusa, it transpired, were the most honest in Sicily. When I asked about his parents he at first said nothing about them as individuals but rather described in detail his mother's cooking. She was from Naples not Sicily and you might imagine from the way he spoke that her cuisine was therefore as different as if she had come from China. He then compared her cooking with the food we were now eating, which he explained was not typical of this part of Sicily. The family who owned the restaurant came from a village near Palermo, the 'Arab' side of the island he said, not here on the 'Greek' side. As the Greeks arrived here well over two thousand years ago and the Arabs nearly a thousand years ago I found his characterisation of the island extraordinary. I came to realise that in Sicily everything is informed by history.

Among the few personal facts we managed to glean were that his parents had met when his father served in the *Carabinieri* in Naples. His father had then left the *Carabinieri* to return to Sicily and join the family business.

'Had you not thought of joining the *Carabinieri*?' I asked.

'No, I am a Sicilian. If I joined the *Carabinieri* I would have been posted somewhere else. That is the way the *Carabinieri* work.'

In answer to Julia's persistent questioning he told us he had come to Syracuse from Ragusa for unspecified family reasons, that he was unmarried and that he had acquired his flawless English from what he described as a 'young lady from Cheltenham' who had spent a year on the island. And, as he made a point of telling us, he was a detective not a run-of-the-mill policeman. As our plates were cleared away I discovered he was rather a good detective.

'I am confused,' he said, sipping at the sweet limoncello that the owner of the restaurant had just produced unbidden and which had apparently been made by his mother. 'And most of all I am confused by you two.' He turned to Julia.

'You are in love, which is clear. You are on your honeymoon. Your aunt disappears and you are upset, you are close to your aunt so you decide to come down to Sicily to see if you can find her. But your loving husband stays behind in Rome, that I find odd but then people are odd. But then he arrives but how does he get here? I know the time of the flights from Rome, if you came from Rome you certainly did not come here directly from the airport. So perhaps you stopped off to see the mysterious Mr Morgan, your friend who just happens to be a businessman working in Catania although his car has diplomatic licence plates. A very well-informed man, Mr Morgan. I mention the 9th Parachute Assault Regiment, *il 9° Reggimento d'Assalto Paracadutisti*, and despite me talking rapidly in Italian and despite the fact that Mr Morgan is clearly no linguist he knows right away that I am talking about *Il Nono*, and he knows just what that means. The truth is that Morgan is a British spy, and not a very good one. It has just taken me one phone call to discover that he is working at the American airbase at Sigonella.

'And you, Julia, do you contact the finance police who are coordinating the search or the Coast Guard? Do you perhaps try to contact the SID who are examining the wreckage to see if you can help identify anything? No, you say you did not, instead you come to see me. I am flattered. But the *Polizia di Stato* are not involved with this case. Your aunt disappeared at sea not here in Syracuse. The only part we have played is to collect some wreckage a fisherman reported to us and pass it on to the SID. Why is your first port of call the *Polizia Municipale* and then me? What's more, how did you know to visit the very police station to which the wreckage was first reported? Could it be that somebody told you to come here, somebody who has a reason for avoiding the other agencies? Somebody perhaps who knows I am investigating the death of Farhad Jahandar?

'Then I have a very strange thought. Perhaps you know what happened to your aunt. Perhaps in Syracuse you just want confirmation. You asked an awful lot of questions about the wreckage, dear Julia. You wanted to work out, I think, what happened to the boat. Did it hit something or did another vessel hit it? Could it have sprung a leak? Could a gas canister have exploded? Were there signs of fire? Well I can tell you what happened, the question is should I?'

He paused. 'If I tell you, who am I telling?'

'You are telling the niece of the woman on that yacht,' said Julia.

57

'Yes I am now sure of that. This afternoon I doubted it. But now yes, you really are who you say you are. You really are married to the man who sits beside you. And everything you say about your aunt is probably true. But there is still something you are not telling me. So let us trade. Tell me what you are hiding and I will tell you how your aunt was almost certainly murdered.'

VIII

There was a moment of silence.

When she spoke Julia's voice was hushed, almost gentle. 'You are sure, aren't you? Bunny is dead.'

Giuseppe Falzone replied in the same tone of voice. 'I am afraid I am. If your aunt was on board that boat when it exploded then she must have been killed.'

There was another silence as Julia made up her mind what to do, glancing across at me for support.

'We really are who we told you we are. Bunny is my aunt and we just want to find out what's happened to her. She's been missing for nearly a week; it was a week ago today that she left Sami. I realise the chances of finding her alive are remote. But murdered, that doesn't make any sense. Everything we've told you is true. The one thing we haven't mentioned because I really don't believe it is relevant is that my husband works in our Ministry of Defence. That's how he knows Morgan.'

He looked directly at me. 'And are you also a member of the Defence Intelligence Staff?'

I was shocked by the directness of the question and the knowledge it implied, just as the DG had been when Behzad mentioned the DIS. We are a small, specialist part of the Intelligence Establishment that even back in the UK hardly anyone has heard of. How did a provincial policeman in Sicily hear about us?

'Yes I am. I am an analyst. I review documents.'

'And yet you are important enough for the Royal Air Force to fly you down here.'

'My wife's uncle is important, not me, he pulled some strings.'

'Perhaps. Perhaps you are all spies, part of a family of spies and that has something to do with your aunt's death.'

'No,' insisted Julia. 'Bunny's death has nothing to do with anything like that. You said you would tell us how you think she died.'

Falzone was silent for a moment, as if still deciding if he should tell us what he knew. In fact, I realised he was deciding how to tell us, how much of the truth could Julia really bear to know. 'I examined the wreckage, what was left of it. Everything smashed. Fragments of metal embedded in the wood. Spirals of metal I have seen once before. It doesn't need specialist forensics. I'm sorry but only one thing can produce that sort of damage: a fragmentation grenade.'

I could sense Julia stiffen. She was thinking of Bunny; like me she knew what awful devastation such a grenade would cause. But it didn't make sense.

A fragmentation grenade at sea? In a small boat? If it had been thrown by someone inside the boat it would have been suicide, the assailant could not have survived. If it had been thrown from another boat they would have needed to be fifty yards away at least to avoid injuring themselves or protected by something pretty solid. I pictured a destroyer pulling alongside and releasing a hail of grenades. The idea seemed absurd.

Giuseppe Falzone was thinking along different lines. 'The question for me,' he said, 'is who would do such a thing? Who would want to kill a surgeon and his wife? What had they done to earn such enemies? Or was it an accident?'

'Accident! How could that be?'

'Well suppose this was not just a relaxing voyage in the sun. There are plenty of people in Italy who would pay for weapons: pistols, rifles, grenades, anything. If the missing yacht was being used to smuggle weapons someone might have been careless.'

'That's ridiculous,' responded Julia angrily. 'Let's get one thing clear. If you are right about the grenade this has nothing to with Bunny and Davoud. They are not criminals, they are not political, they are not anything that would make them a target. It must be a case of mistaken identity.'

She was right but the question was: whose identity? Was the *Mahsheed* mistaken for another boat altogether or was somebody else expected to be on board? Was Behzad the intended target – and not Bunny or Davoud?

Giuseppe seemed to accept Julia's answers. I wanted to think over what he had told us but neither he nor Julia showed any sign of wanting the evening to end. Instead they reverted to the subject of Farhad Jahandar. Giuseppe again asked if we were certain that we had never heard Behzad mention that name. No we had not. I was becoming mildly irritated by the Italian policeman. The lack of progress in his investigation seemed to me to reflect the pace of life in Sicily which seemed to extend to the Italian police. I remembered that the police, *Carabinieri* and SID had just a handful of possible suspects to investigate for the espionage at Sigonella but seemed to have spent weeks getting nowhere.

'Police work in Italy must be difficult operating with so many different police agencies,' I suggested. 'Morgan tried to explain the roles of the *Carabinieri* and the SID, the *Polizia Municipale* and the *Guardia di Finanza* and all the rest. The bureaucracy must be frustrating for you.'

Giuseppe merely raised an eyebrow. 'I am sure it is the same everywhere. You have the famous MI5. Are there not also an MI1, 2, 3 and 4?'

'No there are not.'

'But there is an MI6,' Julia put in unhelpfully. 'They work overseas while MI5 works at home.'

'And what does MI stand for?'

'The letters stand for military intelligence,' Julia told him, 'but neither are part of the military now.'

'But is there still a military intelligence in Britain?'

It was my turn to respond.

'That's us now, the DIS. The Army, Navy and Air Force all used to have their own intelligence arms but they were merged together ten or twelve years ago to form the DIS.'

Giuseppe nodded. 'And my friend from Cheltenham told me that there is a secret intelligence agency there which nobody is supposed to know about.'

'That's GCHQ and it's not a secret any more.' The year before a left-wing journalist had written an article for *Time Out* that lifted the lid on one of the few remaining secrets in the supposedly closed world of British Intelligence.

'And I understand the police in England also have their own intelligence agency, the Special Branch. The bureaucracy must be frustrating for you.'

He smiled innocently and when Julia grinned in support I had to raise my glass in defeat. Perhaps Intelligence everywhere is a mass of competing fiefdoms.

Giuseppe moved on. 'We have left-wing journalists here as well,' he mused. 'You heard about the Borghese conspiracy.'

I nodded. 'The supposed fascist coup a couple of years ago.'

'The failed fascist coup,' he corrected. 'That was uncovered not by the SID but by journalists on the old Communist rag *Paese Sera*. Perhaps we should discuss that another day.' He rose from his seat and shook my hand rather formally. 'Tomorrow you should perhaps talk to your friend Mr Morgan again. I wonder if he is interested in fragmentation grenades. And perhaps he has been able to learn something more about my dead body, Farhad Jahandar.'

He then turned to Julia. 'There are some people I want to talk to in the morning, I would like you to accompany me. Shall we say nine o'clock?' He spoke with a smile but his words sounded like an order.

Our room on the second floor looked out towards the sea. Directly in front of us were the remains of an ancient limestone quarry, perhaps 500 yards in diameter and nearly as deep. The countess had made it into a major feature of her Villa's grounds. She had ordered cartloads of soil to be sprinkled over the base of the quarry so that it was now a mass of green bushes and at one side trees with oranges hanging heavily. Before going to bed Julia insisted that we go downstairs again and out on to the front drive. Leading from the driveway was a promontory of rock left jutting into the quarry and on that Maria Teresa Laudien Politi now sat captured in stone for posterity, book in hand. The sculptor had caught a wistful, youthful beauty in her downcast eyes. The moonlight highlighted the folds of her dress and the shadows it cast on her face revealed an expression of pure serenity. It was possible to imagine the countess sitting here a hundred years earlier smiling happily at the life she had created for herself. That was obviously the picture Julia wanted to conjure up for us. Morgan, however, had told me on the way down from Sigonella about another famous feature of the hotel. As a consequence I suspected that the promontory on which we now stood hand-in-hand was originally intended not to encourage honeymoon thoughts of romance but for something far more brutal. Here no doubt the overseers had stood looking down as 7000 Athenian prisoners of war had been worked to death hacking out the quarry in 425 BC. The disturbing thought of how Bunny and her husband had died remained with us as we returned to our room.

Giuseppe arrived promptly at 9.00 the next morning and he and Julia left me to my own devices. I phoned the DG in London. He was already in the office and I told him about Giuseppe's suspicion that a fragmentation grenade had exploded on the *Mahsheed*. He didn't respond immediately and I wondered if he had put the phone down. When he finally spoke his voice had a note of resignation, as if he had just given up hope of finding his sister alive. 'They must have been after Behzad who they thought was on the yacht,' he said, 'but who are they?' There was another silence.

'Morgan told me about Farhad Jahandar. I've never heard of him but I'm getting his name checked. It's too much coincidence that two Iranians are killed within hours of each other. Something is very wrong here. If the Shah's people were involved the Americans would have known but we're getting nothing from them. I spoke to Stansfield himself and he assured me they are not involved. And we're getting nothing from anyone else. If an Italian policeman can recognise grenade damage why have SID forensics still not produced anything? Why can't the Canadians produce something on Ramone? We gave them an address; we don't even know if it's real. I'll phone Ottawa myself when they wake up.'

I left him no wiser. The DG must have used all his personal influence for Stansfield Turner, the new head of the CIA, to take time out from turning the Agency upside down to talk to him about his missing sister. He was pulling every string he could but clearly to no avail.

I then tried to phone Morgan without success and left a message asking him to call me at the hotel. I toyed with the idea of driving Julia's hire car up to Sigonella to find Morgan. Instead I sat at the bow window of what the hotel called its music room. I was alone except for an ageing waiter with a perfectly upright body but perpetually bowed head, as if a lifetime of being obsequious had caused a permanent deformity to his neck. He appeared to have nothing to do and was happy to spend time telling me all about Winston Churchill, who had stayed at the hotel after resigning in 1955. He had apparently sat peacefully painting at this very spot. I wondered what Behzad would have made of that, given his conviction that Churchill shouldered the blame for the very existence of the hated Shah's regime.

The same waiter reappeared to announce that there was a phone call for me. It was the DG again. He was in sombre mood.

'The Italians think they have found Bunny's body,' he said. 'A frigate is taking it into Augusta and I want you to go there. Don't take Julia.' He paused. 'They can't be sure it's Bunny, the head is missing.' He was clearly having difficulty speaking but continued in his usual methodical way. 'Morgan will be there. He will have all the papers you need to ensure the Italians let you into their base. They won't allow you to send the body home yet, they need to do an autopsy. I want to know how she died, anything you can find out let me know right away.'

He put the phone down and I was left imagining what he must be feeling. The Grimspounds were a close-knit family. Losing a sister was bound to be painful but losing her like this seemed barbaric. I considered trying to send a message to Julia but decided to wait until I could confirm that this really was Bunny and could break the news to my wife in person.

I took the keys of Julia's hire car and drove north. Augusta, one of the best natural harbours in Italy, is about halfway between Syracuse and Catania. It was an important naval base before the war and during the war had been heavily bombed. The Royal Navy took it over after the invasion of Sicily, then in 1949 an oil refinery was built, followed in the fifties and sixties by all sorts of gas and chemical plants, heavy engineering and a massive power station. The result was an unappealing industrial jungle surrounding the port where the Italian frigate had just docked. I followed the signs for the *Marina Militare* and arrived to find Morgan waiting inside the gate.

Morgan led me into a shed containing various pieces of marine equipment and then into a room at the side. Bunny was lying under a sheet on a table in the middle of the room. Beside the table stood two uniformed Italians. The first was a naval captain who came forward and shook my hand.

'I am so sorry,' he said, in English. 'Are you sure you want to see what is here?'

I nodded and he removed the sheet. The body underneath was missing not just the head but the left shoulder and arm. It occurred to me that I could identify Bunny neither from her face nor her rings and was shocked that such a callous thought could come into my mind. There were still some clothes on the body although they were largely in shreds. There had clearly been a massive explosion.

The Italian naval captain was following my chain of thoughts. 'This was no accident,' he said. 'There is no possibility that a collision or fire caused this death. And there is one other thing.' He pointed at a wound at the top of the right leg. 'I think that is a bullet hole.'

'No doubt at all,' said Morgan.

'We are passing the matter to the *Carabinieri*, they will be in charge now,' said the captain. He turned towards the *Carabinieri* officer beside him who nodded and, after introducing himself in Italian, replaced the sheet.

There was really nothing more that Morgan and I could do.

'I need a drink,' I said as we stepped outside but decided that if I was going to drive back to Syracuse and break the news to Julia it had better be no more than an espresso. We found a café near the medieval fort that overlooked Augusta and I slumped into a seat. I had not known Bunny very well and had already reconciled myself to the fact that she was probably dead but nevertheless seeing her laid out in that way had been a physical shock. It was not something I ever wanted to see again.

'What now?' asked Morgan.

'I'll go back to Syracuse – hopefully Julia will be back. Could you call the DG?'

'Of course. There's something else I should tell you. I saw Romney this morning and asked him what he knew about an operation called Tortellini. He replied that he had never heard of it but I wasn't sure that I believed him. I then asked about whether he had ever heard the name Ramone. He really did look shocked. I can't imagine how he became so senior in the Company if he is so incapable of hiding his feelings. Anyway he again insisted that he had never heard the name Ramone but this time I was quite sure he was lying. He wanted to know where I had heard the names.'

'What did you say?'

'I told him the truth. That the DG had asked me if I had come across either name, Tortellini or Ramone. I don't think he believed me any more than I believed him. He kept asking if the DG had said anything else, what the context had been. He said he would ask around but that if I could provide more information that would help.'

I wasn't surprised that Romney might know more about Tortellini than he let on, but that he should react to the stranger who visited Behzad was unexpected. Had the Americans been keeping Behzad under surveillance in Kefalonia? It seemed highly unlikely. They had other priorities. But somehow they had known about my visit to the island.

'How's the hunt for the Russian mole going?' I asked.

'Of course I should have told you about that as well. There's been great excitement at Sigonella, with Romney running all over the place. There's a KGB man by the name of Yevgeny Kapustin on the island. One of their trade officials at the Embassy in Rome, who we had tagged as probable KGB, flew down to Palermo and then disappeared from sight. He travelled on his diplomatic papers which is how the SID picked up the flight, but by the time they did that he had already gone to ground. That was two days before the DG's sister set off from Greece. We have no idea what he's been doing here. Romney's getting the man's photo sent down from Rome.'

That was real news and gave a new urgency to the work Morgan had been sent down here to do, although I couldn't see that it had any bearing on Bunny's death.

'Other than Kapustin's sudden appearance the mole hunt is going absolutely nowhere,' Morgan continued. 'The Company have had the FBI crawl over the backgrounds of the Americans on the suspect list and nothing at all has come up. There's not even a whisper of suspicion. The SID have done the same for the locals with the same result, although I think Romney still believes that is where the leak must be. They are talking about sending all the Americans home and moving the suspect locals off the base. That would stop any more leaks from here at least but make it near impossible to find the mole.'

IX

As I arrived back at the hotel Inspector Falzone was just dropping Julia off. 'See you tomorrow Giuseppe,' I heard Julia say with a smile as he drove away. Julia turned and as she saw me I'd like to think her smile increased. Unfortunately the smile would not last long.

'I have news for you,' she said.

'And I have news for you as well,' I replied. 'We had better go inside.'

She cast me a puzzled look and we said nothing more until we had reached our room.

I then told her about the DG's call this morning and my trip to the naval base at Augusta. She insisted on hearing the details but took the news remarkably well.

'I knew there was no chance of finding Bunny alive. At least now the family can have a proper burial. Perhaps Davoud will be found as well.' She walked over to the window and stood looking out for a few moments. 'I must speak to Uncle Gordon.'

It took some time to reach him and after that call was over she looked more upset than she had been before. 'He's taking it really badly,' she said. 'They were very close.'

'As you were,' I said.

'That's true but, as Bunny would have said, life must go on. Let me tell you my news and then we should drink a large gin and tonic to her memory.'

She opened a bottle of mineral water and sipped it absent-mindedly.

'Giuseppe and I spent almost all day talking to fishermen and visiting the bars and cafés around the dock. Nobody said anything. I thought this was the usual response to a visit from the police but Giuseppe said it was something more. Some of the people had seen the article in *La Sicilia* this morning and were clearly sympathetic to me, which is why Giuseppe wanted me along, but still they had nothing to say. To Giuseppe it was what he called *omertà*.'

I knew the word, the film *The Godfather* was still fresh in my memory. *Omertà* meant silence and was a term I immediately associated with the Mafia.

'Are you suggesting the Mafia are involved in Bunny's death?' I asked incredulously.

'Well, that has to be possible,' Julia said. 'Giuseppe doesn't want to believe it. He says that the Mafia have always been part of life in the western side of Sicily but here in the east the influence of the Mafia is relatively new. From the way Giuseppe talks you would think everyone in Sicily is corrupt. It seems the Mafia own some of the big construction companies and totally control industries like road building and refuse collection. But they haven't been interested in small-scale operations like fishing. His worry is that because the Mafia are now so heavily into drug smuggling there may now be some connection with the fishermen here. He's gone off to talk to the *Guardia di Finanza* and the *Carabinieri*. He says there isn't a major drugs problem in Syracuse. But who knows?

'Anyway I haven't finished my story. We were getting absolutely nowhere when we crossed over the bridge into Ortygia which is the old city, really run down now, and started talking to people there. It was the same *omertà* until Giuseppe approached an old woman standing outside her doorway. I am not sure she really understood what we were asking, she seemed to think we were enquiring about an ambulance that had been in the port three days ago. That was on the day we think Bunny and Davoud's boat was attacked. The woman told us that a fishing boat had come in with injured men on board. She was upset that they had had to wait a very long time for the ambulance to arrive.

'We tried to find out which fishing boat she had seen but all she could say is that it wasn't from here. She was able to tell us where the boat had been docked while it was waiting for the ambulance to arrive. We had visited a bar right there earlier and learned nothing. Now, when we went back again Giuseppe played the hard man. He threatened to drag everyone in the area down to the police station and eventually managed to piece together what appears to have happened last Thursday.

'It seems that a fishing boat arrived that was badly damaged and had two wounded men on board, one quite badly injured. Nobody would say anything at all about these two men which made Giuseppe think the unthinkable: that they really might have been gangsters of some kind. Nor would anyone say much about the boat's owner. He had stayed on the boat when the man who was least injured rushed ashore and phoned for an ambulance. That man had only minor injuries to his arm. The other man was laid out on the deck and what Giuseppe found incredible is that apparently nobody went to offer any assistance. He says that in a community like Sicily the only reason that people would not rush to help a badly injured man is fear.

'Eventually an ambulance appeared and the two injured men left, one of them being carried from the boat on a stretcher. The fishing boat, despite being quite badly damaged, also left. We couldn't get a name for the fisherman but eventually somebody whispered that he came from Marzamemi down the coast. Giuseppe and I are going there tomorrow morning.'

I shook my head. I simply could not believe that the Mafia would be involved or that Bunny and Davoud could have anything to do with drug smuggling. I told her about the mysterious Russian spy who had appeared in Sicily and then disappeared. This was becoming totally surreal. None of it made sense.

I phoned Morgan and told him what Julia had discovered but he was as mystified as I was.

'I'm still trying to accept that somebody is using fragmentation grenades,' Morgan mused, 'even though I saw the evidence right there on the slab in Augusta. But who? There is so much Second World War ordnance floating around in Sicily that anybody could have got hold of something like that, although I really can't see why you would want to. Start throwing those sorts of things at anyone and you'll really get a war going. Incidentally the SID have now come back and confirmed that judging by the wreckage they found the damage to the boat was indeed caused by a fragmentation grenade. I don't know what took them so long. I have been promised that the report from the autopsy on Bunny's body will be ready tomorrow.'

No sooner had I finished speaking to Morgan than Janet, the DG's assistant, phoned. When she put him through the DG came straight to the point. 'Farhad Jahandar was Moscow's man. After I went over his head Ffortiscue sent me their file. Jahandar's a born and bred Communist who's been floating around the Iranian exile community in Paris for years. Behzad must have come across him.

'Jahandar's file goes right back to Operation Boot, the MI6 attempt to organise a coup in Iran in the early fifties. Boot was taken over by the Americans to become Operation Ajax which Behzad told you all about. The parallels between Jahandar and Behzad are uncanny, it can't be a coincidence. After the Second World War Iranians had to choose sides and both Davoud and Behzad's father and Jahandar's father chose losing sides. Davoud's father went with the liberals. Jahandar's chose the Tudeh, the Communists.' He stopped for a moment and seemed to be casting his mind back thirty years, trying to imagine a world in which wealthy young men in Britain as well as Iran could decide that the future lay with a bloodthirsty tyrant in Moscow.

'Stalin had manufactured an image of himself as the great liberator, the man who had defeated the Nazis. Some people in Iran thought he would stop the British and Americans taking their oil. Of course it was nonsense. At the same time that things were collapsing in Iran Stalin was using his tanks to put down a popular uprising in East Germany. But men like Jahandar's father didn't want to see that. They wanted to believe the Communist propaganda. Just like Philby, Burgess and Maclean and all the others here.

'The Tudeh had widespread support within Iran. Communist officers in the military formed their own network, the TPMO. Some people think they were getting ready to stage a coup of their own but Allen Dulles and Kermit Roosevelt pre-empted them. Once the CIA put him back in power the Shah had the TPMO rounded up. Jahandar's father was one of their leaders but when the proverbial hit the fan he wasn't there. General Jahandar was in Moscow with his family. He never went back to Iran and died in 1956. His son Farhad was brought up in Russia.

'Farhad spent fourteen years under the tutelage of the KGB. They made him. Ten years ago he moved to Paris. First as a correspondent for the Soviet News Agency TASS, then as a freelancer. He wrote for various left-wing journals around the world. We think that the KGB were using him to keep tabs on various exile groups. He wasn't a spy, everyone knew where his allegiances lay, more a conduit, a fixer. He helped people who wanted favours from Moscow but didn't want to be seen asking for them. He became an unofficial channel, a messenger, someone with his ear to the ground. He must have remained on the Russian payroll because he couldn't have been living on his earnings from journalism.'

'I suppose it's possible,' I suggested, 'that he had nothing to do with Bunny's disappearance. If he's a KGB man he could be here to handle the spy they seem to have in the American base at Sigonella.'

'Perhaps, but as your Italian policeman says, it's one hell of a coincidence for two unconnected Iranian exiles to be murdered at the same time in the same place. If Jahandar is connected with Sigonella, who killed him? The Americans? Harry Bastamente wouldn't hesitate for a minute if he thought it suited American interests but it doesn't. Bastamente wants to catch the mole in that base, if he thought Jahandar might lead him in that direction he would have kept him alive.

'No, if the Russians are trying to help their asset in Sigonella then there's a better bet: that Russian diplomat who's turned up in Sicily, Yevgeny Kapustin. We've also got more on him. He's certainly KGB, one of their hard men, brawn as much as brain. We think he started out in Kaskad, one of the KGB Special Forces units. After that he spent six years in Berlin and Dresden in some sort of role with the East German Stasi. Then back to Moscow and briefly Prague. This is the first assignment we know about in the West. He's been posted to Rome with his wife which means he's trusted and senior. Ffortiscue thinks he may be responsible for security at their Embassy.

'The truth is we have no idea what either he or Jahandar were doing in Sicily but again it's too much of a coincidence to think they aren't connected. Two KGB assets turning up in the same place at the same time.'

I tried to find an underlying logic in what the DG was saying but that only seemed to lead to one conclusion. 'So we're saying it's too much of a coincidence to think that Bunny's brother-in-law Behzad Sadeghi and Farhad Jahandar are not connected and too much of a coincidence to think Jahandar and this Russian Kapustin are not connected and too much of a coincidence to think that Kapustin is not connected to the Russian mole in Sigonella. Doesn't it follow then that Bunny's disappearance is somehow linked to the Sigonella spy?'

I could almost feel the DG shaking his head on the other end of the line. 'That just doesn't make sense. Bunny and Davoud were on holiday, there's just no way they could be connected to Russian spies. It all comes down to what Jahandar was doing in Syracuse. I bet Behzad could tell us that. Politically the two of them were miles apart but surely they must have known each other, even if not very well. The world of politically active Iranian exiles in Paris can't be that big.'

I wondered if the DG was just seeing what he wanted to see. The implication of what he was saying was obvious. If one Iranian dissident was murdered at almost exactly the same time as the yacht of another dissident was blown up the chances were that whoever had attacked the boat had been targeting Iranian dissidents not a London surgeon and his wife. Behzad was the real target, the DG's sister just happened to be in the wrong place. The one conclusion he could not accept was that somehow Bunny and Davoud had brought the attack on themselves.

When the call was over Julia and I were left with the feeling that we must have missed something in Kefalonia. The DG was surely right that Behzad undoubtedly knew far more than he was willing to admit. And now we were left feeling we ought to be doing something here in Sicily but knowing that there was nothing practical we could do.

We tried to clear our heads by strolling through the town but the same thoughts kept churning in our minds. The cool limestone buildings with their basalt steps and careful shading spoke of another less hurried age. We crossed the bridge into Ortygia and Julia showed me where she and Giuseppe had been that morning. We reached the Duomo, the impressive eighteenth-century cathedral. Like so much in Sicily first appearances were deceptive, the pillars of what looked like a typical baroque fantasy were actually Greek and probably two and a half thousand years old and the interior was laid out by the Normans a mere seven centuries ago. Julia wanted to see the Caravaggio hanging in the Church of Santa Lucia alla Badia almost next to the Duomo. The painting, *The Burial of St Lucia*, was not, Julia concluded, one of Caravaggio's finest. The sombre browns that dominated the canvas did nothing to raise our spirits. The calm of the interior of the church had at first seemed welcoming but the Stations of the Cross with their images of the tortured Christ inevitably reminded us of Bunny's broken body. By now it was nearly six o'clock. Although the July sun was still beating down the evening was approaching.

'Let's have an early dinner and then go to bed,' said Julia. 'After all, we are on our honeymoon.'

Never, I thought, had such romantic words been spoken with such little enthusiasm.

X

Our spirits were raised a little by another amazing Sicilian meal. Pasta with an aubergine and tomato sauce followed by mussels removed from their shells, wrapped in lemon leaves and then grilled. The pasta was a type I didn't know although the name was familiar. It had been rolled into S-shaped lengths about the same size as penne: casarecce. I wondered why the Americans had called their spy network after such an insignificant item, at least tortellini had something inside it. Perhaps they just happened to be Harry Bastamente's favourite dishes.

'It is amazing how the world moves on,' said Julia. 'Here we are talking about different types of pasta when just twenty years ago the BBC ran the famous April Fools' Day news story about the success of that year's spaghetti harvest.'

'Yes, and people phoned up to ask where they could buy a spaghetti tree for their garden.'

We gave each other a superior smile and raised our glasses. The wine was local and mediocre but that did nothing to dampen our appreciation of the food and I was looking forward to bed when we arrived back at the hotel. As we crossed the reception, however, a man not much older than me approached. He was dressed casually in jeans and T-shirt, not the attire the Grand Hotel Villa Politi encouraged; I noticed the ageing waiter with the permanently bowed head was frowning in disapproval. He obviously took exception to hippy types but this man was clearly no hippy. His hair was cut alarmingly short and his jeans and T-shirt were spotless. In his hand he clutched a copy of *La Sicilia* with the picture of Julia uppermost. When he spoke it was with a strong American accent.

'May I speak to you ma'am?'

'Of course,' replied Julia, curiosity mixing with caution.

Checking that I was following her she led the way back to where the man had been seated, waiting for us. The three of us sat down. Without any sort of introduction the stranger started talking.

'I saw the article in *La Sicilia* about the disappearance of your aunt and the *Mahsheed*. I don't know if this helps but there is something you should know. The paper says that nobody knows what happened to the boat or even where it happened. But they do. The US Navy knows. They tracked that boat all the way from Greece. There were two planes up all the time maintaining surveillance. They knew that it had almost reached Syracuse but they let people believe it was much further north. They reported that a US destroyer had heard an explosion somewhere up there but there was no US destroyer in that area. You should find out why they were tracking the boat.'

He spoke in short disjointed sentences as if repeating words he had rehearsed over and over. Now it seemed the speech had been delivered and our visitor started to rise out of his seat as if he were going to leave.

'Wait,' said Julia. 'Who are you? How do you know this? Can't you at least tell me your name? How do I know if I can believe you? How do I find out if you're telling the truth?'

'Go up to the base at Sigonella and ask for Jack Romney or Harry Bastamente. They can tell you. I can't tell you anything. I don't know what's happening. All I know is that the planes were up, two P-3 Orions, and I know they reported back to Romney and Bastamente on the progress of that boat. They used the code word Tortellini.'

He got up again; he was plainly keen to move on quickly. 'I am an honourable man; I always have been. When I see something that stinks I have to do something about it. But I must go now. Please don't try to find me. I don't want to be involved but something nasty is going on here and you have a right to know.' With that he walked out of the hotel.

'What was that all about?' I asked.

'No idea,' said Julia. 'Who is he? That was an odd phrase, an honourable man. He looked like an American serviceman.'

'That's what I thought.'

'And he had the sort of detail only a military man would have, like the type of plane he says was watching Bunny's boat.'

'There's one thing that's odd though. I noticed him when we came in, he was sitting there reading the paper.'

'What's odd about that?' Julia asked but then answered her own question. 'I see what you mean. How many American servicemen understand enough Italian to read a newspaper?'

'And how many are interested enough in what's happening in Sicily in the first place to go out and buy the local paper?'

I jumped to my feet. I was irritated with myself. I should have followed the man right away then I might at least have seen what sort of car he was driving. Now he would almost certainly be out of sight.

He wasn't. He was standing at the bottom of the drive, about 100 yards away, talking to a tall, grey-haired man. As I watched the older man put his arm around our visitor's shoulder and guided him into the back seat of a large black car that had clearly been waiting in the street outside and had drawn up beside them. The older man then climbed into the car himself and both were driven away.

I returned to where Julia was still sitting puzzling over what the man had told us. When I described what I had just seen she looked even more confused, as was I.

If our visitor's story was true then both Bastamente and Ffortiscue had been lying to us back in the meeting at Heathrow. The CIA were running something called Tortellini, MI6 knew enough to open a file on it and whatever it was it involved tracking Bunny and Davoud across the Ionian Sea. But was the man's story true?

'That depends on who he is,' said Julia. 'I don't believe a kind-hearted American sailor, who happens to be linguistically gifted, just saw my picture and decided to come and tell me things that must be covered by whatever the Americans call their Official Secrets Act.'

'The 1917 Espionage Act.'

Julia smiled weakly. 'Trust you, Mr Know-it-all, but that was not the point I was making. I was asking a rhetorical question.'

She looked serious again, so I thought it best not to point out that she had not actually been asking a question. Julia continued. 'Let's assume he is American, he is a serviceman and he didn't come here out of the goodness of his heart. Who would send him? Presumably whoever met him when he left here. The ONI?'

Morgan had mentioned that the US Office of Naval Intelligence had a team at the base and that they didn't get on with Romney. Was the CIA up to something the ONI wanted to stop? The suggestion was faintly ridiculous. Even if there was some sort of demarcation dispute going on between the two organisations what would they gain by involving us? Nothing at all.

With some difficulty we managed to get through to the DG in London and I described the evening's events. He was as perplexed as we were by our mysterious visitor but seemed less surprised by the story the man had told us.

'It has the ring of truth about it. The Americans were tracking that yacht and MI6 knew. But why? Something to do with drug smuggling perhaps, but if it had been that I'm sure Stansfield Turner would have told me. He's only been there a few months but everyone agrees he's straight as a die. Why would he risk alienating one of America's closest allies by lying to me about something with no national security implications? We're all on the same side when it comes to the drugs trade. But we're obviously not all on the same side when it comes to Tortellini. Think about that. There's some sort of project or operation out there code-named Tortellini. We haven't been told anything about it but Six clearly know what it's about because you saw that Ffortiscue had a Tortellini file. Judging by Romney's reaction when Morgan mentioned the name to him it's not a secret to the Americans. And your visitor tonight seems to confirm that. We appear to be the only people not in the loop. Now why is that? Why are Six and the Company so keen to stop us finding out anything at all about Tortellini? It can't be just a case of "need to know". There has to be more to it and there's only one explanation I can think of. It's about me.'

I was starting to understand where the DG was heading. 'It's not that Ffortiscue and Bastamente don't want the DIS to know what's going on,' he continued. 'It's that they don't want me personally to know. And that has to be because something or someone connected with me is involved.'

'Behzad Sadeghi.'

'That's right. Either Behzad himself is doing something that's been code-named Tortellini or someone else is doing something that's been labelled Tortellini and it will affect Behzad. Perhaps the Iranians really are after him. Or he's become involved in something the Americans are planning. Or the Russians. Or even us, MI6. Somebody somewhere out there is running an operation with Behzad at its core and Bastamente and Ffortiscue believe that if I find out I might tell Behzad.'

The DG paused before saying as much to himself as to me, 'Behzad is the key. If only we could find out more about his mysterious visitor, Henry Ramone. The Canadians must be able to find out something about him.'

'If that's his real name.'

'True. We have to do something, Thomas. I think we need to rock the boat. Go and see Jack Romney. Tell him we know Tortellini involved tracking Behzad's boat. Tell him our Navy says there was no US destroyer where we were told it was. And try to get access to the records of US servicemen at Sigonella. If your visitor really was someone from the base, and I very much doubt that he was, we need to find him before Romney twigs that he has a conscientious objector in his ranks. But I do think it's more likely that someone is playing silly buggers.'

'The Russians?'

'Possibly, but what have they to gain? Why would they want to draw attention to Sigonella if they have a man on the inside?'

Nothing made sense. The idea that the Russians were connected to Bunny's death seemed crazy but somehow the idea that the Mafia and the drugs trade might be involved was even more absurd. After the DG phoned off I turned to Julia.

'Come on, let's have a nightcap in the bar and then up to bed. You can tell me how sad you were to spend the morning without me and with an ugly Italian policeman instead.'

Julia laughed and when we went back to our room demonstrated where her affections lay. But as we lay silently afterwards I knew she was thinking about Bunny, as was I. The sight of that mangled body on the table in Augusta would stay with me for a very long time.

XI

The immaculately dressed Inspector Falzone arrived promptly next morning and departed with Julia in a police car for Marzamemi. Over breakfast we had again tried to make sense of events with no success. As Julia later told me she had continued to puzzle over them on the drive south. The people she and Giuseppe had spoken to the previous day were clearly frightened. Since the film of *The Godfather* had been released in 1972 the whole world knew what happened when anyone crossed the Mafia but she didn't get the impression that anyone yesterday had been directly threatened. There were no burly gangsters loitering nearby, nobody in a shiny suit sitting out of place amongst the fishermen. And yet she had felt fear. She and Giuseppe had been resented but they were not feared. The silence they faced, what Giuseppe described as *omertà*, sprang not from fear of the police but from fear that someone would see them talking to the police.

When Giuseppe had finally broken through and learned about the boat from Marzamemi it had not been because witnesses suddenly decided that they should be more scared of Giuseppe's threats than of anyone else's. It was because people realised we already knew about the men who had disappeared with the ambulance. It was only then that anyone mentioned Marzamemi. Julia suspected that one thing they were not going to find in Marzamemi was the Mafia; their informants knew the man in the boat and were confident that they had no need to be scared of him.

Something else struck her. 'You know,' she said, thinking aloud, 'we were not the first ones to be asking questions in the docks. Nobody yesterday was surprised by our questions.'

Giuseppe seemed unsure. 'Is that just feminine intuition or did someone say something?'

Julia smiled. 'Perhaps just intuition, but that doesn't make it untrue. Someone had been there before us.'

She returned to her earlier thoughts. 'This may be naïve but something puzzles me. Everyone appears to know who the Mafia are, the papers even name the Mafia bosses, the Mafiosi, and yet they still seem to be able to carry on unmolested. Is nobody trying to destroy the organisation once and for all?'

Now it was Giuseppe's turn to smile. 'Leaving aside the fact that the Mafia is not an organisation, it is a collection of warring clans, people have tried to destroy them. But it is not as simple as it would be in a quiet English village. Let me tell you a very famous story. I think it could have some relevance to our investigations today.'

'Intriguing, go on,' encouraged Julia.

'There is a town in the mountains south of Palermo called Piana dei Greci. A century or so ago the whole area was a political hotbed with peasants rebelling violently against their landlords. It was known at one time as Piana la Rossa, or Red Piana. The socialists won control of the local council despite the landlords paying a local Mafioso called Cuccia to murder two of their leaders, indeed they won every seat. That, I think, was in 1914. Then one day all the councillors resigned and they resigned for one simple reason: the Mafia had threatened to kill every single one of them and nobody doubted that they meant it. In the next elections no socialists stood and Cuccia became mayor.'

'And nobody did anything?' asked Julia, incredulously.

'I'm just coming to that. Not only did nobody do anything but Cuccia was congratulated on getting rid of the socialists. The king, Vittorio Emanuele III, visited Piana dei Greci and personally presented Cuccia with one of our country's highest medals.'

'But that's awful!'

'Wait, I haven't got to the point of my story yet. A few years later the Prime Minister of Italy also visited Piana dei Greci. Cuccia laid on a magnificent feast as he had for the king but the circumstances were a little different. The prime minister was a man you may have heard of: Benito Mussolini.'

'Of course I have heard of him,' said Julia a little sharply.

Giuseppe smiled again; he was enjoying his story. 'Mussolini arrived with his usual bodyguard of fascist thugs as well as a contingent of police. Cuccia was not impressed. "Why do you need all those men?" he asked. "This is my town; I provide protection here." He couldn't have said anything more stupid. Mussolini was about to appoint himself Il Duce, the new Roman emperor, and a petty provincial gangster makes a remark like that. Mussolini reacted furiously and Cuccia then made matters even worse. To show who was boss he cleared the town square where Mussolini was due to speak. Mussolini never forgot the insult and when he took total control of the state he gave orders that the Mafia be smashed. Thousands of police and *Carabinieri* and fascist vigilantes set to work. More than ten thousand men were thrown into jail. Their property was confiscated, many were tortured. It seemed to work. The big names like Gambino emigrated to the United States. The protection rackets ceased. The murder rate declined dramatically. Civilised life returned.'

'Success! Marvellous. Then what happened?'

'You arrived, well you and the Americans in 1943. The British landed here in south-eastern Sicily and had to fight their way north. The Americans wanted a smoother passage when they arrived further west, they wanted the Italian troops facing them to melt away. And they did, thanks to the Mafia. The Americans released Mafia leaders from prison in the United States and brought them to Sicily. After the war the Allies controlled the island and they were determined to root out all the fascists. So they looked for people who could show that they had never been allied with the fascists and installed them as mayors and councillors. And who do you think had the strongest anti-fascist credentials? Why of course the Mafia. And they are still there, thirty years later.'

They continued in silence. The sun was blazing down, it was going to be another very hot day.

Like fishing villages all over Europe, Marzamemi was in a period of transition, its character undergoing fundamental change without anyone understanding where the change would lead. The tuna factory which had dominated village life as much as the church had closed but the tourists with their seafront restaurants had yet to appear. The working fishing boats still outnumbered the motor boats and yachts that one day would cram into the new marina on the southern side of the harbour.

On the narrow beach which formed one side of the harbour of Marzamemi a couple of fishing boats were drawn up near some crude wooden sheds. A road bordered the beach and across it stood a few one and two storey official-looking buildings, home presumably to the bureaucrats who attach themselves to every sign of human enterprise. At right angles to the beach a long quay, dominated by the old tuna factory, pointed eastwards out to sea. Harbour walls provided protection for boats unloading their catch. The village itself lay behind the tuna factory and the fish market. Julia remarked that it reminded her of John Steinbeck's *Cannery Row* and the sense of community that Steinbeck had so brilliantly captured. She was both surprised and impressed when the Italian policeman nodded in agreement, telling her Steinbeck was one of his favourite foreign writers.

'What are we going to do now?' Julia asked.

'As you English say we shall play it by ear. First of all we look for the damaged boat. The damage can't be too bad or it would have had to remain in Syracuse. On the other hand I doubt if it will have put out to sea again already. If we can find the boat we find the owner. You had better stay in the background, we will not be trading on sympathy for a grieving relative this time.'

In the event there was no need to play anything by ear. As they drove towards the sea, the village at first looked idyllic with its thirteenth-century church and jumble of small houses; however the flash of blue lights could not be missed. Giuseppe was waived through a police cordon and parked beside two police cars and an ambulance on the seafront.

'What's happening here?' he asked a uniformed policeman standing beside the ambulance.

'There's a body down there,' came the reply.

Giuseppe moved off in the direction the man had indicated, leaving Julia to follow in his wake. Two men in civilian clothes were standing outside a rough wooden shed. Julia was surprised to see Giuseppe warmly welcomed by the elder of the two. Then the two strangers turned to look in Julia's direction and her rudimentary Italian was good enough to understand that Giuseppe was introducing her merely as an English visitor. Giuseppe called her over and introduced her to his two colleagues explaining that one of them, Vittorio Milliceni, was an old friend. They all shook hands but then the men seemed to lose interest in her and the three Italians started an animated and rapid conversation that she could not follow. After a few moments they went into the hut and Julia followed.

The hut was open at one end and she realised that it was actually a small boat shed. A fishing boat was taking up all the space inside the hut and Julia was struck by how small it was, barely thirty feet. She could see that much of the woodwork on the port side was missing but it was something else that grabbed her attention. Lying face down in front of the boat was the body of a man. The sparse black hair on the back of his head was now matted with congealed blood. He was a small man made smaller by death and dressed in working clothes that had clearly been mended time after time. On his feet he wore rubber boots of the kind worn by fishermen the world over. There was no obvious sign of any struggle, just one bullet to the head.

The three Italian policemen continued their conversation and then Giuseppe seemed to remember Julia was there. He turned to her and explained in English that the man's body had been found by his wife. His name was Giacomo Conti. He had gone down to work on his boat very early this morning and she had expected him back for breakfast. When he did not appear she had gone looking for him.

That seemed to be all that was known. The local police were speaking to everyone in the area but so far nothing. Most of the other fishing boats were at sea and this part of the beach was completely empty. A woman in the village had reported seeing a large car driving rapidly away from the seafront but she could say nothing about who might have been in it. She couldn't say what sort of car it might have been and she certainly could not remember the licence number.

They were just waiting for the medical examiner who had to come from Syracuse and then the body would be taken away.

'Vittorio has suggested that he and I go to talk to the widow once again,' said Giuseppe. 'It might be useful for you to come with us. You could use that female intuition again. But I won't be able to provide a running translation.'

The dead man had lived in Via Santoro Romeo which ran from near the fish market at right angles to the quay. Low buildings lined each side of the street. Some were a single storey while the rest had another upper floor each with a balcony and tall windows hidden behind green shutters. When they arrived at Giacomo Conti's home it appeared to Julia that the house was entirely inhabited by women. Giuseppe and Inspector Milliceni cleared the tiny front room which led directly on to the street, leaving just the dead man's wife and his daughter. It was difficult to gauge the age of his widow. She looked well over sixty but the young woman who was introduced as her daughter could have been eighteen. The two women and the two policemen filled the whole of the room. Julia had not been introduced and felt very much an intruder as she leaned against the open front door. The feeling was exacerbated as the conversation was conducted in rapid-fire Sicilian and only later did Julia learn the details of what had been said. The emotions, however, needed no translation.

Signora Conti was in shock. Tears had left her eyes red but her appearance now conveyed not grief or anger or bewilderment but resignation. Her husband had been murdered but she seemed to be saying that such is life. What could she do? There was no point in saying anything more. Her daughter's reaction was quite different. There was real anger, although where that anger was directed was unclear. Was it against the murderers or against her mother or even against her dead father? It was hard to tell. The daughter seemed to be haranguing her mother and turning to the two policemen for support. She fired a question at Julia and when Julia was unable to respond carried on regardless. At one point Julia thought they were talking about Piana dei Greci, the place Giuseppe had mentioned on the way down, but that seemed unlikely. She edged out of the door and stood in the hot sun.

When Giuseppe and Vittorio Milliceni emerged the daughter was still shouting to them from inside the house. Milliceni responded animatedly but eventually the two policemen walked away and back towards the boat shed. Julia followed, still with no idea of what the conversation had been about. It was not until five minutes later that Giuseppe finished with his friend and seemed to remember that Julia was still there.

'Come on,' he said. 'I'll explain as we drive back to Syracuse.'

It appeared that at first Conti's wife would tell the police nothing. Her husband Giacomo was just a peaceful family man who went to church on Sundays and did nothing at all illegal. She would say nothing more but simply kept repeating the same refrain. He was a good man. He was an honest man. He was always faithful to her. He loved his daughter. He had no enemies. The perfect husband. Then why, Milliceni asked, did somebody kill him? They must have been trying to steal his boat. But his boat was damaged, Milliceni replied, why would anybody choose to steal that boat? Then it was a mistake, she insisted, the killers must have been looking for somebody else.

'Had he met with any strangers?' Giuseppe had asked.

'No, Giacomo didn't speak to strangers he talked to nobody outside the village.'

'Don't you want to catch whoever killed him?' asked Milliceni.

'Giacomo is gone. There is nothing we can do. Go away and leave us alone.'

It was then that the daughter had lost control. 'You must tell them, Mama,' she shouted. 'Tell them about the visitors.' But Signora Conti just retreated even further into her shell and said nothing. It seemed clear that she was not going to change her mind and nothing more would be learned from her.

'Then the girl declared that she would tell us,' continued Giuseppe as the car swung on to the main Syracuse road. 'At that the mother suddenly came alive and the two of them started screaming at each other. The old woman shouted that her daughter didn't know what she was doing. She must be silent, everyone must be silent. She begged us to go away.

'But the girl would not be silent. "You knew them," she had shouted and the mother screamed back that she didn't know them, she didn't know men like that, she had left all that behind. Left what behind, we wanted to know, what had she left behind and where?

'Eventually it all came out. As a young girl Signora Conti had left her home town, Piana dei Greci near Palermo, to come to Syracuse. She was looking for a new life away from the poverty of peasant life. After meeting Giacomo she had settled instead for the poverty of a fisherman's life. She had very little contact with her family in Piana dei Greci until a few weeks ago when two men turned up. We don't know who but they clearly came from Piana dei Greci. She won't tell us and her daughter didn't meet them. They wanted to speak to her husband but she won't tell us what about. We do know from the daughter that Giacomo Conti met the men and that he and his wife had a massive row about it. Suddenly he had money and insisted he would soon have more. Just one day's work, he insisted, that's all. Then back to life as before but with a new boat and new clothes for his family.'

'And he never said what he was expected to do?'

'Well if he told his wife anything more she won't tell us. There is one other thing and I don't know what it means. The daughter said that her father talked about meeting a foreigner, and it was the foreigner who had given him the money.'

'What sort of foreigner?'

'I've no idea. Her father would have been speaking to her in Sicilian and he might just have meant someone from Rome but I don't think so.

'I suggested to Vittorio that this might all be about heroin,' continued Giuseppe. 'Over the last twenty years smuggling has provided a big part of the Mafia's income, cigarettes into Italy and heroin via Sicily into North America. It's become a massive problem for us. In the fifties the American Mafia were under a lot of pressure, the FBI started really hurting them and then what nearly killed them was Fidel Castro taking power in Cuba. They needed Cuba as a base from which they could smuggle drugs into the US. When the Cuban Revolution happened they had to find somewhere else and they came back home to Sicily. These days most of the heroin smuggled into ports on the American East Coast comes from the Sicilian Mafia. The problem is getting worse. You must know the film *The French Connection*.'

'Of course, I had just moved to London when it came out. Somewhat melodramatic.'

'Melodramatic perhaps but based on a real French connection. The Corsicans used to control a big part of the American drug trade but now that the French have smashed all that the Mafia have no competitors. They've even started setting up heroin refineries here in Sicily.'

'Did your friend Vittorio think Conti could have been involved in smuggling drugs?'

'No, Vittorio is very sceptical. He knows this area and says that he's never heard any rumours about the fishermen here being involved with drug smuggling. He thinks Conti was exactly what he seems to be: just a fisherman. Vittorio is a friend, but he's not always right. Or he might have reasons for keeping, as you would say, his cards close to his breast.'

Julia wasn't about to explain the difference between breast and chest.

Giuseppe had glanced across at her. 'Conti's murder is Vittorio's case and even friends don't always tell each other everything. You, for example, have you told me everything? Your husband yesterday was with Captain Morgan, did he learn nothing new? And did you just spend last evening enjoying our wonderful Sicilian food?'

Julia toyed with the idea of telling him about our mysterious American visitor but decided against it. Giuseppe, she was sure, wasn't being completely open with us. How was it, for example, that a provincial policeman could make one quick phone call and discover that Morgan was a British spy?

When Giuseppe dropped her back at the Grand Hotel Villa Politi she had a lot to tell me, but I wasn't there.

XII

I had no sooner finished speaking to the DG that morning than the phone rang again. It was Morgan. Just the man I wanted if I was going to rock the boat as the DG had instructed.

'Are you busy?' he asked.

'Not at all, I was just going to call you.'

'Good,' Morgan interrupted. 'I've just realised it's the anniversary of Primosole Bridge. That's about half an hour from here. Let's meet near there for lunch. You have a car?'

'I do.'

'Good, write this down. It's a new place north of Augusta.' He gave me directions to a restaurant with the improbable name of *Chateau d'Or*. 'If you leave now you'll be fine. Must rush.'

With that the phone went dead and I was left bemused. I had no idea what Morgan was talking about nor why he had been so abrupt. What or where was Primosole Bridge and why did it have an anniversary? I left a note for Julia and grabbed the keys to the hire car.

As I later discovered, at that very moment Julia was looking at a dead body. Morgan's odd behaviour was the least of our worries.

When I reached the turning to the *Chateau d'Or* restaurant, Morgan's car was at the side of the road. Before I had a chance to park he signalled for me to follow him and set off at full speed. He led the way along a road that paralleled the coastline. Suddenly he turned off, following a sign indicating Vaccarizzo. It was more of a lane than a road, bordered by orange trees and cactus plants and the occasional small house. When we reached the sea there was nothing but a small bar with a few tables and a sandy beach. Morgan parked and approached as I was getting out of my car.

'You'll think I'm being paranoid,' he said without any sort of greeting, 'but we may need to be careful. I think I've been threatened.'

'Who by?'

'By our American cousins.' Before I could respond he led me into the bar and we sat down.

'You know I asked Romney yesterday about Tortellini and Ramone? Well, as soon as I got to the base this morning his sidekick came in and started asking the same questions Romney had asked. Why was the DG asking about Tortellini, where did the name Ramone come from, who had the DG been talking to, was George Ffortiscue involved, was there supposed to be a connection between Tortellini and Ramone? Obviously I couldn't tell him as I don't know, but he wouldn't accept that. He became really quite aggressive. Had I mentioned Tortellini or Ramone to anyone else? What exactly had the DG said to me? He was convinced that we must have more than just the two names. Eventually he changed tack. I should find out more from the DG. He wanted me to phone London there and then.'

'Did you?'

'Yes I did. I got hold of the DG's assistant, Janet, but he wasn't there. I said I would call back. Our American friend then changed tack again. He calmed down and seemed to decide that it might be better to have me on his side. He announced he was going to take me into his confidence. We were all on the same side. But I had to understand that it was all top secret and he didn't want me talking to anyone here about it. Then he explained that Tortellini was part of an operation that the Company was running in Rome. It was all to do with the Casarecce network which had been in place for years. Tortellini was one of their agents and had helped recruit their source in the Russian Embassy.

'I asked for more details but he told me it was all "need to know" and that I didn't need to know. Tortellini was internal Agency business and I should tell London that there was nothing there for them to get involved with. As to Ramone he had never heard of him and if I heard anything myself I should tell him right away. Then he gave me the most extraordinary lecture, the gist of which was that I was here at a US facility at the invitation of the US government and any information London had or I had about Tortellini or Ramone should be passed over to the Agency as soon as possible. If he had any reason to believe that we were not cooperating fully then I would be off the base quicker than the piss hits the pot. I should remember that this was their territory and they would know everything that I did here. I shouldn't think that just by phoning London from the apartment I had rented in Catania rather than my office at the base I could keep any secrets. They were not about to have two-bit foreign agencies interfering in the network they had so carefully put together over the last thirty years.

'There was something about the way he spoke. I'm convinced they are really watching everything we do, intercepting my office phone for example. That's why when I called you from the base I suggested that other restaurant and then switched. I thought they might have planted somebody to listen to our conversation.'

Instinctively I looked around but the bar was almost empty. We each ordered a beer.

Part of me thought that Morgan was more than a little neurotic. Playing at spies. The CIA people I had worked with were certainly aware of their own importance but they had a subtlety about them that was very different from the approach described by Morgan. If the CIA wanted us to keep out of the way the message would be delivered discreetly at a senior level in London or Washington, not crudely like this.

I nodded non-committally. 'And what was the stuff you mentioned about the Primosole Bridge?' I asked.

'That was just to distract anybody listening, put them off the scent,' Morgan replied. 'You know the film that came out a couple of weeks ago *A Bridge Too Far* about the raid on the bridge at Arnhem after D-Day. Primosole was another bridge too far and it's near here and I just thought visiting it sounded plausible if anyone was listening to our conversation.'

It all sounded a bit melodramatic. Morgan, I concluded, had been reading too much John le Carré. It was time to change the subject and tell him about the mysterious visitor Julia and I had received the previous evening. But then Morgan suddenly mentioned a name that made me jump.

'I really don't understand why Romney seems to give Harry Bastamente such a free rein. You would think Bastamente was in charge of operations here.'

'Harry who?' I asked.

'Harry Bastamente, the man I'm talking about, Jack Romney's sidekick. I'm not at all sure what his role is supposed to be, he seems to come and go as he pleases. He's clearly something to do with the set-up in Rome.'

'Bastamente is here?'

'Yes, you know him?'

'Yes I do. I met him with the DG in London just a few days ago. He's one of the most senior people in the Company, been there since Dulles' days.'

Now it was Morgan's turn to look confused. 'Are you sure? This chap can't have been around that long and I'm pretty sure he's been here for the last week. I'd have known if he'd been away long enough to meet you in London. Romney described Bastamente to me as his assistant, he calls him Junior, but he seems to have taken over the investigation. Romney had left the interrogation of the locals on the suspect list to the SID but Bastamente reinterviewed them all again himself, apparently his Italian is pretty good.'

'How old is he?'

'Difficult to say. Around forty.'

'That's not the Bastamente I know but it's too much of a coincidence to assume they're not related.'

It was odd but not nearly as mysterious as our visitor from the previous evening. I told Morgan what had happened. He was clearly amazed first at the thought that Romney had apparently been tracking Davoud and Bunny's voyage and second at the fact that someone perhaps from the base would come and tell us.

'What did he look like?' he asked.

The description I gave him could have fitted half the Americans on the base, as Morgan pointed out.

'Then we had better get to the base and start looking around,' I replied.

'It won't be difficult for me to get pictures of all the US servicemen at Sigonella,' said Morgan. 'There's a set of handbooks with mugshots which they're very good at keeping up to date. I've got a set in my office; the Americans don't seem to think the photos are very secret. But finding anything more than name and number is going to be a problem. There was a long debate about even giving me the files on the men who might have leaked information to the Russians, I don't think they'll give me the files on anyone else without a really good reason.'

'And we can't give them a good reason,' I said. 'The last thing we want is Romney realising that someone from here is leaking information to us about his Tortellini operation, whatever that really is.'

I paused and could sense we were both thinking the same thing. Our visitor had said Tortellini was an operation involving US Navy planes flying surveillance missions over the Ionian Sea. Bastamente Junior had just told Morgan that Tortellini was a CIA agent in Rome. There was surely no way they could both be telling the truth, but if one was lying then which one and why?

Everything seemed to point to Bastamente being the liar. How would our visitor have come across in Sicily the code name for an American agent supposedly operating 300 miles away? And even if he had, why would he throw it into a conversation about Bunny's disappearance?

'You seem pretty sure that your visitor was from the base,' said Morgan.

'No I'm not sure. He looked like an American and he talked like an American but that doesn't prove that he was an American. And even if he was, I have no evidence that he came from the base. It just seems to me that for an American to have information about the flight paths of US Navy aircraft he's likely to have something to do with the US Navy facility here. Who else would have it?'

Over lunch we tried to make sense of what we had learned but without having any blinding new insights. Eventually the conversation turned elsewhere.

It seemed that Morgan had only been in the Department for a few months and the Embassy in Rome was his first appointment. He had clearly been looking forward to life as a spy but was already starting to realise the sheer boredom of most of what we did. 'I took over from an RAF chap,' he said, 'who told me that nothing ever happened. I was beginning to think he was right. The Italians keep inviting us to receptions and meetings but never have anything new to say. The Americans treat us like amateurs and the Russians are so paranoid that we never see anything of them. The Communist Party in Italy is still a major force and that could be interesting but they're really MI6 hunting ground not ours. The Communists have some MPs in the European Parliament and a couple of them actually invited me to lunch to discuss what they described as military matters. My official title is assistant military attaché.'

'Did you go?'

'Yes I did. It was bizarre. These two chaps turned up, both wearing beautifully tailored and very expensive suits, and insisted on taking me out to an expensive lunch where we discussed just about everything except military matters. I think all they really wanted was to persuade me that the Italian Communists are good Europeans and that Russia is not a threat to anyone. They did go on about the CIA, insisting the Americans were behind the Borghese fiasco and just about everything else that has gone wrong in Italy since the war. But even then they seemed more interested in what they were eating than what they were saying. Very Italian.'

'All very different from what you were used to,' I commented. 'I assume you were in Northern Ireland.'

He nodded. 'That's right. The paras always get the shitty jobs.' He started telling me about Primosole Bridge and I realised that he wanted to change the subject.

'Thirty-four years ago this month the 1st Paras set off from airfields in North Africa as part of the invasion of Sicily. Half the planes got lost or were shot down by the enemy or by our own Navy. Our paratroops arrived at about the same time as German paratroops and the whole thing was an enormous mess. By the time we eventually took the bridge the front had moved on and it hardly mattered.'

Morgan was keen to go and look at the bridge now, as we were so close, but I wanted to get to the base and as the DG put it, rock the boat. It seemed to me that Morgan had been here for weeks and had not felt the need before so he could wait a little longer.

Reluctantly he agreed. 'I thought you might want to go to the base again so I've got you a vehicle pass so you can park near my office; unfortunately they only give out day passes for that area so we will need to get one every time you come up.'

When we reached Sigonella we found that the boat had already been well and truly rocked. Another body had appeared, this one with a recent bullet in the back of the head.

The message on Morgan's desk had simply told me to phone Julia at the hotel, urgently. I rang her right away. She picked up the phone immediately and had clearly been waiting for my call.

'What's happening?' I asked.

'Well we found the man we were looking for but unfortunately last night somebody put a bullet in the back of his head, Mafia style.'

'What?!'

She started speaking again but I was beginning to be infected by Morgan's paranoia. If Romney and Junior were really listening in to Morgan's phone calls on this line I was not sure I wanted

Julia saying any more. 'I'll be back in Syracuse as soon as possible,' I interrupted her, 'but things are getting a little hairy here.'

It occurred to me that if we were being bugged I should take the opportunity to start rocking the American boat a little more and spread some confusion. Perhaps I could convince Romney and his friend that our Navy had discovered something to do with the *Mahsheed*'s disappearance.

'Morgan is being fed a load of bollocks by our American cousins,' I told Julia. 'Either that or we can't trust our esteemed Royal Navy as much as we thought we could. If there is a drugs connection here it would seem that Uncle Sam is determined that we don't find it. I'll see you soon.'

'Don't you want to know what happened in Marzamemi this morning?'

'No, don't tell me now. There is something I must do here first.'

We wished each other love, Julia somewhat miffed, and I put down the phone.

'Right,' I said to Morgan. 'Let's find Romney and his pal.'

That proved easier than I expected. We were just leaving Morgan's office when Romney appeared.

'What the hell is going on?' he demanded.

'That is just what I was going to ask you,' I responded.

'What's this about Mafia executions and drugs?' Romney asked. He was red in the face and clearly very angry. He seemed completely oblivious to the fact that he was making it very obvious that he had been listening in to our phone call. 'Who's dead? Where? How? And what the fuck do you think Uncle Sam's got to do with drugs? We've got nothing to do with the Mafia, not now, not ever.'

He slurred the last few words, 'nonow nonever' he seemed to say. I realised that although it was only early afternoon Romney had already been at the bottle. The veins on his nose suggested that this was not unusual. I remembered a comment that Morgan had made the day before that he was surprised that Romney had managed to survive in the Agency and reach such a senior position. The man might not be a raving alcoholic but he was going that way, and yet he had been put in charge of investigating a Russian spy ring inside an American airbase.

I shouted back. 'What the hell is happening indeed? You've been feeding us bullshit. You were tracking Eveline Sadeghi's boat. That was all part of Tortellini.'

'Who told you that?'

'It doesn't matter who told us, the important thing is that it's true. You've been lying through your teeth. Even making up stories about a US destroyer hearing the *Mahsheed* blow up miles away from where it was actually attacked.' Suddenly out of nowhere a thought struck me. 'Does Stansfield Turner even know what you're doing?'

Romney went rigid at the mention of the CIA's new director. 'You're crazy.' With that he swung around and almost ran out of the office.

XIII

Morgan and I simply stared at each other, not sure what we had just witnessed. If there was any sort of Company operation going on here Washington would know about it. The CIA is a very bureaucratic organisation. Operations might be run on a strict need to know basis with regard to those outside the chain of command but if Tortellini was big enough to risk endangering the Intelligence links between Washington and London then Romney's boss, the Harry Bastamente I met in London, would have needed authorisation from the very top.

It was time to see Julia and find out more about the murder in Marzamemi that she was clearly keen to tell me all about.

Before leaving his office Morgan unlocked a filing cabinet and removed four fairly large ring binders and managed to jam them into his briefcase. He said nothing to me but I could see that the folders contained a collection of mugshots. I led the way to where we had parked our cars and as we got there a man approached from the direction of the main gate.

'Junior,' shouted someone from behind us. It was Romney who came running unsteadily from the opposite direction. 'Junior don't let them leave.'

The approaching figure stopped with a puzzled expression on his face. There was no need for Morgan to tell me who he was. He had the same deep brown eyes and heavy eyelids as his father and the same broad shoulders. He too was wearing an expensive Italian suit with white button-down shirt and dark striped tie.

'What's going on?' he asked of no one in particular.

'Someone's been killed,' said Romney, 'executed by the Mafia apparently. These Brits seem to think it's something to do with drugs. And that we are involved. They've been asking about Tortellini again.'

Romney seemed to have pulled himself together. He spoke slowly in a flat level voice.

Bastamente Junior looked away from him and turned to Morgan. 'I thought we had said all there was to say on that subject. I told you: Tortellini is just a code name for one of our sources in Rome.'

It was a bizarre reaction. Romney had just told him that someone had been murdered but that seemed to be of no interest to him. 'You don't need to concern yourself with Tortellini,' he continued. 'It's purely Agency business.'

'That's bullshit,' I responded and Bastamente looked up as if he had just seen me for the first time.

'Ah the new boy,' he said. 'Dylan Thomas is it or Thomas Dylan? You have been getting around. Kefalonia one day, Sigonella the next. Shame you didn't pick up some manners in your travels. I've told you all you need to know about Tortellini now drop it.'

'You didn't tell us that Tortellini gets around as well: one day he's apparently a source in Rome, the next day he's flying a P-3 Orion tracking the Sadeghis all the way from Kefalonia.'

Now it was his turn to respond in the same way. 'That's bullshit, pure bullshit. Has Jack Romney here been letting the booze get to his tongue?'

'I haven't said anything, Junior,' put in Romney. 'These guys have done all the talking. They say that somebody has been killed in a place called Marzapani or some name like that. A Mafia execution, something to do with drugs, and they claim it's connected to us.'

Bastamente looked at me curiously. 'What's all this about drugs and the Mafia? Sounds like you've been watching too many Hollywood movies. All that Godfather stuff is just made up you know. It's not Marlon Brando you gotta be looking for – it's Behzad Sadeghi.'

'What makes you think this has anything to do with Behzad Sadeghi?' I asked. 'It was his brother who's disappeared. I'm down here to find out what happened to Davoud Sadeghi and to his wife. We're not talking about Behzad Sadeghi.'

'Is that right? Well let me tell you fellow, Behzad Sadeghi's got to be at the bottom of all this. He's practically a Commie and he's dangerous. If anyone has been involved with drug smuggling it will be him, it's his boat that seems to have exploded. That's who your DG should be investigating, not wasting his time sending you two down here.

'And now,' he continued, 'Di Benedetto tells me that your wife has been asking questions about a murder down in Marzamemi. God knows what she thinks that has to do with her aunt disappearing.'

He looked at Morgan. 'You are supposed to be helping us to find a spy on this base. If you want to join in your DG's family games instead then perhaps you should pack up your office and go do that.'

With that he turned and walked away with Romney at his heels. I turned to Morgan. 'Well that's one man who doesn't need an introduction. He has all his father's subtlety. The odd thing

106

was that he paid practically no attention to Romney telling him that somebody had been killed, absolutely no curiosity about that.'

'Because he already knew,' suggested Morgan. 'Di Benedetto from the SID had told him.'

'That's what he said, but the SID are an intelligence agency. How would they become involved in the murder of a fisherman? There must be some security connection we haven't spotted and Bastamente knows what it is. Let's see if Julia can work it out. We need to find out what's happened in Marzamemi.'

I returned to my hire car and followed Morgan out of the main gate. I soon gave up trying to keep up with him. I wondered what the DG would say about him using the protection of his diplomatic plates to break the speed limit every time he floored his Lancia. When I reached the hotel he was already in the bar with Julia.

'What kept you?' he asked.

'The law,' I replied. Julia grinned and mouthed 'Typical' to me.

'I was just telling your wife about Romney and Bastamente Junior's extraordinary behaviour,' Morgan said.

'Any fresh ideas?' I asked Julia.

'None.'

'Well then, let's hear about you and loverboy in Marzamemi.'

Julia affected a dreamy look. 'Yes, Giuseppe is rather gorgeous. Handsome, intelligent and more than a little patronising. Just like my husband, in fact.'

She pecked me on the cheek and pushed over the glass of white wine she had waiting for me.

'It's a Sicilian variety, a grape called grillo. Giuseppe recommended it.'

'Did he really? How fortunate he had the time.'

'Come on children,' said Morgan. 'Let's hear what happened in Marzamemi.'

Julia recounted the morning's events. When she had finished Morgan and I tried to put the pieces together.

'So on the day Bunny disappeared,' I said, 'a fishing boat arrives in Syracuse. On board are two injured men who are taken away in an ambulance and a third, whom we must assume was Giacomo Conti, who then sails home in his damaged boat. Three days later somebody shoots him. We have no idea who but it could be someone from this village, Piana dei Greci, his wife's birthplace near Palermo, or it could be a mysterious foreigner.'

'Or it could be somebody else entirely,' said Morgan.

'I favour the foreigner theory,' said Julia. 'Giuseppe phoned me this afternoon. I had this feeling yesterday that we weren't the first people to be poking around the docks asking peculiar questions. Giuseppe was sceptical but it seems he went back there after he dropped me this morning and I was right. Apparently a foreigner had spent the day Bunny was due to arrive lounging around the docks.'

'Why is that significant? There are plenty of foreigners here,' I interjected.

'Of course. But the next day he was back asking lots of questions. Had anybody seen anything unusual? Had there been any strangers acting oddly? Were any boats missing? Had anyone seemed to have more money to spend than usual? He said he was a journalist.'

'Well, perhaps he was.'

'Yes, but he first appeared the day before Bunny disappeared. And why would a journalist ask if any of the fishermen had been spending more lire than usual? Apparently his Italian was pretty awful but that's a really odd question. And he was offering to pay for information. Giuseppe thinks everyone was too scared to tell him anything but who knows, he was offering a lot. Somebody could have told him the same story they eventually told us; they might have mentioned Marzamemi. He hasn't been seen back at the docks since.

'And that's not all,' added Julia, with an air that she had been keeping the best to last. 'When Giuseppe phoned me just now he casually added that he had taken a photograph of a possible suspect along with him and it had been positively identified as the supposed journalist.'

'Suspect! What suspect?' said Morgan and I in unison.

'That's what I asked him but Giuseppe wouldn't say. He did say that he's now going back to Marzamemi to see if he could find anyone there who had seen his suspect.'

This was a bombshell. I was totally perplexed. How had Giuseppe identified a suspect? Had his friend Inspector Vittorio Milliceni discovered something about Conti's murder that we had not been told? Or had somebody said something to Giuseppe in the docks yesterday that Julia had not been able to understand?

Morgan cut such speculation short. 'I don't know how Inspector Falzone has managed to identify a suspect,' he said, 'but I know how we might do so. I have the mugshot books from Sigonella. They aren't the sort of thing to read in a bar so let's go up to your room.'

I had forgotten all about the American who had come to warn us that US Navy planes had been tracking Bunny's boat all the way from Greece.

We went up to our room where Morgan produced four white folders containing head and shoulder shots of every serviceman on the Sigonella base, four rows of three on every page. 'That's two books for each of you,' he said. 'Best of luck.'

I was not optimistic. Although I had a clear picture in my mind of the man we were looking for, the black and white photos of young men in military uniform had, unsurprisingly, a remarkable uniformity about them. The fact that they all wore headgear that seemed to hide much of their face did not help. I was halfway through my second book when Julia let out a cry.

'That's him,' she said.

I looked at the photograph she was pointing to and there was no doubt, we had found our man.

'SCPO Robert Milan USN,' Morgan read.

'Now we just have to find a way to pull his records and then track him down,' I said.

Morgan replied quietly. 'No we don't. I know all about Milan. He's one of the thirteen Americans who were in a position to leak the information that was passed to the Russians.'

XIV

'You mean our visitor could be the Russian spy?' said Julia. 'I don't believe it.'

We looked at each other for a moment in silence. None of us knew what to say. Julia was the first to break the silence. 'I need a long, cold drink.'

We all really needed something to eat as well so we put off any further questions until we had settled into a local fish restaurant. Over *linguine alle vongole* I tried to assimilate what we had learned. If our visitor was not a clean-cut American with a conscience but a Soviet spy could we believe anything he had said? And if he was being deliberately misleading, why? Why would he come to see us and risk exposure in order to make us think that the Americans had been tracking the *Mahsheed*? What was in it for the Russians?

'What can you tell us about Milan?' Julia asked Morgan.

'A lot,' he replied, 'although I'm not sure any of it helps. I must have been through his file twenty times. I can probably recite it by heart.

'Robert Anthony Milan. Born in 1947 in New York. His father died when he was a few months old. His mother remarried and had two more children, two girls. The family moved to Chicago and then to Omaha, Nebraska. His stepfather worked on the production line at a furniture factory. His mother worked on and off at a local supermarket. She became quite sickly and died when Robert was sixteen.

'Then the Vietnam War came along and Robert enlisted in the Navy. I don't think he had any great love for the sea but enlisting in the Navy might have seemed safer than being drafted into the Army. He did one tour in Vietnam as part of Operation Game Warden patrolling the Mekong Delta. After that he was based in Hawaii for some years. While there he met a local girl and two years ago they got married. That didn't work out and they started divorce proceedings before he was posted to Sigonella.'

'When was that?' Julia asked.

'In January. His service record is good without being outstanding. He's what the Americans call E-8, a senior chief petty officer. He's never shown any ambition to climb any higher. His job here includes access to some pretty sensitive stuff but he's never had any problem getting the highest security clearance.'

'So he could have leaked some really damaging material,' I suggested.

'Absolutely. If he is the spy, and that still has to be proved, he could have passed on classified information that the Russians would find a lot more useful than the files Bastamente's source managed to get hold of. And perhaps he has.'

'Because we don't know what was in the latest batch the Russians received.'

'That's right. But there's nothing in his file to show any connection with Russia or with Communism. His politics seem pretty conventional by US standards, conservative Republican. The FBI have crawled over his family and found nothing. His stepfather moved back to New York and died last year of natural causes. His half-sisters have both married and live blameless lives in Middle America somewhere. There don't seem to be any women in his life now, he's married to the Navy. His soon to be ex-wife has been interviewed at length in Hawaii and she was placed under surveillance for nearly a month, but there is absolutely nothing there.'

'Has Milan himself been under surveillance?'

'Everyone on the suspect list has been under surveillance at some point but it's a waste of time. In the early days one of them might have done something revealing but now they all know they're under suspicion. The spy will assume he's being watched. You can't interview people over and over again without them working out why they're being questioned. And anyway we don't have the manpower to keep thirty people under round-the-clock surveillance.'

'Well if he knew someone could be watching him why did Milan still come to see us I wonder,' said Julia. 'Was he being watched that night?'

'I doubt it. Romney is convinced the leak must have come from one of the locals, mainly it seems to me because that's what he wants to believe. All the Americans on the list are being posted somewhere else so he's now throwing all his resources at the Italians.'

There wasn't much more we could say so we agreed that Morgan would find out where Milan was living and we would try to think of a way to approach him again. He was almost certainly living on the base, which might make contacting him more difficult.

'You know what we should do now,' said Morgan, 'talk to Romney. If Milan is leaking stuff to the opposition he could be doing enormous damage. There is a lot of material here that we are as anxious to keep secret as the Americans are. If we try to approach Milan again we may spook him; if he then does a runner that's the end of any special relationship between the DIS and the US of A.'

He was almost certainly right. He was here first and foremost to catch a Russian spy. Bunny's murder was a family matter that couldn't be allowed to take priority. But the Bastamentes had really pissed me off: Senior by his behaviour in London and Junior with his bullshit this afternoon. Of one thing I was certain: they were not being straight with us. And I didn't like them listening in to our phone calls. Even if Milan had been lying about them tracking the *Mahsheed* I was sure they had been up to something.

Julia was in no doubt. 'We can't talk to the Americans. Unless we are absolutely sure Milan is the spy we've been looking for, we need to find him, he must know more than he told us. I'm sure the DG will back us up. He told us to rock the boat so let's think about ways of doing that.'

Morgan look surprised. I think he had assumed I was in charge and Julia was along for the ride. In fact Julia and I were the same grade but as she had been with the DIS for longer I suppose strictly speaking she was the more senior. In any case I agreed with her.

We arranged to meet at lunchtime the next day at the bar in Vaccarizzo to which Morgan had led me before. Morgan would spend the morning trying to find a way of approaching Milan and Julia and I would track down Giuseppe and find out more about his sudden discovery of a suspect.

Julia phoned the DG at home before we went to bed. He was in sombre mood. He had just got off the phone to Ottawa. 'Henry Ramone seems to exist,' he told her.

'So the Canadians have produced something.'

'Not much and at this stage it doesn't take us very far. The name and address you found in Kefalonia are real but the RCMP know nothing about the man. No criminal record, not even a speeding ticket. But there is one curiosity. At the request of the Americans there's a POI tag on him.'

A Person of Interest tag meant that if Ramone's name cropped up in any investigation whoever put the tag on would be notified.

'I've gone right to the top,' the DG continued. 'If the Canadians can find anything more I will be told. They owe us some favours.' There was a moment of silence and Julia thought her uncle had finished with the subject, but he hadn't. His voice suddenly sounded unusually flat. 'When I say Ramone seems to exist it's not because of anything the Canadians have told us. We've found his name much closer to home, in the last place I would have expected: Harley Street.'

'Harley Street?'

'Yes. Janet found it at Davoud's clinic. In my brother-in-law's appointment book. Eight months ago there was an entry for Henry Ramone. It was down as Davoud's last appointment for the day. Later than his usual hours. But there were no details, just the name. And we've been through everything else in his office, in his home, in the house in Bosham, on their boat the *Bunny Hopper*. There is no mention of Ramone at all. He certainly wasn't a patient.'

'Does Davoud's secretary remember anything?'

'That was my thought but the woman there now is just standing in and can't help. His usual secretary has just got married, in fact on the same day as you, and is now somewhere in India on her honeymoon. We're trying to find her but we may have to wait until she gets back.'

'So what does it mean?'

115

'I have no idea. I know Davoud. He is, he was, absolutely above board. Nothing at all suspicious.'

'Except this.'

'Yes except this. We've obviously checked that name everywhere. There's no Henry Ramone mentioned anywhere in this country. There actually is a Harold Ramone but he's seventy-two, lives in a home in Edinburgh, has apparently never married and has no family. I'll have someone interview him to see if he knows of a Henry Ramone but I'm not optimistic. Other than that nothing and crucially no record of anyone of that name entering or leaving the UK. The man doesn't exist.'

'But Davoud met him.'

'Quite. But why? What does it mean?'

We could not help him with that question. Julia told him about the day's events. He agreed we should tell the Americans about Milan but also agreed that we wouldn't do so yet. 'Bastamente Senior may be an arrogant thug but he's good. He's been their top man in Europe and the Middle East for a very long time and knows everyone. If we can't get to Milan by tomorrow evening we must give the Company his name.'

As it turned out we didn't have to give the Company Milan's name. We had just finished breakfast the next morning when Morgan phoned. 'All hell's just broken loose. One of the Americans on the list of suspects has disappeared. A man called Robert Milan.'

He said the name as if it were the first time he had heard it. Clearly Morgan was worried that Romney might still be bugging his phone. For that reason I didn't want to press him for details but the news was too important to just hang up and wait until we could meet face to face.

'When?' I asked.

'Some time in the last two days. Milan has been off duty since Wednesday evening and was due to start again at 0700 this morning. He didn't turn up. Somebody was sent to find him and his quarters were empty. I mean empty. Most of his personal possessions had gone. Look, I don't know all the details. I'll call again as soon as I know any more. If I don't phone we'll meet for lunch as arranged. Romney's just received a mugshot of that KGB guy, Yevgeny Kapustin, and is running off hundreds of copies. I'll bring some along.'

With that he put down the phone.

'What do you make of that?' I asked Julia.

'I'm not sure. Milan's shift ends Wednesday evening. Twenty-four hours later he comes to see us. Then thirty-six hours after that he's gone. When did he decide to do a bunk? I'm certain we didn't say anything which might have spooked him. Either he had decided to do a runner before he came to see us or something happened after that.'

'Something to do with the man I saw him talking to,' I suggested.

'Perhaps. Would you recognise the man again?'

It was a good question. I might recognise him in the right circumstances. He had been quite a distance away and there must be a lot of well-dressed, grey-haired men in Syracuse.

'Pity you didn't get the car's number.'

'Yes it is. I was too far away. I am pretty sure it didn't have diplomatic plates but that's not much help. It looked official though.'

Julia looked dubious. 'Big black cars with a driver waiting could be anyone, it could just as easily be gangsters as government. Something else strikes me. How easy is it to do a bunk from military quarters inside a US naval base? It's one thing to just walk out but it's another to take all your clothes and paraphernalia. I wonder if he took things like his record player and television. You can't just stroll out with all that under your arm.'

'No. And our mystery man from Moscow can't just drive in and pick it all up.'

'Hang on a minute. Milan must have had a car. I wonder what's happened to that. If it's parked at the base does that mean somebody brought him here?'

'Another good question. I am sure Romney will be on to that. We should phone the DG.'

'First of all,' insisted Julia, 'I am talking to Giuseppe. Who is this suspect he's talking about? If he's got a name for this man claiming to be a journalist, the one who's been poking around at the docks, I have a right to know.'

'You have a moral right. I am not sure Giuseppe would agree you have a legal right. Why didn't he give you the name yesterday? Why be so mysterious?'

'That's what I intend to find out.'

But Julia didn't find out. Inspector Falzone was not in his office and nobody would suggest where he might be. To my surprise, Julia produced a card on which the inspector had written his home number but there was no answer there either. I then called the office in London thinking that the DG might be there. He wasn't but his assistant Janet was. She explained he was taking the weekend off which, knowing the man, struck me as odd. 'What are you doing there?' I asked.

'Trying to check a bank account,' Janet replied. 'The DG phoned Ottawa again last night and they came up with a bank account in the name of Ramone at a bank in Rome. Apparently that's where the money came from to buy the apartment in

Toronto six years ago. There's an estate agent who handles the rents from Ramone's tenants and any expenses using a local account at the Toronto Dominion bank. Then the balance of that account is transferred once or twice a year to an account in Rome. I can give you the account details if you want as you're in Italy. I am getting absolutely nowhere with it here. I tried the SID in Rome, our embassy there, MI6, MI5, the Bank of England and anyone else I can think of. Everyone seems to think that as it's the weekend there's no chance of learning anything today and as it's Italy there's probably no chance of learning anything anytime soon.'

To make Janet feel better I jotted the account number down. She didn't really seem very concerned about her lack of success. The DG had said that she wasn't likely to learn anything but he was determined to rock the boat in every way possible.

'Did Ottawa tell him anything else?'

'No, nothing, which is what upset him. There's nothing. No birth registered. No passport. No tax records. The driving licence used in Greece was phoney.'

'What about the Toronto property purchase? Ramone must have given a previous address.'

'Yes in Rome. The address doesn't exist. Somebody's created a legend.'

'Looks like it. And yet there is a POI tag out there.'

'Yes, it would be good to know why the Company issued that,' Janet agreed. 'It's been in place for four or five years.'

That was interesting. Five years ago a phantom named Ramone appeared in Toronto and almost immediately the CIA registered him as a Person of Interest. Why? One obvious answer was that they were watching whoever created the legend and were waiting to see when it was used. Another explanation is that they had created the legend themselves and wanted to find out if anyone else came sniffing around it. But why would the CIA or anyone else want a legend in Toronto who did nothing more than own an apartment and let it out?

'Have his tenants been investigated?' I asked.

'Apparently they have and they are utterly blameless. Nothing there. We've interviewed that Harold Ramone in Edinburgh. Dead end. He arrived in this country after the war with a long unpronounceable Eastern European name and changed it to what he thought sounded English. He's never met anyone else with that surname. The only mention of Ramone we have found other than you finding his name in Greece and me finding his name in the Harley Street clinic is that one of our analysts found a couple of recent articles in obscure French left wing journals attributed to Enrico Ramone. Nothing startling. One on opposition to the Shah inside Iran, and another about the Communists and socialists in France needing to form a broad front. Both articles were well informed but said nothing at all new.'

'Odd though that one of them was about Iranian politics.'

'Yes, we've asked the French to investigate. Now we're in the Common Market we're all supposed to be helping each other. We'll see if Paris comes up with anything.'

I felt sure that what Janet was telling me ought to mean something but I really could not see what and on that note I rang off. There seemed nothing more Julia and I could do. We didn't want to leave the hotel unless Giuseppe Falzone turned up there but he did not. After a morning in and by the hotel pool I suggested that Julia might stay in Syracuse in the hope that her friend Giuseppe would contact her, but eventually we decided that we should drive up to Vaccarizzo together to meet Morgan.

XV

Morgan rapidly brought us up to speed. Milan had left the base at seven o'clock on Wednesday evening when he came off duty. On Thursday evening he had visited our hotel. He had been driving his own car but when he returned at 3.30 in the morning he was on foot and carrying a large suitcase. When asked by the marine guarding the gate what was in the case the guard remembered that Milan had lifted it on one finger to demonstrate that it was empty. How he travelled back to the base was unknown and the whereabouts of his car was also unknown.

The next morning Milan was seen in his quarters by two neighbours. One of them had suggested going for a beer but he had replied that as he was being posted back home he had decided to start packing.

Sometime after that he disappeared. When he failed to turn up for duty this morning his apartment was found to be empty. All his civilian clothes were gone along with all photos, books, records and pretty much all his personal possessions: certainly far more than would fit into a suitcase. In fact Romney estimated two or three suitcases would have been needed. The whole base was being searched in case Milan was still hiding somewhere but that seemed a forlorn hope. He had just vanished.

'But how could that happen?' asked Julia.

From what I had seen of the base it seemed highly unlikely somebody could simply disappear. Morgan confirmed that. 'If he went out through one of the gates there would be a record. There is a fence around the whole place. Now I reckon someone who really knew what they were doing might get over that fence without being spotted, but Milan with a couple of suitcases? No. Even with someone waiting on the other side in the middle of the night it is hard to imagine. But that must have been what happened. The only other alternative is that he managed to hide with his suitcases in a van or truck leaving the base. But we have no reason to believe that he had an accomplice on the base who could drive him out.'

But Julia persisted. 'You seem to be saying that whether he went over the fence or through the gate he must have received help.'

'At the moment nobody has any idea where he's gone or how. And they're all blaming each other. There is an Italian part of the base. Romney says the US section is secure so chances are he slipped out through the Italian section. The *Carabinieri* are saying their section is secure and they would certainly have noticed an American with two or three suitcases. Colonel Castorini, who is the number two or three guy in the *Carabinieri* in the whole of Sicily, turned up this morning and had a massive row with Di Benedetto of the SID. Castorini was overseeing the original leak investigation until Di Benedetto arrived. Castorini clearly saw an opportunity to say I told you so. Romney is saying pretty much the same to the Navy guys which, as you can imagine, is making him even less popular than usual. Bastamente is lurking around looking threatening and waving a stack of photos of this KGB fellow Kapustin. I've got some of those photos for you. There are no reported sightings of him anywhere since he landed in Palermo on the fifth.'

I was incredulous. 'Today is the sixteenth. Surely he can't just disappear, as well. He was travelling on his own papers.'

'This is Italy,' Morgan explained. 'He could be staying openly in a smart hotel in Palermo and the system just wouldn't pick him up. He may never have been within a hundred miles of Sigonella.'

In fact the Russian had been much closer than that, but that was something we would not know until the next day. For now there seemed nothing to do but enjoy our paninis and then return to Syracuse to try to track down Giuseppe Falzone. It was all intensely frustrating. The inspector had a suspect, Milan had vanished, Conti was dead, Bunny and almost certainly Davoud were dead: things were happening all around us but for us it looked like being another afternoon sightseeing or sitting by the pool.

Giuseppe remained uncontactable, as was the DG when Julia tried phoning again. Julia went shopping and I went swimming. She returned to the hotel at 4.30 with only one bag, but still my heart sank. Julia and shopping were a dangerous and often expensive combination. When the bag proved to contain only an extremely nice shirt and silk tie for me I had to concede that I was pleasantly surprised. I kissed her guiltily.

'What shall we do now?' I asked, thinking we might adjourn to the bedroom.

'Well, there doesn't seem to be much point sticking around the hotel. As it happens, next to the shop where I bought that shirt is a place with a darling silk dress. Obviously I wouldn't buy it unless you liked it. It's a bit short but the cut is wonderful and I think you will adore the colour. It would be a fabulous souvenir of our honeymoon,' she finished with a winning smile.

To suggest that this was not the honeymoon I had hoped for did not seem a fair response – after all, Julia's aunt had been murdered and I should be doing everything I could to raise my wife's spirits. So off we went to check out the 'darling silk dress'.

Just after we returned to the hotel, with Julia happily examining her new purchase and trying to decide whether she really needed new shoes to match, Morgan phoned. He had two pieces of news. First Milan's car had been found, in the car park at the rear of our hotel.

'Romney thinks that finding the car at your hotel means you must have had something to do with Milan's disappearance,' said Morgan. 'But Bastamente insisted that you're far too amateur to have reached Milan. Junior is obsessed with the idea that there is a KGB team here who spirited Milan away when they discovered he was about to be posted back to Hawaii. That's where my second piece of news comes in. That Russian, Yevgeny Kapustin, has been found but not here. The SID have just discovered that he flew back to Rome yesterday. He was using his own papers and flew back from Catania.'

Morgan paused to let the news sink in. Kapustin flies into Palermo more than a week ago, he disappears from view and then on the very day Conti is murdered and Milan is somehow spirited out of Sigonella he flies back from an airport just a few miles away. Presumably job done. But what was his job? Did he kill Conti? What role did he play in Milan's disappearance?

'What time did his flight leave?' I asked.

'That was my first question,' replied Morgan. 'He would certainly have had time to murder Conti. Whether he had anything to do with Milan depends on when Milan actually left the base. I have to believe Milan did a bunk in the middle of the night in which case it is highly unlikely that Kapustin was directly involved, he was back in Rome by then. But Romney and Bastamente think he must have briefed a Russian snatch team and are now looking for evidence that it exists.'

I relayed Morgan's news to Julia. Finding Milan's car at the hotel meant that he had come to see us under his own steam. The grey-haired man with whom he had left had not brought him. But he had taken him away. Had Milan gone voluntarily? Milan had been standing near the end of the drive when I had seen him, beyond the entrance to the hotel car park. Unless the other man had a gun it was difficult to see why Milan would have walked on down the drive if he had not wanted to. I had not seen a gun and Milan's companion had both hands in full view. As they were quite a distance from me I could not swear that Milan was being kidnapped or arrested but it seemed unlikely. But why would he arrange to meet someone there and leave his car behind?

If Morgan's call left us puzzled Inspector Falzone's call fifteen minutes later left us simultaneously puzzled, annoyed and alarmed. When the phone rang and I heard his voice I hoped that he was now ready to tell us about his mysterious suspect, but it was soon clear he was not calling for a friendly chat. He spoke in quick staccato sentences.

'I must see you at ten o'clock tomorrow morning. I am sending you a photograph. It will be delivered to your hotel in the next thirty minutes. It is a picture of the foreigner who claimed to be a journalist, the one who was asking questions around the docks. You will recognise him I think. You should talk to your Director General and then be prepared to be completely honest with us tomorrow.'

His tone did not invite any discussion but I picked up on his last phrase.

'Honest with us you say. Who is us? Who will be there tomorrow?'

There was a pause. 'A cousin of my mother's is interested in this matter. You will see tomorrow. You and your wife at ten o'clock.'

'Where? Here at the hotel or at your office?'

'No that will not be suitable. At the Café Firenze in Ortygia. I will give you the address.'

I had hardly written the address down before he had rung off.

A cousin of his mother's! What was he talking about? Giuseppe Falzone was a police officer investigating not only the murder of Farhad Jahandar but the disappearance of Bunny and Davoud and now the murder of the fisherman Giacomo Conti. But he wants to meet us, not at the police station, but at a café and he plans to have his mother's cousin tag along. Things are done differently in Sicily but surely not that differently. What was happening?

'Perhaps we will know that when the photo arrives,' suggested Julia.

Despite Giuseppe promising its delivery in thirty minutes it was more than an hour before a uniformed *Guardia Municipale* arrived with a sealed envelope for which he required my signature on two separate forms.

I ripped open the envelope as soon as he had left. Inside was a photograph I had first seen a few hours earlier. The Russian Yevgeny Kapustin stared blankly up at me. The man who had been lurking around the docks on the day Bunny and Davoud were supposed to arrive, the day before any alarm had been sounded, was someone the DG had described as a KGB hard man.

It seemed that the KGB had been waiting for the *Mahsheed* to complete its voyage from Kefalonia while at the same time the US Navy and the CIA had been carefully tracking its progress. Why? What had been on that boat that was so interesting to both organisations? I suspected that is exactly what Inspector Falzone was planning to ask us in the morning and I had no idea how to answer.

The café where he had told us to meet him was on a narrow street off the Via Roma barely wide enough for two donkeys to pass. The old sandy-coloured three-storey houses crowded in on each other with dark interiors and occasional glimpses of tiny courtyards. The café occupied the ground floor of a building that in every other respect looked like all the other houses in the street. Two old men in shapeless jackets and baggy trousers sat outside nursing half-drunk espressos and glasses of water. The scene was timeless and placeless. We had seen just such men sitting in village squares in Kefalonia a few days before. There must have been thousands of other men sitting in cafés just like this one in the back streets of Istanbul, Damascus or Tehran. With nothing to do but watch the world go by and wonder why their wives now looked so worn out.

The blazing sun struggled to reach down between the buildings. The interior of the café was cool and empty and oddly desolate. Like the scene outside it seemed untouched by the modern world, except for the sound of ABBA coming faintly from somewhere at the back of the house. A woman who could have been the wife of one of the men outside eventually appeared. We ordered coffees and waited. Despite our best efforts we had been unable to contact the DG and had no plan other than to play everything by ear.

The man who entered the café with Inspector Falzone seemed instantly at home but could not have presented a stronger contrast to the two men outside. Although about the same age, around sixty, I would guess, he was tall, upright, elegantly, almost foppishly, dressed. Expensive suit, silk tie, highly polished black shoes, not a grey hair out of place. As he sat down ABBA suddenly clicked off mid-song, 'Knowing Me' sang the voices in harmony but there was to be no Knowing You. An omen perhaps?

'Colonnello Castorini,' said the man, introducing himself first to Julia and then to me. 'Please do be seated.' He was not only immediately at home but also immediately in charge.

XVI

So Giuseppe's mother's cousin was a colonel in the *Carabinieri*. That would explain how Giuseppe, a provincial policeman, could make a quick phone call and discover Morgan worked for British Intelligence and how he had got hold of Kapustin's picture before us.

I looked at the Colonel more closely. This was the man Morgan had told us had conducted the initial investigation at Sigonella and who only yesterday was having a row with the Italian intelligence agency which had taken over his enquiry. He was also the man I had seen with Milan outside our hotel, the man in whose car Milan had been driven away. Before saying anything more he turned and ordered coffees. The woman who had been so slow to emerge when Julia and I had entered the café had reappeared the moment the Colonel arrived.

'My condolences on the death of your aunt,' he said to Julia. 'Giuseppe tells me you were very close. And this was to be your honeymoon. I am so sorry, a tragedy indeed. A tragedy and a mystery, a mystery I have been struggling to understand.'

He spoke quietly, his English slightly accented but spoken with confidence. I noticed another man who seemed to have arrived with Castorini and Falzone seating himself outside, perhaps the Colonel's driver or bodyguard. Morgan had mentioned that Castorini was an important man.

The Colonel was still speaking to Julia. 'When one has a mystery to solve one looks for clues, is that not correct? And in the case of your aunt's death there have been so very few clues. How fortunate then that your husband here works for British Intelligence and your uncle is the head of that organisation. Perhaps they can provide the clues that will help us solve the mystery. But first we have to decide whether we are all on the same side.' It had apparently not occurred to him that Julia might also be working for British Intelligence.

He turned to me. 'Davoud Sadeghi and his wife sail across the sea to Sicily. They do not arrive. But there is a man waiting for them. A spy. A Russian spy well known to the intelligence agencies of my country and yours and of course to the Americans. Why is a Russian spy waiting for that boat? I don't know but you, I think, may do. Have you spoken to your Director General and told him we have identified Kapustin as the man posing as a journalist and asking questions about the *Mahsheed*?'

'I spoke to him,' lied Julia. 'He doesn't know why Kapustin was there.'

'Really? Perhaps there are secrets that he does not share with his family. He is a professional no doubt. Perhaps he has said more to your husband when Mr Dylan went back to London to be briefed.'

'My uncle would say no more to Thomas than to me,' Julia replied. 'I am a DIS officer as well.'

Giuseppe's head shot up. 'You didn't tell me that.'

'You didn't need to know.'

Colonel Castorini smiled at that and stirred his coffee gently. 'Let us for the moment accept that nobody knows anything for certain. Let us use our imaginations. What do you think may have happened? Your aunt has been killed, a fisherman has been killed, this man Kapustin pops up and then disappears. You must have theories. What do you imagine took place on that boat?' He looked enquiringly at me.

My imagination had been working overtime but every theory I had produced seemed hopelessly improbable. I still thought the most likely possibility was that Bunny and Davoud had accidentally come across a Mafia drug smuggling operation. Conti and his two friends had been making a rendezvous at sea to receive or pass on heroin. When I suggested this the Colonel raised an eyebrow and then gently shook his head.

'No,' he said, 'the Mafia smuggling drugs using a fisherman from Marzamemi – that is not possible.'

'How can you be sure?' Julia asked.

'Believe me I can be sure. The Mafia are involved in this affair certainly but drug smuggling, I don't think so.'

Julia pounced on that remark. 'So you do think that the Mafia are involved, what makes you say that? What evidence do you have that we don't?'

The *Carabinieri* Colonel continued as if he had not been interrupted. 'We will come to that. For now let us return to the people on that boat, the *Mahsheed*. I believe they were attacked. They did not stumble across something in all those miles of empty sea. They were not in a speedboat unexpectedly racing over the horizon. They were under sail. Whoever threw a grenade into that boat saw it coming. He had plenty of time to get out of the way if he wanted to. That boat was targeted. The question is who on the boat was the target?'

'Or was the target actually on the boat?' I put in. 'Perhaps it was someone who was not on the boat but who was expected to be.'

'Go on.'

'Davoud Sadeghi's brother, Behzad, was planning to sail. We don't know why he didn't.'

It was difficult to decide how much to trust the two Italian policemen but on balance I thought we needed them more than they needed us. If their investigation of the murders of Farhad Jahandar and Giacomo Conti turned up anything it would almost certainly shed light on what had happened aboard the *Mahsheed*. We needed them to be open with us and for that reason we needed to show good faith by offering something ourselves. I decided to tell them everything we knew about Behzad – even his wild accusations against British Intelligence.

When I had finished the Colonel was quiet for a minute and then nodded. 'If this whole affair is political it would explain why the KGB were waiting for the boat and why the SID are so keen to be involved. The SID are keeping secrets from me and the CIA are keeping secrets from you. It would seem we are not all on the same side.'

At that point Julia said something that sent the conversation into an entirely unexpected direction. Having, like me, come to the conclusion that for now we and the two policemen were on the same side she had clearly decided that there was no point in trying to keep anything back. Almost casually she mentioned a name that would eventually unlock the entire affair.

'When we were in Kefalonia, Behzad had a visitor. A man with fake Canadian papers in the name of Henry Ramone.'

Initially there was no response. 'The name Ramone means nothing to me,' said the Colonel.

I was watching him closely and felt sure he was telling the truth. He repeated the name, Ramone, in the Italian way, rhyming it with pony. 'It could be Italian, Sicilian perhaps.'

It was then that, to my surprise, Giuseppe Falzone intervened. 'Yes, Ramone is Sicilian and it may be a name that means nothing to you but it means something to me.' He spoke hesitantly. 'I've seen that name very recently but it just doesn't make sense. My colleague Inspector Milliceni in Marzamemi showed me his file on the fisherman who had been shot. Giacomo Conti born Marzamemi 1919. Married Palermo 1940 to Chiara Ramone.'

Julia looked at Giuseppe. 'You mean the woman we spoke to, the fisherman's wife, her maiden name was Ramone?'

It couldn't be a coincidence. And yet we were convinced Ramone was a legend, a fake identity. If there was one thing I had been sure of it was that the man whose name appeared in Davoud Sadeghi's appointment book, despite apparently never having entered the UK, and who eight months later had visited his brother Behzad in Kefalonia, was not born with the name Ramone. Now here we discover that not only is Ramone a family name in Sicily but that one of these Ramones is related to the fisherman we were sure had been involved in Bunny's murder.

The Colonel echoed my thoughts, this was more than coincidence. 'It is an odd fact,' he added as if to demonstrate the point, 'that there is a greater variety of surnames in Italy than anywhere else in Europe.'

We told the two policemen about Ramone's address in Toronto, the arrangements with the tenants and the fake papers. We didn't mention the Company putting a POI tag on the Canadian security files and we certainly did not mention that there might be some connection with the DG's brother-in-law Davoud.

When I said London had discovered a bank account in Rome in Henry Ramone's name Castorini's eyes lit up.

'Can you get the account number?'

'I have it. We've tried to find more through the SID but got nowhere.'

'Let me try. I have contacts in the *Guardia de Finanza*. If there is Mafia money involved they may have something.' I wrote the account details down for him. When I had finished he continued. 'There is certainly some Mafia involvement in the deaths of the Sadeghis as I said earlier. Giuseppe tells me that two men disembarked from Conti's fishing boat in Syracuse and left in an ambulance, one of them on a stretcher. It has not been easy to find that ambulance. Nobody is willing to talk. But eventually we discovered that an ambulance from Catania had been summoned to take two men from Syracuse all the way to Palermo. They were admitted to hospital there but one was discharged immediately without giving his name. We still haven't managed to find him and may never do so. *Omertà.* The other was very badly injured. He remained at the hospital for two days and left in a coffin. The autopsy revealed he died of injuries received in an explosion, fragments of metal perforated his body.'

'A fragmentation grenade.'

'Precisely. We have identified the man. He was well known to the *Carabinieri*. A thug from San Giuseppe Jato, a Mafia footsoldier. We will learn nothing more for now. One day perhaps someone will want to offer us a deal: information on this man in return for turning a blind eye to something else but that will be ten or twenty years from now, when it is far too late to do anything with the information. In that part of Sicily *omertà* means *omertà*. He was a member of the Luchareza clan but that tells us nothing, they are what you would call small fry.'

Castorini started to get up as if he were about to leave but then appeared to change his mind. 'Thank you for your cooperation,' he said, 'we will speak again if I can discover anything about that bank account.' He stood looking at us for a moment. 'There's just one other thing. The Americans were tracking the *Mahsheed* all the way from Greece. You haven't mentioned that. Why do you think they were doing that?'

'We have no idea,' I replied firmly. 'I had hoped you would be able to tell us. Perhaps we should all sit back down and have another cup of coffee. Then you could really tell us all you know. How did you know the Americans had been tracking the *Mahsheed*, for example? And what else have you learned from Robert Milan? I saw you with him outside the Grand Hotel Villa Politi.'

'Ah yes. You are right.' The Colonel smiled and resumed his seat. 'We are all on the same side after all. I did meet Mr Milan. I was actually coming to the hotel to see you that evening. I wanted to meet the young lady who had so charmed my dear Giuseppe and to find out what sort of husband leaves his wife on their honeymoon; and not just that but who leaves her just when she most needs him, after she learns her aunt has mysteriously vanished. I wanted to ask how that husband, supposedly left in Rome, can suddenly reappear at an American naval base in Sicily stepping off a military flight from Germany. But when I reached your hotel you were both sitting in the bar with a man I knew in very different circumstances. I had interviewed Milan only a few weeks before about a supposed breach of security at Sigonella. I had found him very sympathetic in that naïve way Americans have. A man who spoke fluent Italian and Sicilian and yet knew practically nothing about contemporary Sicily and claimed not to be interested in his own family story. I decided to make your acquaintance at a later time and have another talk to our American friend instead.'

Castorini was silent for a moment. I was not sure if he was trying to remember what Milan had told him or trying to decide how much he would tell. He suddenly stood up again and went outside. After speaking to the man seated there he returned. 'It is not easy to know where to begin.' There was an odd tone in his voice, impersonal but not completely detached, as if recounting a story of which he was not a part and yet in which he had a personal interest.

'What do you know about Italian history and politics?' he asked.

XVII

Not much, I thought, although remembering Behzad Sadeghi asking me a very similar question in Kefalonia, more than I had known about Iranian history and politics. Without waiting for an answer Castorini moved back into the past.

'Our history is not straightforward but I must describe some of it to you. It will help you understand what is happening now. I believe, in fact I know, that only if you understand our history will you understand that young American. More than that, only if we study this nation's past will we be able to establish who murdered your aunt and uncle.

'I shall try to explain it simply but simplicity is not an Italian virtue. You are an island, you have clear boundaries, you have continuity, you have an identity. Ask two Italians what it is to be Italian and they will give different answers. We are ancient and new at the same time. The *Carabinieri* have been here longer than Italy itself. The history books tell you that the Kingdom of Italy was formed in 1861 just 116 years ago, but even that is misleading. Anyone on this island will tell you that the so-called unification of our country did not stop the Italian Navy subsequently bombarding Palermo and executing hundreds of Sicilian patriots. The MIS, the Sicilian Independence Party, won nearly ten per cent of the vote just thirty years ago.

'And what is true of Sicilians is true of all Italians. We do not bow to authority. And yet fascism was invented here. I know

Giuseppe told you that the *Carabinieri* led Mussolini's war on the Mafia. His dictatorship would not have been possible without us, but remember it was also the *Carabinieri* who arrested Il Duce in 1943.'

He paused. 'I don't suppose you have heard of the author Vitaliano Brancati.'

I shook my head.

'That is a pity. Brancati was born near here and studied in Catania. He wrote brilliantly about the Sicilian character. His most famous work *Gli anni perduti*, The Lost Years, was a satire of fascism and Mussolini's megalomania. If you read that book you would wonder how anyone could have been fooled by a man like Mussolini who was so clearly mad and yet Brancati himself had been fooled. He had been an outspoken admirer of fascism in the early days.

'It is difficult to explain fascism and the war to foreigners. We don't like to talk about our campaigns of conquest in Africa and the Balkans. Now we talk about our war against the Germans after the Armistice in 1943. I joined the *Carabinieri* in Bari then and fought alongside British troops, that's where I learned my English. But in some parts of the country Italians still fought on the side of the Germans. Italy was in turmoil. The Germans were massacring civilians in retaliation for partisan attacks. In addition to the new Italian Army there were all sorts of partisan groups. The biggest were the Communists, the Garibaldi Brigades. Then there were the Socialist Matteotti Brigades and a host of small groups: Catholics, monarchists, liberals, anarchists and more. It was awful. Brother against brother. When the war was over we just wanted peace but that was not easy to achieve. Elections were set for April 1948. They would determine the future of Italy. Now here is a question for you: who do you think won those elections?'

Not Winston Churchill, I thought, remembering Behzad Sadeghi's assertion that Churchill had determined the fate of his beloved Iran. If I closed my eyes I could almost believe I was back on Kefalonia listening to Behzad Sadeghi. The two men were about the same age, the same casual elegance and the same accented but almost perfect English.

'The Christian Democrats won,' replied Julia.

'Yes of course the Christian Democrats gained the most seats, but who *really* won? Not Alcide De Gasperi the Christian Democrat leader. No, two men won that election, two brothers sitting in their offices at the Sullivan and Cromwell law firm in New York. Allen Dulles, who soon after became chief of the CIA, and John Foster Dulles who became US Secretary of State. Those two men settled the fate of Italy.'

It really was like listening to Sadeghi all over again. Two men recounting thirty-year-old stories, tales from their youth, that both believed were somehow still relevant today. It was more than mere reminiscence. There was a gentle urgency in Castorini's voice.

'When the election was called it seemed obvious to everyone that the Popular Front of Communists and socialists would win. They had led the fight against fascism. The old order was thoroughly discredited and people wanted something new. But the Dulles brothers had other ideas. They were terrified of Communism. Stalin had just staged a Communist coup in Czechoslovakia, destroying the other parties and imposing a police state entirely subservient to Moscow. It was unthinkable that Communists should be allowed a foothold in Italy. And the brothers had what was needed to win an election: money. They poured private money into the campaign and persuaded congressional leaders to pressure President Truman into allowing the CIA to intervene. The Christian Democrats received massive funding. Catholic priests were paid to lead a crusade against the ungodly Communists. Dissident socialists were bribed to break away from the Popular Front. The country was flooded with pamphlets and newspaper articles warning that a victory for the Front meant rule from the Kremlin. And it worked. Against all expectations the Popular Front lost.

'Naturally, there were all sorts of local factors in play in different parts of Italy. In Sicily there was one factor in particular, the Mafia. Just six months earlier the Popular Front had won the regional elections here and the Communist leader Girolamo Li Causi was promising to break up the big estates, the latifondo, and give the land to the peasants. That was bad news for the big landowners who were keeping the Mafia in business. Remember, this was long before the Mafia moved into the drugs trade. Back then the Mafia clans were employed by the landowners to keep order.'

The Colonel paused and went off on another tangent. 'You won't know Girolamo Li Causi. One of the grand old men of the Communist Party, imprisoned by Mussolini. He represented Sicily in the parliament in Rome for more than twenty years and died just a few months ago, in April. Right to the end of his life he fought against the Mafia. Just last year he was sued for libel by two leading Christian Democrat politicians. He had accused them of being involved in corruption and in the murder of one of their own Party members who had dared make a stand against the Mafia. I am pleased to say Li Causi was acquitted.'

I was beginning to feel that Italian politics were as incomprehensible as Iran's. My own political awakening came in my first year at university when the Russians invaded Czechoslovakia: Soviet Communism crushing the first stirrings of democracy. Now here was what seemed to be the epitome of an establishment figure, a senior officer in the *Carabinieri* dedicated to the defence of the Italian state, singing the praises of a Communist politician.

'Li Causi's campaigns against the latifondo are what brings us to the Portella della Ginestra massacre. And in case you are starting to wonder what something that happened thirty years ago has to do with us today the Portella della Ginestra massacre leads us to Roberto Milan. Giuseppe you know the story of the massacre, tell our English friends.'

Falzone took up the story. 'I only know what I learned in school. I told Julia the other day about Piana dei Greci, the area was famous for two things: left-wing unrest and the Mafia. In 1947 there was a huge May Day celebration at Portella della Ginestra which lies between Piani dei Greci and San Giuseppe Jato. It was attended by hundreds of peasants with speeches from local Communists and lots of flag waving. People attended from all over the region. It was a traditional family affair, more of an enormous picnic than a political protest. The event was well underway with a local Communist leader making a speech when suddenly machine guns opened fire from the hillside and horsemen started firing into the crowd. Eleven people were killed including four children, more than thirty were injured.

'It soon became plain that they had been killed by a gang of local bandits, Mafia, led by a man called Salvatore Giuliano. His name is about the only thing everyone can agree on. Why did he do it? Was he paid and if so by whom? Theories have circulated ever since. Senior politicians were implicated but nothing proved. You know Mario Scelba?'

I shook my head.

'He is a Sicilian and now he is a senator in Rome and a member of the European Parliament. On the surface a distinguished man, he has been Prime Minister of Italy and President of the European Parliament. He helped found the Christian Democrats here in Sicily. Back at the time of the massacre he was the Minister of the Interior in Rome and he immediately declared that the massacre was not political in any way, it was just a war between local bandits.

'Salvatore Giuliano himself, the bandit leader, was mysteriously strangled. Some of his gang ended up in prison, others simply disappeared. His chief lieutenant, a man called Pisciotta, was arrested and made the fantastic claim that Mario Scelba had been involved in the plot. That may be true but before Pisciotta could give his evidence he was poisoned inside the jail.'

Colonel Castorini took over the account again. 'It was an extraordinary time. We are still feeling the ripples. Millions of leftists took to the streets across Italy to protest the massacre. There was talk of civil war. Passions were raised, especially as the dead included children. But amongst the dead was a young man named Salvatore Lipari. He had left the area as a sixteen year old and emigrated to the United States. In New York he found work, married and had a child, Roberto. Then his mother back in Piana dei Greci fell seriously ill and he travelled home to see her. Why he was at the rally. I don't know – but he was. He died on the spot and is buried now beside his mother and father. Behind him in New York he left a widow with a young child, barely one year old. The widow soon married again, to a man born in New York to parents who had migrated from Lombardy. Her new husband adopted the child and gave him his name.'

'Milan!' exclaimed Julia.

'Exactly. Roberto Lipari became Robert Milan. The baby now had a new father and as he grew up nobody told him that this was not his real father. The family left New York and eventually settled in Nebraska. They spoke Italian in the house and Robert and his mother often spoke Sicilian but to the outside world young Robert became the all-American boy. The American dream had become a reality. But then life started to go wrong. His mother died and her husband quickly went downhill. He couldn't hold down a job, money became tight and his mind started to wander. Robert's younger sisters went to live with an aunt in Florida but the aunt couldn't afford to take Robert and in any case, she said, he wasn't a blood relative. So it was that at the age of seventeen Robert discovered that his father was not his father and his sisters were only half-sisters. You can imagine perhaps what effect that would have. At the very time he needed his family most, with his mother dead and the man he thought was his father dying, he discovers he has no family. Even his young half-sisters have been spirited away.

'As soon as he could he joined the Navy, saw action in Vietnam and moved to Hawaii. It was the end of what you call the swinging sixties. He cut his ties with his old family and started a new life. But that too started to go wrong. He made a bad marriage, was looking at an expensive divorce and realised he was tired of life. He saw some sort of counsellor who told him he needed to find his "inner being" and he could only do that by "returning to his roots". So he applied for a transfer to Sigonella and set about finding himself. I suspect he had been using drugs of some kind but he says not. It doesn't really matter why he came to be here. The fact is he arrived and went looking for his father's family. He had a name Salvatore Lipari and a place Piana dei Greci and that was enough.

'He discovered that his father had been the eldest of eight children, most of whom still lived around Piana dei Greci. They welcomed him home. Everyone in Sicily has family abroad and wherever they are they remain family. One of his cousins worked for a travel agent in Palermo. The tourist industry, she told him, was the future of Sicily. Why didn't he leave the Navy and live here? Anyone fluent in English was sure to find a well-paid job. At first, he told me, he rejected the idea completely. This was not something he had ever considered, he was an American, he would be a foreigner here.

'It was then that somebody in the family said something that changed his whole view of the world. "Why would you want to be American, they killed your father." It seems that his new family were Communists or Communist sympathisers. They told him that the massacre had been organised by American agents. At first he refused to believe it but it was clear that the family genuinely believed the story. The CIA had been in Piana dei Greci, they said. He started thinking about what he had seen in Vietnam and how the American people had been lied to over that war. He remembered that the Communists he had been warned against when he had been posted to Vietnam turned out to be just peasants like his new family in Sicily.'

'So he contacted the Russians,' interrupted Julia.

'The answer is both yes and no,' responded the Colonel mysteriously. 'Let me finish my story.

'There have been rumours about the Americans paying the Mafia to shoot those attending the rally ever since the massacre happened. But there were rumours about the Americans being behind everything. I don't believe it. Money was all that was needed to win elections. The Americans had nothing to gain by creating martyrs. And I'm not sure Milan believed it but he was confused, unsure what to do. His family had mentioned by name an American agent who they claimed had been in Piana dei Greci, and helped organise the massacre, Harry Bastamente. And then one day a CIA agent named Harry Bastamente appeared at the base issuing instructions for a new secret operation, Tortellini. Milan snapped, he collected a great pile of classified folders, put them in a box and posted them anonymously to the Russian Embassy in Rome.

'It was a crazy thing to do and when he thought about it the next day he realised that the Harry Bastamente at Sigonella would probably have been at kindergarten at the time of the massacre. Milan was no traitor but it was too late, the CIA had found out about the leaked documents. He had become a suspect. I interviewed him myself and he claimed to have had no contacts with anyone on the island even though he spoke passable Sicilian. Romney and Bastamente interrogated him. At some point it occurred to him that Romney always called his colleague Junior. Was there an older Bastamente who could have been involved in his father's killing?'

'And so he sent more files to the Russians,' Julia interrupted again.

'He says not. Milan insists there was just one parcel.'

'But we know that the Russians received another more secret batch.'

'Milan says he didn't send that. He kept his head down until your aunt disappeared and he read about you in *La Sicilia*. That reignited his doubts all over again. He came to see you and the rest you know.'

'So where is Milan now?' I asked.

'He's disappeared. I dropped him back at the base at three thirty this morning and I haven't seen him since.'

XVIII

It took me a minute to realise the implication of what he had just said.

'You mean Milan admitted to sending secret information to the Russians and you just let him go?'

The Colonel drew himself upright. 'I formed the opinion that Signor Milan is an honourable man, misguided to be sure, but honourable. He agreed he would give himself up to the American authorities and I trusted him. I saw him talking to the marine guard at the gate. As soon as I learned he had vanished I contacted my opposite number in the *Servizio Informazioni Difesa* and offered the full cooperation of the *Carabinieri*. I reminded him that none of the papers Milan passed on related to Italian military affairs and that I had therefore thought it best for the Americans to handle matters themselves. What was important for us is that, contrary to Mr Romney's assertion, the leak came from the American side not the Italian.'

I could now understand what Castorini and Di Benedetto from the SID had been arguing about. I was not surprised Di Benedetto was angry. When the Company find out that Castorini had allowed Milan to slip through their hands there will be hell to pay. Still the Colonel and Giuseppe Falzone had given us plenty to think about. I wanted a chance to discuss it with Julia and see what she had made of it all, but when Giuseppe suggested she accompany him to Marzamemi for another conversation with

146

the dead fisherman's widow she immediately agreed. Colonel Castorini insisted on giving me a lift back to our hotel where I was left to contact the DG and Morgan and brief them both on what the Colonel had told us.

I couldn't reach the DG but Morgan was in the apartment he had rented in Catania and answered the phone immediately. 'I was planning to go to the beach,' he said, 'and find somewhere for Sunday lunch. Why not join me?'

The idea of a swim followed by an afternoon lazing on the beach was enticing but the thought of Julia's inevitable reproach that we were here to work pricked my conscience. I agreed to meet him in a bar near the base.

On the drive up to Sigonella I thought about Robert Milan. Colonel Castorini had painted a sympathetic picture of an innocent abroad but was that really the case? Milan was a thirty-year-old Vietnam veteran. Was he really the sort of man who would see Julia's face in the paper and decide that he had to help her? He already knew he was one of the people suspected of passing on classified secrets, would he really risk doing it again just because an English woman he had never met was searching for her aunt?

On the other hand I had been impressed by Castorini and was inclined to accept his judgement. When he came to our hotel Milan had certainly sounded more like an innocent abroad than a Russian secret agent. But, I acknowledged ruefully, if I were to start making decisions on the basis of whether someone looked like a spy my friends in MI5 would despair. They had devoted hour upon hour to my training precisely in order stop me judging anything by appearance alone.

When I reached the bar Morgan was not in a good mood. 'I've just had a call from Romney. He would like a chat this afternoon to clear the air. I said you and I would drop into the base later on.'

Morgan's mood was not improved when I told him about this morning's conversation. He was more sceptical than me about Milan's motivation and appalled that the *Carabinieri* had merely dropped him back at the base rather than immediately arresting him. 'What on earth is Colonel Castorini playing at? The man admitted passing classified information to the Russians. We know he's lying about what he passed on. It was certainly more than one batch. And now he's disappeared and I'm betting that was only possible with the help of this Russian Kapustin.'

Morgan had a theory to explain Kapustin's appearance in Sicily.

'The Russians received the stuff from Milan. And forget about him sending it anonymously. Why would anyone do that? He must have given them some way to contact him, and that is assuming we believe his story that he's never had any contact with the Russians before. They send Kapustin down here as his handler. Kapustin flies into Palermo rather than Catania to avoid us suspecting they've got an agent on this side of the island. He contacts Milan and Milan gives him more files, but also tells him about the weird US operation to track a boat coming in from Greece. Kapustin goes down to the dock to see what's happening. When he doesn't find anything he goes to ground again and sends Milan to you to try to find out if you had any idea what the Company was doing.'

It was a plausible theory. Kapustin's appearance at the docks before Bunny and Davoud had disappeared had always struck me as odd. Either he was waiting for the *Mahsheed* because there was something or someone on board that the Russians wanted or, as Morgan suggested, he was waiting because he had discovered that the Americans were watching the boat and he wanted to know why. The problem was that the most likely reason that the Americans were tracking the boat was because they thought the other side, the Russians, had something on board. I was in danger of arguing myself in circles.

'Of course,' I said, 'we only have Milan's word that the Americans really were tracking the *Mahsheed*. Bastamente and Romney flatly denied it.'

'But there,' said Morgan, 'I think I believe Milan. I haven't been able to get hold of any flight plans for the two days the *Mahsheed* was at sea. There is nothing positive to suggest Junior was lying but it is the absence of evidence that is puzzling. There were a couple of P-3 Orions up for the whole time. I know that because I saw them taking off and returning. But what were they doing? If they had been going somewhere, to another US base perhaps, they would have filed flight plans in the normal way. If they had been on routine training that would appear in the training programme. I've checked with our Navy, there was nothing happening anywhere in this end of the Mediterranean that would warrant special surveillance. If they weren't tracking the *Mahsheed* itself I would put money on them watching something or someone who was keeping very close to Sadeghi's boat.'

'Whatever they were watching they won't tell us,' I said, but when we arrived at Sigonella Romney proved me wrong. That is exactly what he wanted to tell us.

'I have been authorised by Washington to tell you about Tortellini,' he started, leading us into an office with views out towards Mount Etna. There were two bottles of bourbon on the cupboard behind his desk but no sign that Romney had been drinking this morning. He looked relaxed and had recovered

149

the control he seemed to have when he met me off the plane. He motioned us to a circular conference table at one end of the room.

'I spoke to Junior's old man,' he said, 'and it seems that our end of Tortellini is going to be wound up, from now on the operation will be run from Washington. Harry has been trying to get hold of your DG to let him know what's been going on but the Admiral's off fishing for the weekend. I guess you guys work a little differently to us – we'd better hope the Russians don't invade on a Saturday night.'

He gave a nervous laugh that belied his relaxed expression.

'Well, Tortellini. The United States is at war. You know that. We are in a cold war with the Russians and whatever the politicians may say about détente, the Helsinki Accords and all that bullshit, we are still in a real war. The KGB haven't changed. They want to destroy us. But there's also another war, the war declared by Richard Nixon on June 18, 1971, the War on Drugs.

'You'll know all about it. The Beatles arrived from England and before we knew it there were long-haired hippies smoking pot and getting high on LSD and now we have heroin. In the last three or four years drug addiction has become an epidemic. We have to stop it. Lots of kids came back from Vietnam addicted because the commies there sold the stuff really cheap. And that's what they're doing in the US right now. Russian heroin made in Sicily. You've heard of the Mafia?'

It was such an absurd question I just nodded in reply.

'The United States used to have its own gangsters but now the Mafia from Sicily have moved in. They control the sale of heroin along the east coast but they need to make the stuff somewhere and get it across the ocean. That's where the KGB come in. They've provided the funds and the equipment to make the drugs here. And then they're shipping it off to places like Panama to be smuggled into the US. It seems Yevgeny Kapustin has been their point man, which brings us to Tortellini.

'Our man inside their Embassy in Rome told us that the reds were planning to deliver equipment to create a whole network of heroin refineries in this part of Sicily. He says that Kapustin was sent down here to supervise the operation. They've been working on it for months. We knew what ship it was coming on but we didn't know where it was unloading and who was receiving it. So we tracked the ship. At first the whole operation seemed to be going to plan. They met a small freighter out of Catania and transferred the equipment. What we hadn't reckoned on was Conti turning up in his fishing boat. It seems that not only were the Russians delivering stuff here but they were picking up a shipment of heroin which Conti was delivering.

'We had to make a decision. We couldnt follow the freighter and Conti. So we tracked the freighter and had a destroyer intercept it when the Russian ship was well out of the way. What happened to Conti after the freighter had steamed off we don't know for sure. Somehow the *Mahsheed* appeared. Conti and the men with him must have panicked. They saw this strange boat heading right towards the rendezvous they were just leaving. They must have decided to eliminate any possible witnesses.

'We thought at one time that Behzad Sadeghi was involved in some way: he's been trying to ingratiate himself with the Russians, maybe the heroin was intended for him to distribute to raise funds. Harry was blindsided because he's been on Sadeghi's case for so long. When we saw that Sadeghi's boat had vanished we jumped to the conclusion that he had something to do with the Tortellini operation, but he didn't. It was just an unfortunate coincidence. They were just in the wrong place at the wrong time.

'When the Soviets discovered what had happened they were left with a potential loose end: Giacomo Conti. Kapustin must have been waiting in Syracuse for Conti to come back with his passengers. When they turned up Kapustin would have realised that something had gone dramatically wrong. The next thing he knows all the world is searching for your DG's sister. Sooner or later someone was bound to connect the *Mahsheed*'s disappearance with Conti turning up in Syracuse with two injured men on his boat. The last thing Kapustin wanted was anybody talking to Conti so he went down to Marzamemi and shot him. Pretty drastic but typical KGB.'

'But what actually happened out to sea?' I asked. 'How did one of Conti's passengers end up coming off the boat on a stretcher?'

Romney at last seemed to show some emotion. 'Dumb ass Italians,' he replied. 'That's the only explanation. The two guys Conti was carrying must have been Mafia types, gangsters with big muscles and no brains. They panic and start shooting. And then one of them has this old grenade he's always wanted to play with so he pitches it at the *Mahsheed* because he's too stupid to realise that it's a fragmentation grenade and he's gonna get his ass blown off.'

Possibly, I thought, but why would even a dumb gangster take a hand grenade out to sea with him? Morgan seemed to have no doubts. 'It all makes sense,' he said. 'It's a pity you didn't tell us this before.'

I wasn't so convinced. 'How do you know that Conti was delivering heroin to the Russian ship? He can't have told you, nor I suppose did the Russians. Did that come from your source in Rome?'

'The SID tested Conti's boat. They found traces of heroin. OK we don't know that he was delivering the stuff but it's a reasonable guess.'

I was still not as satisfied as Morgan appeared to be. 'What about Ramone? Where does he come in?'

'You keep mentioning Ramone,' Romney replied. 'We don't know anyone with that name. Come on, we've been straight with you, tell us where this name comes from.'

'I don't know,' I lied. 'You would have to ask the DG.'

Romney looked disappointed but also relieved, as if he had expected a different response from us.

When we had left his office Morgan drove me back to the beach where I had left my car.

'What did you make of all that?' I asked. 'It leaves a lot of loose ends. Someone in the Company knows about Ramone because they put a POI tag on him. We've still got the mysterious Robert Milan out there somewhere, not to mention Kapustin. That suggestion that the SID have found traces of heroin in Conti's boat is new, they don't seem to have told anyone else, certainly Falzone and Castorini hadn't heard. The local police have completely dismissed the idea that there could have been some sort of Mafia drug smuggling operation in Marzamemi and surely if there was drugs money circulating in a little place like that somebody would have noticed.'

'It seems to me that the loose ends have actually been cut off,' said Morgan. 'Ramone's only in the frame because of Behzad Sadeghi, if Sadeghi isn't involved we can forget Ramone. Similarly Milan is irrelevant. There is no suggestion he has anything to do with the Mafia and drug smuggling. As to the local police dismissing the heroin angle, I think that says something about the police. If you ask me Inspector Falzone and Colonel Castorini are just too good to be true. If you think about it they are perfectly placed to be working with the Mafia themselves.'

When we reached the beach I phoned Julia while Morgan went to buy bruschetta. Julia had spent the morning with her favourite Italian policeman.

'Did you enjoy yourself?' I asked.

'Yes thanks. Giuseppe insisted I try an almond granita in Marzamemi and then we had lunch on the way back to Syracuse. Amazing seafood.'

'Sounds wonderful. Did either of you get any work done?'

'We tried but didn't really get anywhere. Without her daughter there Signora Conti just clammed up. She acknowledged of course that her maiden name was Ramone but insisted she had had no contact with any of her relatives for thirty years. We talked to the local police but they are no further forward. The SID have taken Conti's boat away but I don't know what they expect to find.'

'Heroin,' I said, 'and they found it.' I recounted our conversation with Romney.

Julia's reaction was muted. 'So the Company thinks this chap Kapustin has been down here to run a drug smuggling operation. Their source in the Embassy actually told them that.'

'That's correct. You sound surprised.'

'I am. My one piece of news is about Yevgeny Kapustin. First the police have shown his photo to practically the whole population of Marzamemi. Nobody recognised him. Giuseppe is convinced Kapustin has never been to Marzamemi.'

'But we know that Conti received money from a foreigner.'

'I don't think it was Kapustin who paid Conti,' Julia replied. 'The people we spoke to in the docks in Syracuse all commented on how badly Kapustin spoke Italian. And yet we imagine he was able to have a meaningful conversation with an almost illiterate Sicilian fisherman.'

I tried to think through the implications of what she was saying. 'If it wasn't Kapustin who was liaising with Conti that must imply that the Russians have somebody else down here, perhaps a whole team. I suppose if they have, that might explain how Milan got spirited away.'

Julia was still on the subject of Kapustin. 'We have a much more fundamental problem with Romney's story about the Russians. According to him Kapustin is running the show. But Giuseppe's just received some news that makes me really doubt that. The *Carabinieri* now know what Kapustin was doing between his appearance at the docks and his flight back to Rome on the day Conti was killed. He wasn't spiriting Milan away or dealing with a botched drug-smuggling operation by murdering a Sicilian fisherman. He was on holiday with his wife in Taormina, a hundred miles from Marzamemi.'

XIX

It seems that the Russian had been out in the open all the time. He had made no effort to hide. It was not the tradecraft of a highly trained spy that had allowed him to remain undiscovered but pure bureaucratic ineptitude. Only when his name cropped up on the passenger manifest of his flight back to Rome had the *Carabinieri* been alerted and had then been able to find out where he had been staying. The taxi driver who had taken Kapustin and his wife to the airport in Catania was able to provide the name of the hotel in Taormina where he had picked them up. The hotel staff in turn were happy to confirm that the couple had been staying there for five days and almost certainly had never left the resort. Nor had they received any visitors. Both were using their real papers. Amazingly, the local police had simply not contacted the hotel and Mrs Kapustin's presence on a flight from Rome to Catania six days earlier had been missed by the police who were hunting for a man. It was now clear that Kapustin had flown from Rome to Palermo on 5 July, spent two days who knows where and then turned up in Syracuse where he had spent a couple of days wandering around the docks asking questions. He had then gone straight from the docks to meet his wife at the airport in Catania following which the two of them spent five relaxing days in an expensive hotel on the beach in Taormina.

'Are the *Carabinieri* absolutely sure that the man at the hotel really was Kapustin and that he never left?'

'That's just what I asked. It was definitely Kapustin; the hotel staff identified his photo. He and his wife stood out at the hotel; they don't have Russian diplomats staying there every day. Of course he could have slipped off somewhere at some point but only for a couple of hours at most. I think we can be quite sure he's not been anywhere near Sigonella or Marzamemi since he picked his wife up at the airport.'

I thought back to Romney's words this morning. He had said quite specifically that the Company source in the Russian Embassy reported that Kapustin was here to supervise the operation going on at sea. Kapustin could hardly do that from the beach. The Russians must have thought we were on to him and told him to stay away. They must have put somebody else in charge. Either that or the American's precious source had got things wrong. I needed to hear what Romney made of the latest news.

Julia did not seem upset when I told her that my planned afternoon swim was off and Morgan merely shrugged his shoulders. I was just about to put the phone down when Julia asked me to wait and I heard her talking to someone else.

'Giuseppe's just come back; he wants to talk to us.'

'What about?'

I heard her repeat the question to Giuseppe. She didn't seem to like his answer. 'Giuseppe just says he wants to talk. Apparently it's urgent. We'll meet you outside the base in an hour.' As nothing else the Italian police had done seemed to be urgent I was sceptical but agreed. The priority now was to find out how our American friends would respond to the news that Kapustin had been soaking up the sun when they imagined he was masterminding a Mafia drugs operation.

Morgan drove and we returned to Sigonella, parking inside the base. We walked towards Romney's office and were startled to see a short, impeccably tailored man come flying out the door, clearly not the sort of person who regarded the weekends as an opportunity for casual dress. He glanced towards us and then hurried off in the opposite direction.

'Di Benedetto from the SID,' Morgan explained. 'I wonder what's bitten him.'

As we drew closer we could hear raised voices inside the office. There was obviously an argument going on. It seemed to be about the church, which seemed highly unlikely. Then I heard someone saying quite clearly 'Goddamn bank account, for Chrissake.' It sounded like Romney. Morgan knocked and silence suddenly descended. At first it appeared that nobody was going to answer but then the door swung open and Harry Bastamente Junior stood in front of us.

'Oh it's you two,' he said, 'the James Bond twins.' He waved us into the office. Romney, tie askew, stood by the conference table at one end of the room while sitting behind Romney's desk was the imposing figure of Harry Bastamente Senior. Like Di Benedetto the older Bastamente was not dressed for the weekend, in fact he looked exactly as he had looked in London, his suit unrumpled and shirt freshly ironed. I wondered how long he had been on the island. Romney this morning had said that he had been authorised to tell us about Tortellini by 'Washington'. I had assumed that meant the man now sitting in front of me, who most certainly had not been in Washington.

Junior seemed less relaxed than his father despite his blue jeans and checked shirt. He could have been out on the range but for the identity tag dangling from his neck. Romney, who had seemed unnaturally calm a few hours earlier, now clasped and unclasped his hands nervously. I glanced across the room and noticed the two bourbon bottles I had seen earlier were still unopened.

It was Bastamente Senior who gestured towards the table and invited us to take a seat. He himself made no effort to move from behind the desk. 'How can we help you?'

'You've heard about Yevgeny Kapustin?' I asked.

'Di Benedetto has just told us. It seems that while we've been assured that every cop on the island has been out looking for this guy our Russian friend has in fact been living it up at a hotel on the beach and none of our Italian colleagues noticed. We circulate his photo to every goddamn agency they've got and this guy sits there enjoying martinis and getting a tan. How the hell does that happen?'

I interrupted: 'But what he's not doing is organising drugs deals off the Sicilian coast.'

'Says who? One minute these people can't find a man who isn't even trying to hide and the next they're insisting they can tell us how many times he took a piss. We don't know what the hell Kapustin has been up to, or who with. The Russians have extracted a man and his luggage out of this base right under our eyes and they didn't do that by sitting on a beach rubbing oil on each other's backs.'

He paused for a second before continuing more calmly. 'Listen. You two are here to do two things. One: find out who's been leaking information to the Russians. Well we know that now. Two: find out what happened to your DG's sister. We pretty well know that too. There's nothing more for you here. I suggest you go spend the rest of the afternoon in the sunshine and think about getting back to England. Leave this to the professionals. I'm going to be briefing George Ffortiscue later today and no doubt he will keep your DG in the picture. In fact if anything new comes up I'll be sure to tell your DG myself.'

'But do we actually know what happened to Bunny? All we really have is guesswork. Jack Romney here says you intercepted a freighter, what did you find? Can any of the crew tell us anything more about what happened to the *Mahsheed*?'

'I'm sorry, anything we learned from that freighter really is classified. Jack shouldn't have told you anything about Tortellini, he was just trying to be helpful because of your personal relationship to Mrs Sadeghi.'

I turned to Romney. 'I thought you said you had been authorised to brief us.'

'I must have misunderstood,' he mumbled. 'Sorry.' It wasn't clear to whom he was saying sorry.

'What about Ramone?' I asked.

It was Bastamente Junior who pounced on that, just as Romney had this morning, and using almost exactly the same language. 'Ramone, Ramone. Why are the English obsessed with Ramone? We don't even know if he really exists. Nobody else has heard anything at all about him and you won't tell us why you're asking. Di Benedetto tells us you've now come up with a bank account in Rome that's something to do with Ramone. What the hell is that about?'

'Calm down, son,' said his father before turning to me. 'The point is your DG seems to be the only person who has ever come across that name. Personally I don't think such an individual exists. Nobody we have spoken to, inside the Agency or outside, has ever encountered anyone, male or female, named Ramone.'

'Is that right? Somebody in the Company knows the name because they've put a POI tag on it.'

Bastamente Senior's expression was unchanged. 'I'll look into that,' he said. 'Nobody's mentioned that before.'

I wasn't going to let him brush me off like that. 'You say nobody's come across anyone, male or female, called Ramone, well I've certainly come across a female Ramone.'

Romney had walked across the room and was picking up a glass from the tray beside the two bottles of bourbon. We all jumped as the glass fell from his hand and shattered on the floor.

'For Chrissake be careful,' shouted Junior. 'And it's still too fucking early for bourbon.'

Romney started to kneel down to pick up the fragments of glass but then changed his mind and returned to his seat by the table.

'What are you talking about?' Bastamente Senior asked me. 'What female Ramone?'

'Chiara Ramone. The wife of that fisherman, Conti. Her maiden name was Ramone.'

Bastamente Senior shrugged. 'So? She shared a surname with someone. With a name like yours, Mr Thomas Dylan, you're surely not going to draw any conclusions about people sharing a name.'

'No,' I said, remembering Colonel Castorini's comment, 'but there's a greater variety of surnames in Italy than anywhere else in Europe. It's one hell of a coincidence.'

Bastamente was not impressed.

'Go home,' he said. 'There is nothing more for you here. There's nothing for any of us any more. We've done what we came here for. Jack here's hanging up his badge and marching off into the sunset. Maybe it's even time for me to follow him.'

He looked across at his son with half a smile. 'I'll leave you to carry on the family business.' With that he rose from behind the desk and held out his hand, I was being dismissed again. His handshake was as unflinching as it had been in London. Junior and Romney said nothing, Junior glaring at me and Romney not meeting my eye. There was nothing more to be said.

XX

I had left my hire car at the beach as I had no vehicle pass for the base. Morgan had driven me to Sigonella in his usual boy racer style and I was surprised when he didn't drive that way on the return journey.

'Police,' he explained. 'They've been right behind us since we left the base. I could lose them but I don't want to spark a diplomatic incident. The DG would not be impressed.' That was an understatement.

We had driven four or five miles from the base when the police car drew alongside, blue light flashing, and motioned for us to pull in to a small parking area just ahead. The police car stopped directly in front of us and two uniformed policemen emerged and, in Italian, demanded our documents. Morgan produced his diplomatic passport which carried no weight at all. The two officers just returned to their car with our papers and Morgan's car key. They made no attempt to ask any questions. I suspected that neither spoke much English. Once they were back in their car we all just sat there. I looked around. Beside us there was what looked like a deserted factory or perhaps barracks. Being a Sunday there was no sign of life.

After ten minutes or so Morgan's patience ran out and he approached the police car to try to prompt some action but to no avail. About five minutes later another car pulled up beside us. To my astonishment Julia emerged with Giuseppe Falzone. The inspector approached the police car and retrieved our papers and the car key. The two uniformed police saluted him then got back into their car and drove off, their job done.

'What's going on?' Morgan started to bluster.

Falzone cut him short. 'You are in my jurisdiction now Mr Morgan and if you don't mind I will ask the questions. It is you who should be telling me what's going on. Let's all just stand here in this glorious sunshine and have a sensible conversation.'

Falzone tossed Morgan's car key from one hand to the other. 'Now I am just a simple policeman. I deal with missing pets and stolen cars. Your world, the world of spies and secret agents, is an alien place. But I am not a fool. I know when someone is lying to me, I know when something smells and let me tell you something here stinks. And you know where that stink is coming from.'

I thought Morgan was going to respond but, wisely, he said nothing. Falzone just looked at us and then continued. 'I will tell you how things appear to me. I was assigned to investigate the murder of a tourist, Farhad Jahandar. An unusual event, a regrettable event, but murders happen here as everywhere. Crimes of passion, robberies gone wrong, perhaps even a Mafia execution in pursuit of some vendetta we know nothing about. But then you popped up and told me that the dead man was not a tourist, really he was some sort of Russian spy. A Russian spy, here in Syracuse, that seems very unlikely. But, I think to myself, let's suppose what these English are telling me is true: who is likely to kill a Russian spy? Why of course the Americans. Now we've all seen Hollywood films with bullets flying everywhere and we all know what the Americans have got up to in the past but could they really be responsible for a murder here in Sicily today? I think not but as I say I am just a simple policeman.

'So last night I put that question to my relative Colonel Castorini, a much wiser man than I. Is it possible that the Americans have murdered a Russian agent here in Syracuse? The Colonel tells me anything is possible. The Americans in Italy have been a law unto themselves ever since the war. If Jahandar really posed a threat to the United States then, yes, the CIA could have eradicated him. But personally, he says, he doesn't believe it. Forget all that James Bond stuff, he told me. Spies don't go around shooting each other on sight. He doubts that any of the CIA agents at Sigonella even carry guns. What's more, if what the British have told us is true, such a suggestion makes no sense.

'Remember you told us that Jahandar was a not very important Russian agent operating virtually out in the open. You said he was a messenger for the Russians, nothing more. He lived in Paris and we have established he had never been to Italy before. We have found absolutely nothing to connect him with any matters political or military in Italy. There is no suggestion, for example, that he has ever been anywhere near the American base at Sigonella. What possible reason could there be for the Americans to shoot him?

'And the Cold War is drawing to an end is it not? Nixon and Brezhnev declared "peaceful coexistence". Détente has arrived. There is a treaty to limit strategic arms. Just two weeks ago President Carter cancelled the B-1 Bomber programme. There is no more secret war between Russian and American spies.'

He stopped as if expecting us to disagree but we said nothing.

'And in any case the Americans are our allies now. If the Americans were running an operation in Sicily they would tell the SID, who would tell the *Carabinieri*.

'So Colonel Castorini says that we should all trust each other. So what should I do when I discover something that I simply do not understand, something quite impossible?'

The Italian inspector seemed to puff himself up. He was coming to the real issue, to whatever was causing his newfound belligerence. He continued in a tone of near-theatrical indignation.

'For that is what I have uncovered, the impossible. How then should I proceed? I decide to tell my new British friends. I suggest to Julia that she phones her husband and arranges a meeting. He is with Mr Morgan at the American naval base but dear Julia doesn't want to phone him there. She tells me that Mr Morgan's phone is being bugged. We must drive up to the base ourselves. Really? Am I to believe the Russians are listening to phone calls inside an American naval base? No, that is absurd. If Mr Morgan thought the Russians were listening he would certainly tell the Americans and have the line inspected. It must be that Mr Morgan fears that the Americans are listening to his calls. It seems that nobody trusts anybody. Perhaps Colonel Castorini is less wise than I thought, perhaps he was also wrong to think that the Americans would not murder a Russian spy here in Sicily.

'But he was not wrong. This afternoon I can tell you that Farhad Jahandar was not killed by the CIA.' He paused for effect before asking softly, 'So who do you suppose is the killer?' Falzone looked around at us, letting the question hang in the air. 'My friends it is my belief that the man I have been assured by you is a Russian spy was killed by Yevgeny Kapustin, an agent of the Russian KGB.'

The inspector now had our full attention, even Morgan's irritation had vanished.

Giuseppe Falzone explained that an hour or so after Jahandar had been killed the night manager at his hotel had seen somebody enter the hotel with Jahandar's key and go up to his room. Soon afterwards the man had come down and walked away. The night manager had insisted that he would recognise the man again but unfortunately he had then taken time off to attend a family celebration in Naples. He had returned this morning and had immediately identified a photograph that the police had shown him: Yevgeny Kapustin. That did not prove that Kapustin was Jahandar's killer, it was possible that Jahandar had given the KGB man his room key before he was killed or Kapustin could have arrived on the murder scene later and removed the key from the body, but it seemed more than likely that whoever killed the Iranian had been the person who had gone on to search his room.

Giuseppe had then tracked down the couple who said they had seen someone leaving the area in which Jahandar's body had been found. He showed them both the photograph and they had both been definite in their response. Unfortunately, the woman had been definitely positive and the man definitely negative.

'In my experience, however,' the inspector asserted, 'women are better observers than men. I believe this lady when she says that Kapustin is the man she saw. She had had less to drink than her companion.'

His logic might not stand up in a court of law but I was not about to argue.

'So,' Giuseppe concluded, 'we have a Russian spy in the American base along the road who may or may not be Robert Milan. We have a second Russian spy who I am told is now back in Rome having had a pleasant holiday on the beach in Taormina. And we have a body which is still lying unclaimed in the morgue in Syracuse and which you tell me belongs to a third Russian spy who, it seems, may have been killed by the second Russian spy. What am I to make of that? Oh and there is a mysterious Canadian called Henry Ramone and of course above all there is the tragic death of Julia's aunt and uncle, not to mention the murder of a poor Sicilian fisherman.'

The way Giuseppe put it, nothing that had happened since Bunny and Davoud Sadeghi set sail from Kefalonia fitted in with anything else. But there had to be a way of putting some of the pieces together. Julia and Charles Morgan looked at me. It seemed that the responsibility for responding to the policeman's questions had been delegated to me.

When I was a very young child my mother would sometimes wash the kit belonging to my father's football club. I used to accompany her to the laundrette and watch mesmerised as the clothes whirled round in the little washing machine window. As much as I might try to spot my father's shirt it wasn't until the wash was over, and my mother had taken the clothes from the dryer and started to patiently fold them, that I could see Dad's shirt with the number 9 on the back. Only then could I distinguish his shirt from everybody else's and place it carefully into a bag with the rest of his kit.

'We need to stand back and remember what we are trying to find,' I said. 'We are in danger of allowing ourselves to be distracted by the actions of people like Kapustin, Milan and Ramone. Let's just think about the two murders we started off with. Julia and I are here to find out what happened to Bunny and Davoud on the *Mahsheed*. Giuseppe is investigating the death of Farhad Jahandar. Let's start with a simple question: are the two cases connected or are they not?

'The reason for linking the two is the extraordinary coincidence of two Paris-based Iranian dissidents being targeted

167

within hours of each other. The only other link between the two is Kapustin. We know he had been asking questions about the *Mahsheed* and we know he had Jahandar's hotel key on the night Jahandar was killed. There is absolutely nothing else linking the two cases. And there is one very powerful reason for not connecting them: Tortellini.'

Morgan flashed me a warning glance but I decided to ignore him. I knew he harboured doubts about Giuseppe but I wanted to see how the Italian policeman would react to the suggestion that the Russians were now actively involved with the drugs trade here in Sicily and were helping the Mafia expand their operations in the US. I told Giuseppe and Julia exactly what we had just learned from the two Bastamentes and Romney.

When we had suggested it before, Giuseppe had dismissed any possibility of Mafia drug smuggling being involved in Bunny's murder and I expected him to dismiss Bastamente's story out of hand. He didn't.

'It is possible things happened like that,' he said. 'The Mafia have been increasing their heroin production here in Sicily. And they certainly ship the stuff to the United States. We don't think the new refineries are in this part of Sicily but if they are landing equipment on the island it might make sense to do it here, where we are not expecting them. But this is the first time I have heard anyone suggesting that there is a Russian connection. I will talk to Colonel Castorini. Yes, it is possible, but it still doesn't feel right. The Mafia doesn't need outside help to run their business, they are doing all right on their own. I still think the fact that you tell me Behzad Sadeghi was expected to be on that boat is the key.'

'But that means Bastamente is lying,' I said. 'The whole story of the Americans tracking a Russian ship and seeing it unload cargo at sea onto a smaller freighter off Catania is a fairy tale.'

'The story is too elaborate to be a fairy tale,' Morgan insisted. 'We can check it out. Find out if there was a Russian ship in the area. Did it meet another ship out at sea? What happened to the freighter the Company claims to have intercepted?'

'The story may be easy to check,' Julia put in, 'but would Bastamente expect us to check it? You say he wanted us to go home, accept his version of Bunny's death and go back to London. And how would we check it? If we ask for any more details he will just say we don't need to know, it's CIA business.'

'Perhaps,' said Morgan, 'but that is what we need to do. Go back and ask the Bastamentes how they account for Kapustin searching Jahandar's room, quite possibly having just murdered him, when according to them he was here on an operation that had nothing to do with Iranian dissidents.'

XXI

'No, Captain Morgan,' responded Giuseppe. 'You will not go back and ask our American friends more questions. First because you will not learn anything. With the greatest respect, I suspect Mr Bastamente is more of a professional than you are and is not going to let slip any information he does not want you to have. Second we are talking about crimes committed in Italy and that is my jurisdiction not yours.'

Morgan looked as if he was going to answer back but Giuseppe gave him no opportunity. 'We are all agreed your CIA colleagues are holding something back. They say they know why Kapustin is here and deny it is anything to do with Iran but we now know that is untrue. But where does that get us?'

We were all silent for a moment. We needed to think but I found that standing in an empty car park in the relentless sun, with the occasional car whizzing past, did nothing to clarify my thoughts. Only Giuseppe seemed unaffected by our surroundings.

'Perhaps now is the time for me to talk to our American friends. They have circulated a photo of a man I now believe to have murdered Jahandar, a murder I am investigating. I have a legitimate reason to talk to them.'

Morgan was not happy. 'I think you will find that your jurisdiction does not extend to a US Naval Air Facility. There is no way you can go in there and start interrogating US government officials, especially those officials.'

'We will come to that,' replied Giuseppe. 'Tell me more about the three Americans you spoke to. It seems to me I would be better talking to each of them on their own. The older Bastamente is clearly a professional. He will tell us just what it suits him to tell us. What about his son, Bastamente Junior? He is perhaps in less control of himself.'

He looked at Morgan, who still seemed uncomfortable discussing intelligence matters with someone he considered a civilian, and a foreign civilian at that.

'Possibly,' he acknowledged reluctantly. 'He might let something slip. Junior is a "shoot now, ask questions later" sort of man. But he's no fool. We are not going to catch him out with a few trick questions. He's an arrogant bastard and I suppose that might let him down. Romney is the weak link, if they have a weak link. There are times when he seems to be all over the place, even when he hasn't been drinking, but he's an old hand for all that. He's been with Harry Bastamente Senior for years. He was station chief in Rome in the sixties. He must be close to retirement now and he's not going to jeopardise his pension. You still have the basic problem that there is absolutely no reason for any of them to reveal anything about an American intelligence operation to an Italian policeman. That isn't the way things work.'

I had to agree with Morgan. As Giuseppe had said, we were all convinced the three Company men were holding something back but if they were not going to share it with British Intelligence they would certainly not share it with a provincial policeman.

Nevertheless Giuseppe seemed determined. 'I will speak to Mr Romney.'

'And how do you propose to do that?' Morgan asked. 'Like I said, you've no authority on that base.'

'Captain Morgan, I think you forget where you are standing at this very moment and how you got here. I will arrange matters for Mr Romney in the same way that I have just done for you. Presumably he does not live permanently at the base.'

'No. He and Junior are staying at a hotel somewhere around Catania.'

'So they might be travelling together?'

'I don't think so. Junior has his own hire car.'

'Then we will intercept him. How will my officers recognise Romney?'

'That's no problem. Romney had a car shipped over from the States. Do you know anything about motor racing?'

'Naturally,' replied Giuseppe with more than a hint of irritation, combined with Italian pride. 'Ferrari are back on top where they belong.'

'I was actually thinking about the Le Mans 24 Hours. You remember those American cars that entered last year?'

'Of course. They were a disaster.'

'Well Romney has one of those, a Dodge, painted in the race colours, white and gold. You can't miss it.'

'Then I suggest you and Mr Dylan return to the base and confirm that Romney is still there. If he has left, try to find the name of his hotel.' He passed Morgan a card. 'Call this number and it will be patched through to my radio.' He then turned to Julia. 'Has Romney met you? Does he know what you look like?'

'We haven't met but he may have seen my photo in *La Sicilia*.'

'But he won't recognise you with your sunglasses on.'

'Hang on,' I interrupted. 'What are you expecting Julia to do?' I was beginning to share Morgan's irritation with the suave Italian. Giuseppe's easy assumption of authority annoyed me but that was clearly not a feeling shared by Julia.

'I'll stay with Giuseppe,' she said. 'If we do manage to intercept Romney and persuade him to talk, I may pick up a nuance Giuseppe might miss.'

'But you don't speak Italian.'

'Nor perhaps does Romney,' said Giuseppe. 'We shall speak in English. I am sure your wife can lose her British accent.'

Julia was clearly determined to remain where we were and I could see the benefit of her working alongside the Italian policeman, so Morgan and I set off for the US base. We were nearly there when an official-looking car approached from the opposite direction; as it passed I saw, sitting in the back seat, the MI6 man George Ffortiscue. Bastamente Senior had mentioned his name earlier but I had not expected to see him on the island. What on earth was there to attract him down here now?

Ten minutes later, as we were drawing into a parking space outside Morgan's office, Jack Romney appeared about 100 yards away. He was walking towards a large white and gold American car.

'That's incredibly convenient,' said Morgan. 'I'll go and phone Giuseppe. You stay here.'

Morgan had only just disappeared when Bastamente Junior came running over to Romney, who was preparing to drive off. Romney was clearly not pleased to see him. Bastamente pulled the car door open and seemed to be shouting angrily at his colleague. I was too far away to hear what was being said but Romney was obviously responding in the same tone. He seemed to push Bastamente away and the car jerked forward. Bastamente slammed the car door and Romney accelerated away. Bastamente stood for a moment and then walked over to a black Mercedes which he quickly unlocked. Just then Morgan reappeared.

'We may have a problem,' I said. 'It looks as though Junior wants to talk to Romney but Romney doesn't want to talk to him. If Junior decides to follow him we're stuffed. We'd better tell Giuseppe.'

'We don't have time. We'll do better to follow Bastamente,' said Morgan, slipping into the driver's seat and starting the engine.

I was not convinced but this was no time to start an argument. 'Well hold back. This car stands out almost as much as Romney's. Bright red with diplomatic plates!'

'It's *rosso corsa*,' said Morgan, 'Italian racing red. What could be more Italian?'

I glanced across to see if he was trying to be funny. He wasn't.

Bastamente was directly in front of us at the gates but fortunately turned in the opposite direction to that taken by Romney. 'Shall we follow him?' asked Morgan.

'No. Let's go and see what's happening with Inspector Falzone and Julia. But don't let Romney see this car. Stop well short of them.'

We came out of the base and turned right. The road ran straight eastwards in the direction of the sea. For nearly two miles the road followed the barbed wire fencing designed to keep the public away from the hangars and runways and then the base was behind us. The fields were well tended but there were no signs of human habitation until, after five miles, a jumble of buildings appeared on our right. That was where the police car had pulled us over.

A long row of huts with curved metal roofs interspersed with larger brick structures stretched off at right angles to the road. It looked like an abandoned military facility of some sort, perhaps an old Italian airfield although there was no sign of a runway.

There were no cars in the parking space where we had stood earlier. An old gatehouse with NANCOS stencilled on it faced towards us, its door and windows long gone. I half expected to see more barbed wire fencing stretching along the front of the site but instead there was what had been an ornate shoulder-high wall with curved arches and topped by terracotta tiles. The wall was now crumbling and overgrown.

We had seen a flash of yellow as we had approached and guessed that it was the sun glinting off Romney's car. Morgan drove slowly past the gatehouse and immediately parked the car beside an abandoned hut. Creeping just a few yards round the end of the hut we could see two cars, Giuseppe's and Romney's, parked side by side about 150 yards away. There was no sign of the police car that would have flagged Romney down.

'We could crawl along by the side of the field and get nearer,' suggested Morgan, but there was really no point. We still would not be able to hear any conversation and I did not want to alert Romney to our presence. We returned to the car to wait. We couldn't see what was happening in the two cars but there was no way either could leave without passing the hut where we were parked.

We settled down for a long wait. I wanted to believe that Inspector Falzone would gain some new insight into the affair but, as I learned later, he did not: Romney was a pro. The two police officers who had stopped him took his papers and despite his protests searched his car. In the glovebox they found a .45 Colt automatic, the M1911 model that had been the standard US Army sidearm since the First World War (and would continue to be until the James Bond 9mm Beretta replaced it in the 1980s). Giuseppe had taken the gun and slid into the passenger seat; Julia sat in the rear. There then followed more than half an hour of inaction.

I later learned that Romney was saying absolutely nothing. Giuseppe had introduced himself by announcing that he was investigating two murders, Farhad Jandahar and Giacomo Conti, and then tried to wrong-foot Romney by thanking him for the help he had already provided in finding Jahandar's killer. Romney was too experienced to rise to that bait. He said nothing. 'You provided us with the name of Jandahar's killer, and even provided a photograph,' Falzone continued. Romney still remained silent. 'Yevgeny Kapustin,' prompted Giuseppe. There may have been a flicker of surprise on Romney's face but it passed in an instant. Sitting behind him Julia noticed a slight upward tilt of the head when Giuseppe asked a question Romney was not expecting. It happened on that first question and it happened again when Giuseppe asked what Romney knew about Signora Ramone. But for the rest of the time Romney was unmoving. Only when Giuseppe started asking about the Ramone bank account did Romney jerk his head back sharply.

'Why would a bank account for a Canadian citizen be opened in Rome?' Giuseppe asked. 'You were living in Rome when the account was opened weren't you?'

'That's enough,' said Romney. 'I've told you. If you want to talk about government business then go through the proper channels. I don't know you and I'm not discussing any government business with you.' Romney was genuinely angry. If Giuseppe had not taken the American's car key he would probably have driven off with Giuseppe and Julia still sat in the car.

But Romney did not drive anywhere. Two shots rang out in quick succession. The second struck Romney in the shoulder but he would not have noticed, the first head shot killed him.

XXII

The shots were so totally unexpected that for a moment I didn't understand what had happened. Even when I realised the loud bangs were gunshots I had no idea where they had come from or what, if anything, they had hit. Morgan's reactions were far faster than mine. He turned on the ignition, slammed the Lancia into gear and jammed his foot on the accelerator in one quick movement and we were racing towards the spot where Giuseppe and Romney were parked. My first thought was that Julia was in one of those cars. I expected him to stop when we reach them but he hurtled past.

The killer must have parked on the road and crept along the fence that separated the site from the fields beyond. He could have seen Morgan's distinctive Lancia from the road or might even, like us, have seen the flash of Romney's even more distinctive Dodge Charger. Morgan must have guessed where the gunman had fired from, he could not have seen the flash of the gun, and had decided to go after him. It seemed obvious to me that whoever had fired would escape as quickly as possible but I was wrong, two more flashes came from 100 yards away off to our left. The windscreen shattered and the Lancia slewed around and smashed side on into an old corroding signpost of some sort. The metal pole buckled over under the impact, bringing us to a sudden halt. There was glass and blood everywhere. The blood seemed to be coming from Morgan's nose which looked to be broken.

Miraculously my side of the car was completely undamaged. As I pulled open the door I heard running feet and ducked down but it was Julia; she was screaming my name. Some way behind her came Giuseppe, gun in hand.

'Are you all right?' Julia and I asked simultaneously, flinging our arms around each other in relief when we discovered that neither of us was hurt.

We turned round to the Lancia where it was clear that Morgan had suffered more than a broken nose. Back near the abandoned gatehouse a car accelerated away but there was nothing any of us could do to stop the killer escaping. It was no easy task extricating Morgan from his car and we saw that his chest had been crushed against the steering wheel. Morgan's Lancia was fitted with seatbelts but in those days nobody bothered to wear them, least of all Morgan. We eventually laid him down on the tarmac beside his smashed Lancia. Giuseppe radioed for support and two police cars arrived within minutes. We then waited for what seemed a very long time for an ambulance. Morgan was taken away, a wan expression on his face, and we later discovered that he had two broken ribs. Also, unnoticed by us at the time, there was a small nick on his elbow which may have been caused by the bullet that the police found embedded in his car seat.

The next two hours were spent standing around, answering questions. I wanted to get Julia back to the hotel but we had no car and a stream of Italian officials descended upon us. The first two police cars were followed eventually by a uniformed officer who proved to be Giuseppe's superior, by Colonel Castorini from the *Carabinieri*, by Di Benedetto from the SID and by a rather ' pompous civilian to whom everyone showed great deference but who seemed to have no idea what was going on. The one person to show him no deference at all was Harry Bastamente Senior. He arrived on the scene remarkably quickly, having apparently been driving past when he saw Romney's distinctive car. He started laying down the law as soon as he arrived, shouting at everyone in Italian until Di Benedetto arrived and took him aside. I could not hear what they were saying but Di Benedetto appeared to be unusually assertive and Bastamente, after one last glance at the body of his old friend, simply drove off. Nobody tried to stop him.

Eventually Giuseppe himself insisted on driving Julia and me back to Syracuse. His earlier ebullience had gone. When Julia tried to discuss what had happened he insisted that we would talk the next day. 'We have tests to do. We must wait for the results.' He refused to speculate on who may have fired the gun or even to describe what he himself had seen. 'Wait until tomorrow' was as much as we could get out of him.

He dropped us outside the hotel and quickly drove off. I headed for the hotel bar but Julia pulled me back towards the lift. 'I'm going to collapse,' she said and, true to her word, she gave me a quick kiss and was in bed and snoring gently within minutes of reaching our room.

I envied her capacity to simply switch off. I lay awake for hours trying to puzzle out what had happened. In my mind it all came back to Harry Bastamente Junior. He had followed Romney out of the base and then turned off. I had checked the map in Giuseppe's car as he drove us back to Syracuse. The road Junior had taken would have eventually led him back towards Catania. He would have ended up on the same road as Romney but ten or fifteen minutes behind him. Why take a longer route to the same destination? Junior did not strike me as the sort of man to go out of his way to admire the Sicilian countryside. The only thing that made sense was that he had seen Morgan's racing red car and decided that we were following him. When he discovered that we were not he had turned round and reversed the position by following us. Morgan would not have been looking for a tail and I certainly had not noticed anything. When Junior saw us pull in he probably continued past and then stopped to investigate. Seeing Romney's Dodge Charger would have made him think twice. He had crept up and saw Romney in apparently amiable conversation with a complete stranger. At that point he must have decided that Romney was betraying the Company and shot him. That was the point when my theory fell apart. It sounded plausible in every way except motive. What possible reason could Junior have had to act the way I supposed? Who did Junior imagine Romney was talking to? What secrets did he think Romney might be giving away? Had he really been goaded into action by the sight of our red Lancia on his tail? On the other hand, to fire a handgun that accurately at that distance needed a professional and Bastamente Junior was just that.

Nevertheless, the more I thought about what had happened the less likely it seemed that Junior could have been Romney's killer. Why would Company men fall out so badly that they would want to shoot each other? Romney was family, he had worked with Bastamente Senior for thirty years. Junior could not possibly have imagined that a man like Jack Romney would be working for the 'other side', whoever the other side might be.

Was I jumping to these conclusions simply because I didn't like the Bastamentes? I didn't like being patronised by Bastamente Senior nor bullied by Bastamente Junior. And I didn't enjoy being lied to; the two of them knew far more about Bunny's death than they admitted. But of course they lied. That was their job. The Company existed to protect America's interests and America's secrets. That was far more important to men like the Bastamentes than the death of the sister of the Director General of a foreign intelligence agency. They would tell us only what they needed to tell us and no more.

I really needed to be more dispassionate. There must be another explanation.

A senior American agent had been killed. Question: who is most likely to be responsible for killing an American spy? Answer: the Russians. They had lost one of their own, Farhad Jahandar. Was this retribution? Had the KGB discovered that Romney had something to do with Jahandar's killing? Was Giuseppe completely off target in identifying Kapustin as Jahandar's killer? Had it really been Kapustin who had searched Jahandar's room? And even if it had been, did that really prove he was also the killer? Romney carried a gun. Suppose he had killed Jahandar and Kapustin had been nearby. What could be more natural than that Kapustin would have taken his dead colleague's room key and made sure there was no incriminating evidence left there.

No doubt Giuseppe Falzone or the SID were now testing Romney's pistol. Would they discover that it had really been Romney who had shot the Russian agent? Julia said Romney seemed surprised when Giuseppe announced that the Iranian had been killed by Kapustin, but was he surprised that Kapustin was the killer or merely surprised that the Italian police believed he was?

Or suppose that Giuseppe was right and Kapustin had killed Jahandar. What that showed was that the KGB were up to something in Sicily which they would not hesitate to kill over, although we still had no idea what that might be. Kapustin was now apparently back in Rome. But was he? Had he returned to Sicily again? Or had the KGB sent another team down here. Perhaps they had sent a team down to extricate their spy at Sigonella, Robert Milan, and perhaps Romney had stumbled on something that might have led him to Milan's whereabouts. That, I decided, seemed highly unlikely; I was confident I knew exactly how Milan had been lifted from the base and it was not done by a team of Russian agents. Blaming the Russians for Romney's death was just too simple. Why on earth would they want to kill him?

Ditto the Mafia. If any of the Tortellini story about Mafia drug smuggling proved to be true, then they were possible suspects. After all, who else was more likely to gun someone down in Sicily than the Mafia? There was a Mafia connection in all this somewhere. The man who had died of grenade wounds in a Palermo hospital was Mafia. The fisherman Conti's death certainly looked like a Mafia execution. But again why?

I thought of Morgan, now in hospital in Catania and thanking his lucky stars that the mysterious gunman hadn't had such a clear shot at us as he had had at Romney. Morgan, I suspected, would have included another name on the list of suspects: Inspector Giuseppe Falzone. And he may have added Colonel Castorini as well.

With hindsight the idea of intercepting a man like Jack Romney and expecting him to reveal secret information to a provincial Italian policeman was absurd. We had been carried down that track by Giuseppe Falzone. He was the one who insisted he could produce something new. But both Julia and Giuseppe confirmed that once they cornered Romney in his car it was immediately clear they would get nothing useful from him. Romney just clammed up as he had been trained to do. And yet Giuseppe had continued to ply him with question after question. Was he really expecting to find the one silver bullet of a question that would make Romney suddenly spill the beans? Again with hindsight the whole exercise was totally improbable but Giuseppe had kept on right up until the moment Romney was shot. Had he just been setting Romney up? And if so who for and why? Not for the Russians almost certainly, but perhaps for the Mafia? That had to be possible. But everywhere I turned I came back to the question why? Why would anyone want to shoot Jack Romney? Because one thing seemed certain: Romney had been shot quite deliberately. There was no possibility that the attacker had been aiming for Giuseppe or Julia.

I wanted to discuss my thoughts with Julia but she had pulled the sheet over her head and was fast asleep. In any case, it seemed she would not hear a word against Giuseppe and had come to trust him completely. Julia's judgement about people was usually spot-on, much more instinctive than my own, but this time perhaps Morgan was right. Giuseppe was just too good to be true.

What I really wanted to do was talk to the DG. He was the one man who could take a more objective view and whose judgement I trusted entirely. But where was he? Why hadn't he contacted us? I finally fell asleep imagining what I would have said to the DG if only he had been downstairs in the bar when we arrived back at the hotel. Next morning I discovered that is exactly where he had been.

XXIII

The phone jangled us awake at seven o'clock and when I answered it did strike me that the DG's voice was as clear as if he were next door. He may have been. 'We have a lot to talk about. Breakfast downstairs in half an hour?' It was not really a question.

'Who was that?' asked Julia.

'Your uncle.'

'Well he didn't say much.'

'He didn't need to. He's here, in this hotel. We're to meet for breakfast in thirty minutes.'

I was ready in twenty. More surprisingly, so was Julia.

When we arrived in the breakfast room the DG was already there, seated at a table laid for four. He rose to greet us and I couldn't help noticing that his normally ramrod stiff back was bowed and his smile had lost some of its usual warmth. Although his face as always sported a healthy tan, the skin below his eyes seemed to sag and the eyes themselves had a pale sheen. He had clearly not been sleeping well. The DG was not far off retirement and for the first time I thought he looked it.

The death of his sister had affected him deeply. I could imagine the turmoil he must have been going through. The last time Julia had phoned he had just learned that Ramone's name had been discovered in his brother-in-law Davoud Sadeghi's appointment book. Suddenly he had been faced with the possibility that perhaps his sister, or at least her husband, had some direct involvement in whatever was going on. Far from being innocents abroad they may have been deliberately targeted. That was something I knew he would not want to admit.

The last time I had spoken to him myself, before the peremptory call this morning, he had been taking the whole affair very personally, convinced that Ffortiscue and Bastamente were keeping the details of Tortellini from him because they didn't trust him. They were worried he might leak any information they gave him to Behzad Sadeghi. After a career serving his country that must have really hurt him. His reaction, it seemed, had been to withdraw, to disappear uncharacteristically to the countryside for the weekend, and then without any warning fly down to Sicily. For the head of the DIS to leave London and personally involve himself in an operation in the field was unheard of and showed the strain he was under.

As we arrived he seemed to consciously pull his thoughts back to his immediate surroundings. He kissed Julia warmly and as he lowered himself slowly down into his seat again his back straightened and his eyes foccused. When he spoke his voice held all its old steel.

'What's happening?' he asked. 'I saw Ffortiscue last night. He looked flustered. No tie and no one to carry his bag. What's he doing here?'

'What did he tell you?'

'Nothing. I was just checking in when he marched past. Didn't look too pleased to see me. He said he had an appointment and we arranged to meet here at nine thirty this morning. It seems this is the only hotel worthy of note in Syracuse. Come on, I want a full report. What's going on?'

It took us over an hour to cover everything that had happened since we had last phoned London. It would have taken quite some time even if the DG had not constantly interrupted. He wanted detail and more detail but expressed no surprise at anything we said. Even when we reached Romney's murder he seemed more concerned that Julia had been in the car than that one of the CIA's top men in Western Europe had just been shot. He listened to our theories but offered none of his own.

Glancing at Julia I ventured my growing suspicion that Giuseppe might have set Romney up. To my surprise, she nodded. 'He just kept asking Romney questions that Romney was simply not going to answer. After five minutes it was obvious we would get nowhere but Giuseppe kept on right up until the moment Romney was shot.'

'Perhaps.' The DG was silent for a moment. 'You two want to know who killed Jack Romney, who killed that fisherman, who killed Farhad Jahandar. You want to know whether Robert Milan was a mole or just a naïve young man and where he is now. You want to know how the Mafia come into all of this. You want the whole big picture. I, on the other hand, just want to know who killed my sister. Who, how and why. That's what I have been trying to find out. And one thing I can tell you is that the story of a Russian ship unloading off the coast of Sicily on to a coaster that was then intercepted by the US Navy is total fiction. I've been over the shipping movements for this part of the world with a microscope. It just didn't happen.

'Harry Bastamente made the whole story up. He knows what did happen but plainly he's not been willing to tell us. Nor would George Ffortiscue tell us, although he too knows far more than he's let on. So I had to start elsewhere, where you started, Greece. But this time I was determined that the sainted Behzad Sadeghi would tell us the truth and the whole truth.

'I have friends in Greece. Let me tell you a story.' The DG sat back and I realised that he was about to set off on one of his familiar monologues, meandering apparently aimlessly towards a destination nobody expected.

'Many years ago I was on a course in the United States, at Annapolis, their naval academy. One of the things they make a point of showing visiting Brits is a hideous sarcophagus in the crypt beneath the chapel. It is supposed to contain the bones of the man they call the founder of the American Navy: John Paul Jones. Most of the American officers were extremely nice but there was one chap who just kept on and on about John Paul Jones and how he had single-handedly destroyed the British Navy in their War of Independence. Of course Jones had done nothing of the sort and I patiently explained that he was just a pirate and probable murderer who had fled across the Atlantic to escape justice. The American officer was getting very irate when a Greek chap intervened. John Paul Jones, he said, was a great hero but not for the American Navy. It seems that after the American Revolution Jones got sick of life in America and joined the Russian Navy. At the time Potemkin was pursuing his dream of Russia restoring the glory of ancient Greece and Jones became a real hero fighting the Turks. The supposed founder of the US Navy was actually an American captain but a Russian admiral. The lesson stuck that people are not always whom they seem to be. I thought that was extraordinary and made a point of getting to know the Greek officer. He's now my opposite number in Greek Intelligence. When I asked for his help he was more than happy to oblige.

'My plan was to turn up at the villa with a military escort and convince Behzad that I could have him deported to Iran if he didn't cooperate. My friend arranged for me to meet the police chief on Kefalonia and there I got lucky. He didn't know much about Behzad but he did have something on Behzad's manservant, Shahryar. It's another long story. It goes right back to the war.

'Historians are still arguing over what Churchill and Stalin really agreed at Yalta in February 1945. But we do know what actually happened afterwards. Most of Eastern Europe was taken over by the Russians but in a few places Stalin held back, in Austria for example and in Greece. The Greek Communists had been a key part of the partisan armies that had fought the Nazis but when the Greek Civil War broke out Stalin effectively abandoned them. In 1949, after the Civil War, the Communist Party was outlawed and many of its members went into exile. The Party was not legalised again until the military junta were thrown out three years ago, in 1974. With the return of democracy some real old hard-line Communists came back, old Stalinists who were now completely out of step with everyone. The Communist Party in Greece had changed, it was now controlled by Euro Communists who had no interest in dogmatic adherence to Moscow. Many of those returning became bitter old men with nowhere to go. One of them, after twenty years in Moscow, had grown tired of the dreary Russian winters spent in a dreary concrete apartment block, and his paymasters had allowed him to move to Paris. Now approaching seventy, it was safe for him to return home to Greece, but to do what? He ended up in Kefalonia helping his brothers run the family business in Sami. They had a taverna and each Sunday one of their customers would come in for a beer and to collect post for his employer.

'That customer was Behzad's man, Shahryar. The two men became friends. The old Stalinist and Shahryar had much in common: a feeling of not belonging, perhaps nostalgia for the expatriate life in Paris, certainly nostalgia for what should have been. It seems that a month or so ago Shahryar asked his friend for help. He wanted to pass a message to someone in Moscow but he didn't know how to set about it. He wanted to contact the KGB. His friend offered to help. He still had contacts there. He could pass on a message and he did. Three messages and three replies. What Shahryar did not realise is that his friend was now back in the bosom of his family and he wanted to stay there, so he copied both the messages and the replies and gave them to his nephew, who happened to be Kefalonia's chief of police.

'The correspondence meant nothing to the Greek police. It was just filed away. They had no interest in anyone mentioned in the documents they received, not Behzad Sadeghi, not Henry Ramone, not Farhad Jahandar. They hadn't even had the last message and its reply translated from Russian into Greek. Luckily the police chief was able to have everything translated into English overnight and the correspondence meant a lot more to me than it had to them. When I set off to see Behzad I was well and truly forearmed.

'Behzad was surprised when a truckload of soldiers and a police car arrived at his villa and demanded entry. He was even more surprised when I stepped out of the police car. By then I had a pretty good idea about what had been going on but I wanted him to confirm it. He started in his usual belligerent style but I cut that short. It was time for some shock treatment.

'"No more lies Behzad. No more secrets. We'll start with the man you know as Henry Ramone. What's his real name?"

'"What do you mean, real name? His name is Henry Ramone, he's a Canadian journalist."

'"No he isn't. I've had him checked. He's an invention. Quite possibly an invention of Harry Bastamente." That name got to him, as I knew it would.

'"Bastamente!" Behzad screamed. "What do you mean Bastamente?"

'"Harry Bastamente. The young man who was one of Kermit Roosevelt's merry band in Operation Ajax in 1953. The American agent who organised the murder of men like your father. He's twenty-four, nearly twenty-five, years older now and right this minute he's sitting just across the sea in Sicily and I want to know why."

'For a few minutes Behzad continued to insist I was lying. "It can't be," he kept saying. But then it all came out.

'He had been approached by Ramone in Paris a few months before. Ramone claimed to be a journalist and had an introduction from his brother Davoud in London. It turned out he had interviewed Davoud for a piece on Harley Street which he had sold to a medical magazine in California. Ramone had the magazine with him and had shown it to Behzad. The magazine may well have been just a mock-up but Behzad had accepted its authenticity without apparent question. Now Ramone said he wanted to move on to serious journalism and was looking for a story that would make his name. Change was coming to Iran he said. The Shah couldn't survive for much longer and Ramone wanted to be with the new revolutionary leaders when it happened. But who would the new leaders be?

'The supposed journalist apparently decided to get to know all the different factions. What he soon realised, he claimed, is that united the factions might bring down the Shah, but divided they were bound to fail. So he tried to bring them together.

'Behzad must have seen the look of disbelief on my face, but he carried on anyway. It appears that Ramone convinced him that a grand coalition of the opposition groups was possible, a Popular Front, and that he, Behzad Sadeghi, could lead it. The hard-line Islamists would refuse to cooperate, they only needed God on their side, but the other factions needed something else: money. Behzad confessed that he, for example, was almost penniless. Although,' the DG commented wryly, 'what Behzad meant by penniless might not be the same as what you and I would mean. Only one group of exiles had access to funds: the Communists. And so Ramone had a bright idea. If the liberals, red Islamists, socialists, Kurds and all the other "moderate" groups came together with the Communists in a "Popular Front", Moscow might provide the funds.'

Julia and I were gripped by the DG's story and he continued.

'Behzad said that he had initially been sceptical but Ramone put him in touch with Farhad Jahandar, who was known to be Moscow's man in the Iranian exile community. Farhad was enthusiastic and promised Russian support. More importantly he produced cash for Ramone to send to Behzad – not a lot but a gesture of intent, transferred from a bank in Rome directly to Behzad in Paris. The next step was to be a formal meeting of the various parties, somewhere away from prying eyes, somewhere like Syracuse in Sicily. The red Islamists would send someone and Jahandar would be there representing the Communists. Everything was arranged but then the leader of the red Islamists died in a hospital in England. It was not clear who would succeed him and some of the other groups started to get cold feet.

'"I decided not to go," Behzad had asserted, adding self-importantly, "Without me there was no point in the meeting going ahead. When I told Ramone I wasn't coming he came here himself a few days after to try to persuade me to change my mind. And," he suddenly remembered, "he told me all about you and warned me that British Intelligence is still determined to keep their puppet on what you call the Peacock Throne. He warned me you would do anything to stop the Popular Front bringing down the Shah's regime and restoring democracy.'"

He broke off his story as breakfast arrived. When he resumed the DG's tone was thoughtful. 'Ramone turning up explains how Behzad got hold of my official title and my office number, but it doesn't explain how Henry Ramone got hold of them. There is still a lot more to uncover.

'Behzad sounded so plausible but he still wasn't telling me the whole truth. He was still holding back and I thought I knew why. I decided to be blunt, although perhaps not entirely truthful myself. I told him British Intelligence had no interest in the squabbles of ageing Iranian exiles. We were too busy watching the Russians, which is how we knew about his man Shahryar. We had read the messages he was sending to Moscow.'

"'You clearly knew Ramone was a fraud," I said. "I don't know why, but something he did made you doubt him. So you told Shahryar to check him out and Shahryar did just that, he contacted Moscow. And that's when you received an almighty shock. The Russians didn't know anything about this supposed Popular Front deal. They hadn't sent you any money and weren't planning to send any. And if Farhad Jahandar was pretending otherwise they had no idea why, but they would certainly be trying to find out."

"'I wonder what you thought when Shahryar reported that back to you. Did you realise you had been conned and Ramone didn't want you in Sicily just to cover you in cash? Did you call everything off? Or were you so desperate for his money that you persuaded yourself there must be a reasonable explanation for Moscow's response? Perhaps Shahryar had contacted the wrong people. Russia's security apparatus is as fractured as everybody else's. Perhaps it was not the KGB but the GRU military intelligence who were offering to bankroll you. What had you got to lose by going ahead with the trip to Syracuse?"

"'The answer to that of course was your life. Perhaps the Shah's agents were planning to assassinate you when you got there. Much better to send someone in your place. That way Shahryar could arrange with Moscow to have someone at the dockside to see what happened when the *Mahsheed* sailed in. What did you do? Did you tell your brother someone was expecting to meet you when you stepped off the boat and he just had to say that you had been taken ill and couldn't come? Or did you give him a letter to hand over?"

'Behzad had shaken his head. "No letter. I never thought anything would happen to Davoud. I swear. I would never risk any harm coming to my brother. Even when Julia came to see me I thought he would turn up. That he and his wife had just decided to borrow my boat for longer and had gone somewhere else. Bunny was always unpredictable.'"

The DG fell silent. Julia reached across the table and gently laid her hand on his.

'People see what they want to see,' said the DG quietly. 'Behzad didn't deliberately put his brother and Bunny in danger. He wanted to believe that Ramone was real and that the money Ramone had promised was really there. But Ramone isn't real, he's a legend created by Harry Bastamente.'

'Can you be sure of that?' I asked.

'Oh yes. I've called in favours in Ottawa. The CIA Person of Interest tag on Ramone has been there for years. Any time the name Ramone came up on the radar a notification was to be sent to the Company. The tag specified that notifications were to be addressed to Mary Jane Schiavetti, room D-127, CIA headquarters Langley, Virginia. Mary Jane Schiavetti has been Bastamente's assistant for nearly twenty years. He authorised that tag. Usually of course you put a POI tag on someone because you want to keep track of what they are doing. But occasionally you want to find out what other people are doing, is anyone sniffing around the subject? It's a standard procedure. If you create a legend you want to know if someone starts prying into their background. We would have done the same thing. I don't know who Ramone is but I'm damn sure Harry Bastamente does, and I'm damn sure George Ffortiscue knows as well. Six are in it up to their necks.'

XXIV

As if on cue at that moment George Ffortiscue appeared in the doorway and the DG waved him over. Ffortiscue seemed surprised to see Julia and me but sat down and summoned a hovering waiter. He ordered Earl Grey tea with lemon.

Without any preamble he turned to the DG. 'I think, Gordon, you had better tell me what's going on. Jack Romney was murdered last night and I gather he was talking to your niece when he was shot.'

The DG had no intention of letting Ffortiscue control the discussion.

'Yes George, he was. The Company's Tortellini project does seem to have exploded in their face. I understand Romney was a good man. Let's start at the beginning shall we? When did you and Harry Bastamente first cook up a plan to kill Behzad Sadeghi?'

'Come now, Gordon. You know we don't go in for that sort of stuff these days. Tortellini is an American operation; I have only just learned about it myself.'

'Oh really? And yet you brought your Tortellini file to our meeting at Heathrow. Quite a thick file even by then. Dammit man, it's my sister who's been killed and clearly it's no accident. I deserve to know what happened and believe me I will not rest until I've uncovered every last detail.'

Ffortiscue seemed unmoved as he considered how to respond.

'Gordon, Her Majesty's Government is not responsible for your sister's death. I gather Harry Bastamente has explained what happened. He has spoken to your man here,' he nodded in my direction.

'Harry Bastamente has lied through his teeth,' the DG interrupted. 'And now you are doing the same. You've been up to your neck in Tortellini from the start. Playing your silly games with your absurd stories about Mafia drug smuggling. Tortellini wasn't about the war on drugs it was about Operation Ajax all over again, keeping an ageing megalomaniac on the Peacock Throne so you can carry on pretending that the British Empire isn't over. Don't start denying it. I know you planned to lure my brother-in-law's brother to Sicily. I know Ramone was Harry Bastamente's man and I know he wasn't delivering cash from Moscow. If Moscow wanted to give cash to Behzad in Paris, they wouldn't have done it via a bank in Rome. And I know why Yevgeny Kapustin was there waiting for the *Mahsheed* to arrive.'

The first flicker of surprise crossed Ffortiscue's face. 'If you know what Kapustin was doing here then you know more than I do,' he said. 'And I am not going to discuss Her Majesty's foreign policy with you. I think you'll find that determining who is and is not worthy of the British government's support is the role of the Foreign Office not the Ministry of Defence. HMG's policy is that the strategic interests of the United Kingdom are best served by ensuring that Iran stays firmly in the Western camp and does not fall under the control of the Soviet Union nor of a bunch of mad ayatollahs. Your job is to execute policy not make it.'

'That's as true for you as for me, of course,' the DG responded, 'but let me tell you something. MI6 may carry more weight than the DIS in the corridors of power back in London, and no doubt you're confident your minister will outrank mine, but I am not without friends. I've known Stansfield Turner for years, long before Carter appointed him to run the CIA. I have spoken twice to him in the last week and if it comes down to your clout in Whitehall against Stansfield's in Washington my money is on Washington pulling the strings.'

This time Ffortiscue did look shocked.

'You've spoken to Turner? You've spoken to the head of a foreign intelligence service about one of my operations? You'll jeopardise everything. That's close to treason. You don't know what Turner is capable of.'

Ffortiscue was really angry now and the DG responded in kind. 'I talk to him as one honourable man to another, as one naval officer to another. The Americans are our allies for heaven's sake. I want to know about Tortellini and Tortellini is their operation.'

'It is now,' said Ffortiscue. The MI6 man paused, unsure how to continue. 'This will finish Harry. You've given Turner all the ammunition he needs. Don't you realise that Harry's networks are fundamental to the security of the United Kingdom? He has agents right across Europe and the Middle East. Nobody has a better understanding of events on the ground. And whenever he can, he shares his information with us, we work together. His enemies are our enemies, his friends our friends. And all that is under threat, first Church and now Turner.'

Suddenly I realised what the fragment of argument Morgan and I had overheard outside Romney's office was all about.

The Bastamentes and Romney had not been arguing about the church but about Church, Senator Frank Church.

We all knew what Ffortiscue was talking about but he continued anyway, talking to Julia and me as if we were not in the intelligence business and never read a newspaper.

'When President Truman set up the CIA after the war he wanted it just to collect intelligence but Eisenhower understood that it was no good collecting intelligence if you didn't then act on it. Allen Dulles created an agency that acted, sorted problems out and took the battle to the enemy. Italy, Iran, Indonesia, Chile, all over the world the Company acted to keep the West safe. And it worked. Communism has been contained everywhere.'

'Cuba?' suggested Julia.

'Nearly everywhere. Threats were eliminated.'

'You mean elections were overturned and leaders assassinated.'

Ffortiscue glared at her. 'Occasionally. Men had to be taken out.'

'But the point is,' the DG interrupted, 'that while we all knew what the CIA were doing, the American public didn't. At least they didn't know until a couple of years ago when the US Senate set up a committee to investigate some nasty newspaper allegations. Once the Church Committee got going all sorts of dirt came pouring out. The Company's dirty tricks during the Vietnam War, how it installed a sadistic military regime in Chile. Church even published Allen Dulles' personal instruction to murder Lumumba, the Congolese Prime Minister. Things had to change.'

'Perhaps,' agreed Ffortiscue. 'President Ford appointed a new director, a Republican politician he knew he could trust, a man called George Bush who was supposed to make a few cosmetic changes. Then Carter was elected and he wanted more thoroughgoing change so he put Stansfield Turner in charge. That's when the problems started. Your friend Turner doesn't begin to understand what we do. It's all ridiculous jargon with him. He wants to replace "HUMINT" with "SIGINT", replace human intelligence with signals intelligence. It's nonsense. Look at what Harry's done here in Italy. Casarecce is amazing. We know everything that goes on in this country before it even happens. Harry was right on top of the Borghese Coup business long before anyone else. Do you think signals intelligence would have been able to tell us we had a Russian spy at Sigonella?'

'So you and Harry Bastamente are saving us all from the red menace,' said the DG. 'How does killing my sister help that?'

'Don't be ridiculous Gordon, that was an accident. Behzad Sadeghi was supposed to be on that boat. He was supposed to be intercepted in the middle of the Ionian Sea and sent back to Iran. Nobody was supposed to get killed. That was the whole point. If he had been assassinated in Paris there would have been an outcry but if he vanished at sea that's unremarkable.'

'What do you mean intercepted? Who by?'

'By the Iranians of course. One of their naval ships was waiting for him. I don't know what happened. It was night-time. Shots got fired. His boat sank.'

'Rubbish,' responded the DG. 'Even now you can't tell me the truth.'

'It is the truth,' Ffortiscue insisted. 'Believe me I wish it hadn't happened that way. Harry has gone ballistic with the Iranians, heads will roll. You can't apply Royal Navy standards to a Middle Eastern navy.'

If Ffortiscue thought the last remark would mollify Admiral Lord Grimspound he was very wide of the mark.

The DG just looked at him. 'George, I think you really believe that bollocks. Let me tell you I've been through the shipping movements in the Ionian Sea with a fine-tooth comb. There were no Iranian ships of any sort anywhere in the vicinity. What's more, I've had my man in Tehran working on this since the day Bunny vanished and every Iranian naval vessel is accounted for, they didn't even have a rowing boat within a thousand miles of the *Mahsheed*. Something you could easily have checked if you tried cooperating with other British agencies as closely as you cooperate with Harry Bastamente. Bastamente never meant Behzad to live. He hired Mafia hitmen to sink the *Mahsheed* and everyone aboard.'

Before Ffortiscue could respond the DG attacked from a different angle. 'What did you mean when you said that Tortellini is an American operation now? Why now?'

Ffortiscue was shaken by the DG's onslaught but he smiled wryly at the last question. 'Do you really think Bastamente could come up with something as subtle as that? This should have been our operation. It was our idea. Harry just took it over and gave it that stupid name, Tortellini. Junior would have cut us out altogether but he needed us.'

'Why did he need us?' I asked. 'What did we have to contribute?'

'Jahandar of course. He was ours. We turned him years ago. Gave him a few shekels and he let us know what Moscow was up to. Low level stuff. He was just a bagman, never produced anything really useful. Expendable if things went wrong. But the Iranian exiles all knew him, they all thought he was Moscow's man. If we could use him to get them all to Sicily perhaps we could grab the lot of them. Junior had ridiculous plans to kill them all. He expected to persuade people that there had been a falling out of thieves and they had ended up shooting each other. But when the other groups pulled out we were just left with Behzad Sadeghi apparently sailing over in his boat. I wanted our Navy to pick him up at sea but my permanent secretary insisted that if the Royal Navy was going to be involved we had to consult you. And of course I knew you would never agree; not only was he your sister's brother-in-law but we all know you have this ridiculous aversion to anything you deem "political". So I asked Harry to get US Navy support but he was in the same position as us. Just as we needed agreement from you he needed agreement from the Office of Naval Intelligence. Normally they would have jumped at the chance of playing pirates but Harry had turned up a spy at their base and then made the mistake of letting Harry Junior go down there and start throwing his weight around. The ONI refused to cooperate. That's when Harry said he could persuade the Iranians to send a gunboat. It didn't seem unreasonable to me, why the hell shouldn't the Shah contribute something? We were doing this for him.

'If Behzad Sadeghi hadn't fallen ill and stayed in Kefalonia this could all have ended so very differently,' Ffortiscue concluded, almost smugly.

'Yes,' spat Julia, 'he could have been murdered as well as my aunt and uncle.'

Ffortiscue glared disdainfully but said nothing, mercifully.

'Behzad didn't fall sick,' said the DG. 'Moscow told him to stay away. I've seen the cables between them.'

Ffortiscue looked startled at that and then the implication sunk in. 'You've seen what? You've seen cables between the KGB and Behzad Sadeghi? How did you do that?'

'You don't need to know,' replied the DG with what in other circumstances might have been a smirk.

'You must show me the cables,' snapped Ffortiscue, his voice rising.

'I will not risk you compromising a DIS source, you're too close to a certain foreign agency,' riposted the DG, steely eyed.

The two men glared at each other before Ffortiscue pushed back his chair and stood up. He strode off without any sort of farewell.

XXV

The DG ordered more coffee. 'Ffortiscue's becoming insufferable. A pompous fool who, because he thinks he knows everyone worth knowing, imagines he knows everything worth knowing. Bastamente's fairy tales simply don't stand up and Six should have realised that right from the outset. Harry Bastamente's losing it. He used to be on top of everything that happened in Southern Europe and the Middle East. Now's he's spouting fantasies about the Mafia and the KGB drug smuggling. And that ridiculous story about the Iranian Navy intercepting a boat in the Ionian Sea, only an idiot like Ffortiscue would have bought that. Bastamente is acting like a rank amateur and he's not. Something has really rattled him.'

'But at least now we know what happened to Bunny,' said Julia, visibly upset, turning to her uncle. 'It's as you say. Bastamente tried to lure Behzad to Sicily and hired the Mafia to kill him. What a mess. They ended up killing the wrong people and seem to have blown themselves up in the process. And when the Russians found out that Farhad Jahandar had come over to us, they killed him.'

'We will probably never know why Jahandar was killed,' replied the DG, 'Kapustin and his wife left Rome yesterday and flew back to Moscow. Kapustin may have confronted Jahandar and wasn't satisfied with his answers, perhaps he thought Jahandar was holding something back. Or perhaps he had been told to send a message to anyone who accepted Russian gold that if they tried to earn a little more on the side from us they were playing with fire. It could even be that the KGB simply don't like traitors.

'There are still a lot of loose ends. Who killed the fisherman Conti and why? It certainly wasn't to protect the two Mafiosi who killed Bunny, one of them is dead and the other probably unreachable. What's happened to Milan? What's happened to Ramone? And above all who killed Jack Romney? I would like to think we will find answers to all of those questions but I think we'll need to leave that to our American cousins. Stansfield was already planning to send over a team to investigate the entire Tortellini saga and now with Romney's murder half of Langley will be here.'

However it wasn't to be investigators flying over from America who filled in the blanks but investigators much closer at hand. We had only just finished our coffees and started walking across the lobby to the lift when two men entered the hotel and came purposefully in our direction: Colonel Castorini and Inspector Falzone.

I introduced the DG to the Colonel and watched with mild amusement as the two men weighed each other up. They were similar in many ways: roughly the same age and both accustomed to command. Both were tall, straight-backed and suntanned, although the DG was heavier and his hair materially thinner. Today he was wearing what he would probably refer to as his country casuals while Castorini, as always, was impeccably dressed in an expensive suit, white cotton shirt, plain silk tie and highly polished shoes. They both seemed to like what they saw.

'I think we should talk,' said Castorini. 'Perhaps we could take a walk, the Villa Politi is not the place for private conversations.'

He and the DG headed outside and strode briskly away, it seemed that their private conversation was not to include the rest of us. Julia and I followed and discussed the previous day's events with Giuseppe Falzone. There were no further developments. Romney had been shot by a .45 automatic similar to his own. A possible witness driving along the road to the base claimed to have seen a large black car driving away from the scene but could offer no further detail. The police had not yet spoken to Bastamente Junior and so had no accounting for his actions after leaving the base. He may or may not have turned around and followed us. Julia and Giuseppe were convinced that Junior was Romney's killer but I preferred to keep an open mind. I was still puzzled by Giuseppe's own behaviour the previous evening; why had he wasted so much time asking Romney questions to which he knew he would not receive any answers?

When I asked him his response was straightforward. 'The officers who stopped Romney took his address,' Giuseppe told us. 'They then radioed it to a team in Catania who went to Romney's hotel and arranged to listen to his calls and bug his room. That's why I kept him busy. All a waste of time of course as he never went back to the hotel. My man did discover that both the Bastamentes were staying at the same hotel but he'd only been told to listen in to Bastamente Junior's calls, the fool didn't have enough initiative to listen in to Bastamente Senior's. I sent him back to the hotel this morning but both the Americans have checked out. One of the staff reported that he heard them having an almighty row last night when Bastamente Senior got back but we have no idea what about.'

After walking for fifteen minutes or so the Colonel and his new friend, the DG, stopped. 'We must escape the sun, only mad dogs and Englishmen go out at such a time.' Castorini led us into a courtyard café with tables and chairs arranged under enormous umbrellas. Without asking anyone he ordered five espressos.

Once the coffees had arrived I expected Colonel Castorini to start by asking Julia and me about the shooting of Jack Romney but it was the DG who took charge of the conversation.

'Colonel, you have six deaths to explain.'

'Six?' Interjected Giuseppe in surprise.

'My sister, my brother-in-law, Farhad Jahandar, Giacomo Conti, Romney and the man who died in hospital in Palermo.'

'Oh yes,' conceded Giuseppe, 'I had forgotten him.'

'I can explain some of those deaths,' the DG continued. 'Let me tell you what I know then perhaps we can discuss the other murders and pool our knowledge. It is time for all of us to be completely open.'

To my surprise the DG then proceeded to tell the two Italians the full story of Bunny and her husband's murder. He even told them how he had been able to see the cables between Shahryar and Moscow, something he had refused to discuss with Ffortiscue just a few minutes earlier. He started right at the beginning with the visit Julia and I had paid to Behzad and our sighting of the mysterious Ramone, apparently forgetting that Julia and I had already told the Colonel and Giuseppe all about that. Then he recounted at length his own experience in Kefalonia. As so often with the DG his account ambled off at tangents. His story of meeting his Greek opposite number at the sarcophagus of John Paul Jones left Giuseppe bemused but appeared to delight Colonel Castorini.

Despite declaring he would be completely open, the DG omitted a few details. There was no mention of the part played by MI6. The DG asserted that the cable exchanges between Shahryar and Moscow had revealed that the Russians had somehow discovered that Jahandar had been turned by the Americans; there was nothing to be gained by admitting that Jahandar had been a British asset, a fact that he himself had only just discovered. Nor was there any mention of Ffortescue's absurd belief that the *Mahsheed* would be intercepted by the Iranian Navy in the Ionian Sea.

'It was a classic false flag operation. Behzad believed he was dealing with the Russians because he knew Jahandar was their man. But he wasn't, he had become Bastamente's man. And when the KGB realised that Jahandar had been working for the Americans they eliminated him.'

When he had finished Castorini nodded. 'Unfortunately that all makes sense.'

The DG fell silent for a moment. 'I now know how Bunny died, and I know why, but I don't have justice. I don't think I ever will have. Those who planned Tortellini are untouchable. I don't believe Tortellini was ever authorised in Washington. This was Harry Bastamente acting on his own, but the Company will have to close ranks now. Turner will make changes, big changes, and Harry Bastamente will never be able to do something like this again, but they won't want do anything that might disrupt Casarecce.'

The DG stopped. He watched Castorini's reaction carefully; he needed to know how much the *Carabinieri* actually knew about the Americans' Casarecce network. It was, after all, supposed to be highly secret, especially from the Italians. But across the table Colonel Castorini simply smiled. 'I can assure you, Admiral, I know far more about Casarecce than you do.'

The DG looked intrigued but continued. 'Turner doesn't like HUMINT and he might not approve of something like Casarecce, but he won't want it to become public knowledge that one of the CIA's biggest spy networks was actually targeting a NATO ally like Italy. Whatever the Company do they will do nothing in public. Bastamente Senior will probably be pensioned off to live happily ever after in a condominium in Florida. Junior will be transferred to El Salvador or Angola. There's only one thing that might make the Americans really go after either of the Bastamentes and that's if they're connected in some way with Romney's murder. Where that fits in I still don't understand.'

The DG spoke gently and the *Carabinieri* colonel responded in the same way. 'Admiral Grimspound, I have to tell you that there is a great deal you do not yet understand.' He paused and then continued. 'Thank you for your candour, Admiral. I will try to respond in the same way. I too seek justice. Whatever you may have heard about Sicily not all of us are accustomed to letting killers walk free. But my interest in this case does not start with anyone's death. I set out to catch a spy.

'It started when I received a call from the *Servizio Informazioni Difesa* in Rome, from our friend Di Benedetto. The Americans, he said, had discovered that there was a Russian spy at the Sigonella base here in Sicily. As the *Carabinieri* are responsible for security at the base I was to be in charge of the Italian side of the investigation. Di Benedetto himself would fly down in a few days and a man called Romney, who was already there, would head up the American side. The Americans had a secure facsimile machine in the base and Di Benedetto was sending down copies of the documents the spy had stolen. Our first task was to find out where exactly they had been taken from and who therefore had had access to them. The Americans, said Di Benedetto, suspected there might be a network of spies at Sigonella, KGB moles who had established themselves inside the US Naval facility. I was to make catching these spies my top priority. Naturally I asked how the Americans had found the stolen documents but I was told I did not need to know.

'When I received the facsimile copies of the documents I was mystified. They were classified documents but low grade. Some were too old to be of any use to an enemy. It hardly looked like the work of a trained KGB mole. Would a professional spy not have stolen something more useful? And then would you believe when I am shown the room where the stolen documents had been kept I find they are not there!'

'Of course,' exclaimed Giuseppe, 'they had been stolen.'

'But think about it, Giuseppe. I discover that the files are empty. The spy seems to have stolen the original documents and sent them off to his masters. Have you ever heard of a spy doing such a thing? Taking the originals is an absurd risk, sooner or later one of the documents must certainly be missed. A professional would surely take copies, he would be equipped with a camera. And yet the Americans are suggesting there could be a full-blown Soviet spy ring in Sigonella. They must have more to go on than the discovery of one batch of stolen documents. I put this to Di Benedetto when he arrived. He consulted Romney and they called me in to tell me their great secret. The CIA actually had an agent inside the Russian Embassy in Rome. This agent had told them about the spy ring and had managed to copy the stolen documents.

'It still seemed to me that whoever had passed those documents to the Russians had been an amateur, but what do I know about espionage? Then suddenly the spy becomes a professional. The source in the Russian Embassy reports that a second batch has arrived, sadly he cannot tell us what that batch has contained except to say that some of the items are top secret. They have immediately been sent to Moscow.

'But think about it. How was that second batch stolen? When Di Benedetto told me about the first batch, I assure you security at Sigonella became watertight. My men were on full alert. Romney and his assistant Bastamente Junior were everywhere. Everyone was watched. There were frequent searches. I can guarantee no more documents have gone missing. So are we to understand that our spy has obtained a camera and learned how to use it? That he has suddenly acquired the expertise to transfer these documents on to microfilm and smuggle them out of the base?

'And if that does not seem strange enough, some weeks later and thanks to the appearance of you, Signora Dylan, in *La Sicilia*, we encounter Robert Milan. He insists that he did not send a second batch. When he tells me that I believe him. So we have a problem: the Americans say there was a second batch, Milan says there was not. Either one of them is lying or another spy has popped up, two unconnected spies within a few weeks of each other. I don't think so. No, I will tell you: there was no second batch. That was another Bastamente invention designed to enhance his own reputation. I will tell you something else my friends that will surprise you. There is no American agent in the Russian Embassy!'

'But there must be,' I said. 'How could the Company have found out about the first batch? That batch was real, Milan admits he sent them.'

'Yes he did, but the Russians never received them!'

XXVI

The DG and I looked at each other in disbelief. That simply did not make sense.

The silence was broken by a quiet voice at my side. Julia had got there before me. 'The SID,' she said. 'Di Benedetto.'

Castorini nodded with a smile. 'Yes indeed, *bella Signora*: Di Benedetto.'

I still did not understand and Castorini was clearly enjoying my confusion. 'Consider,' he said, 'Milan really is an incredibly naïve young man. He has watched enough films to know that when he removes the documents he must wear gloves to hide his fingerprints. He carefully disguises his writing on the package. But then he simply puts the package in the post addressed to the Russian Embassy in Rome. Doesn't he realise that the SID monitor everything going to that address? No he doesn't. The SID intercept the parcel and it arrives on Di Benedetto's desk. So what does Di Benedetto do? He goes to his friend Bastamente and Bastamente comes up with the fiction of an agent inside the Embassy. And to make this agent sound really important he invents another batch of truly top-secret documents as well.'

Again we were silent until the DG conceded, almost to himself, 'It could be. It could make sense. Harry Bastamente was under pressure to show that HUMINT was producing the goods. This would have been a golden opportunity for him to demonstrate that his Casarecce network was worth all the money that must have been invested in it.'

'But why would Di Benedetto go along with such a story?' I asked. 'Why not take the credit for discovering the stolen documents himself?'

'Now that is a good question,' said the Colonel. 'The SID are under pressure; the organisation is not popular in certain circles. There are those in Rome who would very much like, as you say in English, to trim their wings. If that is so why did Di Benedetto not use the opportunity to improve the reputation of the SID? He could have shown that his organisation was protecting Italy against the activities of foreign agents rather than, as many believe, protecting the interests of a few corrupt politicians and neo-fascists.

'How do I explain? Perhaps I should go back just a few years, to 1970. It was a difficult year for Italy. Protests on the streets. Bombings. The hard left seemed to many to be close to seizing power. Then along came Junio Borghese. A man on the surface not unlike Admiral Grimspound here, a naval man, an aristocrat, a warrior but underneath very different. Many regarded him as a hero. In the war he took his submarine right into the harbour in Alexandria and his frogmen all but destroyed two British battleships.'

'I know,' said the DG, '*Valiant* and *Queen Elizabeth*.'

'A hero then but after Mussolini was seized by the *Carabinieri*, and most Italians had welcomed the Allies, Borghese continued to fight alongside the German SS. He waged a dirty war against the Communists: the Yugoslav and Italian partisans. The troops he commanded were largely destroyed by the partisans. Borghese himself would have been executed by the Communists but he was rescued by an American who dressed him in an American uniform and personally drove him to Rome. There he received just a token sentence for aiding the enemy. That American was James Angleton. You know him.'

Of course we knew him. Borghese had acquired a very useful friend. Angleton had probably been the most powerful man in the CIA. For two decades he had been the head of counterintelligence and spent much of that time fighting what he saw as a vast Soviet conspiracy to take over the world. Amongst the foreign leaders he alleged to be Russian agents were the Prime Ministers of Britain, Canada, Sweden, Australia and the Chancellor of West Germany, but only when he began to insist that the CIA itself had been comprehensively infiltrated by the KGB was he forced to resign on Christmas Eve 1974.

'After the war Borghese became a leader of the neo-fascists and by 1970 he had decided that democracy had to go. You know about his planned coup. On the night of 8 December fascist activists, parts of the Army and, here in Sicily, some of the Mafia clans were supposed to kidnap the president, murder the chief of police, occupy official buildings and take over the government. It didn't happen. Nobody seems to know why. Borghese may have thought he needed more time. But a few months later details of the planned coup started to leak out and the government was forced to respond. A few arrests were made but Borghese himself escaped to Spain. As is typical in Italy, nothing happened quickly. Then in March 1974, just three years ago, the SID finally prepared a report on the attempted coup. They produced not just a report, but a very good report, a report, in fact, that was so good that it became clear that the SID itself must have had some involvement in the coup. In October 1974 Vito Miceli, the head of the SID, was arrested.

'Now, you may be wondering, what has all this got to do with Di Benedetto and Bastamente? The answer is that I don't know for certain. But some things we do know. We know Di Benedetto was close to Vito Miceli and almost certainly therefore close to the coup organisers. And we know that the CIA knew about the coup before it happened. People say that President Nixon insisted on being briefed personally as the coup plans were developed. The truth about the Borghese Coup is still emerging, everything may never be known. But I am willing to wager that Di Benedetto and Bastamente were together in there somewhere. They know each other's secrets. They need each other.'

I remembered Ffortiscue's comment that Harry Bastamente had been right on top of the Borghese Coup business long before anyone else. There was a plausibility about the Colonel's remarks but what he said next took the conversation in a totally new and unexpected direction.

'I am a humble colonel of the *Carabinieri* many kilometres from Rome. I am not part of the Borghese investigations; I am not privy to the secrets that may or may not one day become public. I know the SID is in turmoil but you are probably closer to the shifting currents in my country's intelligence community than I am. I just follow the information I have that seems to relate to crime here in Sicily. And one such piece of information you provided: the details of a bank account in Rome held by Signor Henry Ramone. Now normally obtaining any banking information in this country is very difficult, obtaining it quickly is impossible and to try to obtain it at the weekend is not even worth considering. But I have an old friend in the *Guardia di Finanza* in Rome. My friend's wife has been unwell for some time and I phoned him to ask after her health. Sadly it is still not good. We talked about our families and of course about our work. I mentioned I was looking for information on a bank account in the name of Henry Ramone. Perhaps he could direct me to someone at the bank who might be prepared to help.

'I have known my friend for many years but I was puzzled by his response. It was formal, cold. He would look into it if he had time but I should not be surprised to hear nothing from him. But I did hear something, just one hour later, and not from him but from his superior, one of the most senior men in the *Guardia di Finanza*. Where had I come across that account he asked. Of course I told him but as soon as he had his answer he ended our conversation. Then first thing this morning he phoned me back. I think he must have checked up on me and decided I could be trusted. He was suddenly very friendly and he had a lot more questions. About you, for example. He suggested a bargain. He would send me full details of the account if I let him know if any of the entries made any sense at all to me. It seems he knew very little about the account other than that there had been large and frequent cash deposits over sixteen years, especially around the time of the Borghese Coup, and there was a regular stream of income from Canada. The Canadian authorities, he told me, had been most unhelpful. There were also a few large disbursements. One disbursement in particular is what had brought the account to his attention. A significant payment had been made in October 1970, just at the time Borghese was finalising the plans for his coup. It had been made to a local lawyer who confirmed that the money had eventually been used to buy a modest apartment for a young teacher; that teacher is the son of our friend Di Benedetto.'

I struggled to make sense of all that the Colonel was telling us. He seemed to be implying that Di Benedetto was being investigated for suspected involvement in the Borghese Coup and that as part of that investigation Ramone's bank account had popped up almost by chance.

The man using the name Ramone was, in my mind, a shadowy figure on the periphery. Perhaps a freelancer Bastamente used for covert operations that he did not want to advertise to those back in Washington. If this man wanted his real identity hidden it was quite plausible that Harry Bastamente had gone to a drawer and pulled out the passport of a legend he had created in Canada years ago for just such an occasion. It would have been easy enough to change the photograph. It was odd that Giacomo Conti's wife also bore the name Ramone but as Harry Bastamente had pointed out, coincidences happen. However, from what Colonel Castorini was saying it now seemed possible that the primary purpose of the legend was not to provide a fake identity when needed for something like Tortellini but to provide a legitimate but untraceable bank account. That account, I guessed, was some sort of slush fund operated by Bastamente Senior. Having the account in the name of a fictional Canadian would make it difficult for anyone to trace the funds back to the Company. And if anyone did start asking questions the Canadian authorities would alert Bastamente's office in Langley because of the POI tag.

Abruptly Castorini stood up, looking at his watch. 'There is more,' he said, 'but I need to return to my office now. I am expecting a call from Rome. Can I suggest we talk again later? Perhaps we could meet for lunch and I will bring the Ramone bank statements along? I believe Giuseppe introduced you to a restaurant in Ortygia. Let us meet there in two hours.'

Without waiting for an answer he shook hands with each of us and walked off. Outside an official car pulled up for him and I wondered how the driver had known where he would be. The Colonel, I concluded, was a careful man.

Giuseppe too excused himself and Julia, the DG and I walked slowly back to the hotel. For once the DG was not in the mood for conversation. When we got back to the hotel he announced he had phone calls to make. We gave him the name of the restaurant in Ortygia and agreed to meet there.

Julia and I decided we might as well do some sightseeing, first collecting a sun hat from our room for Julia. When we came down we were just in time to see a hotel porter carrying Ffortiscue's luggage to a waiting taxi. The MI6 man himself caught sight of us and snarled that he was going back to London to salvage what he could from the mess created by the DG. We said nothing. Instead we wandered around the ancient Greek amphitheatre and marvelled at the sophistication of the people who built it and performed there. The works of Aeschylus, Sophocles and the long-forgotten Achaeus of Syracuse were enjoyed by thousands of people seated right here while in Britain our own Iron Age ancestors were doing no more than erect a few crude hill forts to keep each other at bay.

When Julia and I reached the restaurant the DG and Colonel were already there, sharing war reminiscences over a bottle of red wine. Giuseppe arrived soon after and it became clear that the two older men had been waiting for us before getting down to business. In Sicily the first item of business had to be deciding what to eat, an easy task as the Colonel was firm in his recommendations which included fritelle, arancinette, olives, lemons, sardines, calamari fritti and beautifully cooked aubergines mixed with wild fennel. He also insisted we should be introduced to the joys of Sicilian cassata to finish.

Once the most urgent item on our agenda was in hand, he produced a dozen printed pages and placed them on the table in front of the DG. 'I have spoken to Rome and been authorised to show you Henry Ramone's bank statements,' he announced. 'This copy is for you but I can summarise. The account was opened fifteen years ago. It's a *conto estero*, a US dollar account.

There is a lot of form filling needed to set up an account like that but all the original papers have disappeared. We suspect someone in the bank was paid to make that happen. All we know is that the original address given for the account holder was an office in Naples in a block that was due to be demolished. That was soon changed to a post office box in New York. Payments were made into the account at roughly monthly intervals in dollars in cash. The sums increased over the years until by 1970 there was a considerable balance. Until then there had not been a single withdrawal. Then the sum of 36 000 Canadian dollars was transferred to a lawyer in Toronto. Shortly afterwards the account's address was moved to Toronto and bank transfers started coming into the account from Canada. We guessed, and you have confirmed, that the 36 000 was used to buy property which produced a rental income. At the same time the monthly cash deposits started to increase. By 1974 they were around US$5000 to US$10 000 per month. That is a lot of spare cash.

'Then came the next disbursement, the one that allowed Di Benedetto's son to purchase his apartment. After that the monthly deposits never fell below US$10 000. It continued like that until the beginning of this year, money in each month and nothing going out. As a result the account had a very healthy balance. Then four months ago everything changed.' Castorini pointed to the last page of the bank statements in front of the DG. 'First there was one enormous transfer in and then two payments out. The payments out I think I can explain. The first was to a lawyer in Palermo who we know has Mafia connections. The other just two weeks ago was again to Palermo and this time it seems to have been another property transaction. A house between Piana degli Albanesi and San Giuseppe Jato was acquired in the name

218

of Daniela Ramone. And then this morning I heard that another withdrawal has been made in the last few days. Almost all the money in the account has gone. All but a few hundred dollars was transferred to a numbered account in Switzerland.'

He stopped and looked around the table. The DG said nothing, leafing through the bank records as if looking for inspiration. Julia and I started to speak at the same time. I waved her to continue.

'Who is Daniela Ramone?'

It was Giuseppe who answered. 'Daniela Ramone appears to be the sister of Chiara, the wife of the fisherman who was killed in Marzamemi. She moved to Palermo in 1934 and there is no record of her after that. There may have been records that were destroyed in the war. She could have gone anywhere, perhaps to the mainland, or she could have died. But I don't think she has been living in Sicily, certainly not under that name.'

I mulled that over before asking my own question. 'You mentioned an enormous deposit four months ago. What do you know about that? How much was it?'

Castorini looked at me and smiled. 'I wondered when you would ask that.' Before he could say any more the DG interrupted, he had reached the entry on the bank statement that I was asking about.

'Half a million US dollars. Bank transfer received on 1 June.' He pointed at the entry and pushed the page towards the Colonel. 'What does this mean: Melli?'

'I suppose that does look Italian,' said the Colonel, 'but it is not. It is the name of the bank that sent the money. Melli is one of the biggest banks in Iran.'

XXVII

At that point lunch arrived and Colonel Castorini held up his hand. 'My friends, we are in Italy, here we treat food with respect. As my mother used to tell me, the lamb who bleats goes hungry.'

Giuseppe raised an eyebrow as if he had never heard the expression before and suspected that the Colonel had just invented it. He contributed another saying of his own: '*Uno non può pensare bene, amare bene, dormire bene, se non ha mangiato bene.* One cannot think well, love well, sleep well, if one has not dined well. An old girlfriend used to tell me that.'

The Colonel nodded his approval. 'That is the spirit of Italy.'

'Or the spirit of Cheltenham Ladies' College,' murmured Julia. 'I believe that is a line from Virginia Woolf's *A Room of One's Own.*'

The Colonel said nothing more until his plate was wiped clean. We likewise ate in near silence, not just out of respect to Castorini but as he had said, out of respect to the food. Julia clearly relished the sardines; for me, the cassata was sublime, even more delicious than my favourite trifle at home.

It was the DG who returned to the bank account as coffee arrived. 'The entries are the wrong way round,' he said. 'If this is a slush fund there should be large payments in and small payments out. And as to the half million dollars from Iran, there is only one explanation for that. Ramone was being paid to kill Behzad Sadeghi.'

'You're right,' said Colonel Castorini. 'Let me tell you what I think.'

He reached across the table and poured the last of the red wine into the DG's glass.

'One possibility is that there really is a man called Henry or Enrico Ramone born in Sicily. I can't find any trace of him but what does that prove? When the Allies invaded in 1943, Palermo was bombed, records were lost. It was a time of chaos. If a man wanted to make himself disappear or invent a new identity he could do so. So much of the old city was lost, beautiful palaces that had stood for three hundred years gone for ever. And you know what was different about the bombing here, different to the bombs in your country or Germany? Now, more than thirty years later, the heart of Palermo stands as it was in July 1943, ruined staircases leading just to the empty sky, walls still upright with their shattered windows staring into space both inside and out, weeds where once bejewelled ladies danced and princes held court.'

It looked as though the Colonel was about to launch into one of those tangents that both he and the DG seemed to love but this time the DG brought the conversation back down to earth.

'Behzad Sadeghi told me that Ramone was in his late thirties or forties. If that's the case Ramone would have been a child in 1943.'

'True, but we don't know that the man calling himself Ramone in Kefalonia was the same Ramone as the man I am imagining.'

Giuseppe responded first. 'That would be an enormous coincidence. Two untraceable people called Ramone.'

'No,' said the Colonel, who had obviously been thinking things through. 'Just imagine someone in Sicily in 1943 wants to disappear, a Mafia man perhaps, a fascist, or a German collaborator. He establishes a new identity. Years later he wants to open a secret bank account that could not be linked to his new identity, so he uses his original name. Perhaps he still had papers in the name of Ramone, papers the bank would accept. And then later again he hires someone to infiltrate the Iranian community and lure their leaders to Sicily. That someone needs an identity, what you people call a legend, and out comes the old Ramone name.'

The DG was not impressed. 'But who is this mysterious man? What has he been doing since the war? Are you suggesting that it might be Di Benedetto?'

'Di Benedetto? No. I am sure that the *Guardia de Finanza* have put his life under a microscope. There are no skeletons there. No, I have another name in mind. A man who was in Sicily after the war, the man you suggested created the legend of Henry Ramone: Harry Bastamente. We know that right after the war the Americans were eager to hire anyone who would help them fight the Communists whatever their background. Suppose they had found an ambitious young Italian who had somehow already proved his ruthlessness. They give him a new identity as Harry Bastamente and enrol him in the Agency. The young Italian becomes a young American and claws his way to the top.'

It was possible, I thought, although Harry Bastamente struck me as very American. No trace of an Italian accent. Only his penchant for expensive Italian suits distinguished him from millions of native New Yorkers.

The DG smiled. 'Vincenzo, I applaud your logic, but you are wrong. I had the same thought myself. My staff have been working on it and that was the call I received just before lunch.

Harry Bastamente is exactly who he says he is. He was born in New Jersey and his parents arrived in the United States from Bologna after the First World War. We've seen his school records. He was in the US Army and then with Allen Dulles in the Office of Strategic Services. There is no doubt at all about it. I'm sorry.'

The Colonel looked crestfallen. 'I am sorry too. It seemed such a neat explanation. But let me move on to a subject I am much more confident about. I will tell you what that bank account really is. My friends, that account is Harry Bastamente's pension. It is his own personal savings account. But more than that, it is Casarecce.'

The DG voiced my own thoughts. 'What do you mean? How can a bank account be Casarecce? Casarecce is an intelligence network, the Company's main asset in Western Europe.'

Once again it was Julia who understood what the Colonel was saying. She spoke slowly, as if unravelling her thoughts aloud. 'There is no Casarecce network. There are no agents. No agents in the Russian Embassy. No agents anywhere. Or at least no Company agents. Casarecce is really the Italian secret service, the SID. Bastamente's only agent is Di Benedetto. The SID are everywhere. They are inside the fascists. They have informers in the Communist Party. They have infiltrated the protest groups. And whatever the SID learns Di Benedetto passes to Bastamente and Bastamente passes it back to Washington as his own Casarecce product. Everyone in Washington is naturally very impressed. Why, Nixon himself insisted on a personal briefing on the Casarecce material. So Langley no doubt funnelled more and more funds to Bastamente and Bastamente simply put them in the Ramone bank account.'

I was suddenly sure Julia was right. The name should have made me think. When I saw the project name Tortellini back at the meeting with Harry Bastamente at Heathrow I had thought it slightly odd to name an operation after a type of pasta. After that it seemed unremarkable when the name Casarecce, another sort of pasta, came up. But of course Casarecce had really come first, the Casarecce network had been around much longer than Operation Tortellini. And casarecce is not just an unusual type of pasta, the name also implies something else: *casereccio*, meaning homemade. The Casarecce network the Company was so proud of was homemade, Harry Bastamente had created it himself. No doubt he would have found the name very amusing.

Julia was still musing over the revelation that the Casarecce network was really no more than the collected reports of the Italian intelligence service. 'But why would Di Benedetto cooperate? Was it just money?'

'I don't know why Di Benedetto acted the way he did. Perhaps it was ideological. Perhaps Signor Bastamente had something on him. Eventually they became partners in crime and Bastamente paid for that apartment in Rome for Di Benedetto's son. When the Borghese conspiracy was being planned Washington upped the money being sent for Casarecce. They did the same again when Di Benedetto discovered that there was a spy at Sigonella. Langley no doubt demanded action and Bastamente was able to demand even more funds.'

The DG nodded slowly and took up the story. 'But things were working against Bastamente. The new CIA management were wary of cavalier operations like his. Sooner or later the spotlight would fall on Casarecce. He was reaching retirement but the Langley bureaucrats could not be guaranteed just to let his son take over. What would happen if the accountants back home decided to start digging? Harry Junior didn't have the status Harry Senior had acquired, he wouldn't be able to block them.'

'And then,' I added, 'there was Jack Romney. He must have been the one actually handling that account, paying in the cash. Harry Senior was flying around all over the place, his base was back in Langley. He needed Romney as station chief in Rome to keep the fiction going. Somebody had to do the paperwork, produce the phoney records that purported to show lots of cash payments being distributed to Bastamente's supposed agents. But Romney too was thinking about his future and the risks, perhaps he wanted a piece of the cake. He started drinking, which must have made both the Bastamentes nervous.'

'All that makes sense,' said Giuseppe, 'but why buy an apartment in Canada?'

'Who knows?' I replied. 'A bolt-hole in case things went wrong. Perhaps he didn't want all his money in one place. He wanted a safe investment that produced a steady income and he thought that real estate was a better bet than the stock market. Investing in the United States was too risky if he ever needed to disappear so just across the border in Canada would have seemed sensible.'

The DG took up the story again. 'So we have Harry Bastamente at the top of his game and suddenly we have Frank Church and Stansfield Turner causing chaos in Washington and Italian investigators homing in on the Borghese conspirators, including Di Benedetto. He wants a way out and he is greedy. How does he find one big last contribution to his pension pot?'

'Tortellini.'

'Yes. Tortellini. He's worked closely with the Iranian secret police, SAVAK, for more than two decades. They are having problems. When the Iranian economy was booming everyone was happy but now things are not so good. The bazaars are getting restive. The ayatollahs are whipping up a frenzy again. The poor see the obscene opulence of the Shah's court and contrast that with the shortages they face themselves. The middle classes who have been living very well start listening again to men like Behzad Sadeghi. SAVAK needs to act. Bastamente is willing to act. An anxious buyer meets an anxious seller and half a million dollars appears in our infamous bank account.'

'Then,' put in Giuseppe, 'Bastamente hires a couple of low-grade Mafia thugs and Tortellini is ready to roll.'

'Exactly.'

We all had a lot to absorb. The idea that Casarecce was entirely fraudulent, just a way for Bastamente and Di Benedetto to enrich themselves, would have seemed absurdly far-fetched just a few days ago. Harry Bastamente had been one of the titans of the US Intelligence establishment for more than two decades. He had brought down governments the US opposed and pulled the strings of those it claimed to support. His reputation was as high in London, Paris and Bonn as it was in Washington. As the DG had said, he was untouchable.

'So what happens now?' asked Julia.

'I am going to interview the two Signor Bastamentes,' the Colonel announced. 'Tonight.'

'You think they will both be at the hotel?'

'I know they will not. Both of them checked out of their hotel in Catania this morning. They first went to their office at Sigonella and then travelled west.'

'You're having them followed?'

'No. There was no time to arrange that. But I know they checked out of the hotel and I know from the base log when they arrived at Sigonella and when they left. I also know they have not left the island by air. Just give me one minute.'

The Colonel left the restaurant briefly. When he returned there was a smile on his face. 'My men have been watching the main routes to the west of the island. A Mercedes car hired by Signor Bastamente Junior passed through Enna an hour ago. There were two men inside. I think we have them.'

'You think they are going to leave from Palermo?'

'That could be. But I think it is more likely that they are going to the house that has just been purchased by Daniela Ramone. You tell me that the CIA are sending a team to investigate the death of Signor Romney. We all believe that the younger Bastamente killed Signor Romney do we not? If the Bastamentes leave Sicily they are effectively admitting their guilt. I don't think they will be ready to do that. Signor Bastamente will want to regroup. See what cards he has. What can be negotiated? Who can be negotiated with?

'Bastamente is an important American government official remember. If I try to arrest him my superiors will demand one hundred per cent concrete proof. Suspicion will not be enough. Even if I just go after Bastamente Junior, which will be my tactic, it will not be easy. I might be able to arrest him but unless I find the gun used to kill Romney I won't be able to hold him for long. The American Embassy in Rome will be on the case right away. And if, on the other hand, the Americans themselves try to arrest the Bastamentes here in Italy I'm sure the Bastamente lawyer will soon have them tied up in knots.'

'The Company will never let Harry Bastamente appear in open court,' said the DG. 'He knows far too much, too many dirty secrets. But they would have to do something, they couldn't risk him defecting. Moscow really would have something to celebrate. Either the Americans will allow him to retire gracefully or he will simply disappear.'

'You want justice for your sister,' Castorini said to the DG. 'Justice is what we must all hope for. That is why we must act now. If Bastamente is able to negotiate an agreement with his superiors we are lost. Then he and his son will have CIA protection. If that happens I tell you now that whatever their crimes, once they have left Italy no Italian government will try to extradite them back to this country.'

He rose from the table. 'Giuseppe will take you to your hotel. I have business to attend to. If you wish to come with me to Piana degli Albanesi I will call for you in one hour.'

XXVIII

We were being dismissed but the Colonel did so with effortless charm, there was none of the gracelessness that characterised the way Bastamente Senior signalled that a conversation was over.

Giuseppe took the DG, Julia and me back to the Grand Hotel Villa Politi and I was surprised when he then shook our hands. 'Your friend Morgan spoke about the complexity of policing in Italy. He was right. Piana degli Albanesi is not within my jurisdiction and in any case this is now a matter for the *Carabinieri*. I hope we meet again.'

He departed, although not before kissing Julia on both cheeks.

The DG disappeared to his room but we were all back in reception when Castorini's big black Fiat 130 appeared. The Colonel sat beside the driver while Julia, the DG and I piled into the back seat.

By the standards of the 1970s it was a luxurious car but it was still a tight fit. The thought of driving across the mountainous heart of Sicily cramped into the back seat was not attractive but the journey was better than I had expected. We were fortunate that two years earlier a motorway linking Catania and Palermo had been completed. We set off for the 150-mile journey and it was soon obvious that there would be no meaningful conversation on the way. Within five minutes the Colonel had fallen asleep and the effect of a heavy meal and copious red wine seemed to be having a similar effect on the DG.

Julia decided it would help pass the time if we tried to identify all the trees and plants we passed. At first that was easy: orange, lemon, prickly pear, olive. When Julia then moved on to sorghum, agave, sword grass, wild fennel and buckthorn I was not so sure. But the Colonel was asleep and his driver appeared to speak no English so she could not be contradicted.

After Enna the motorway turned north over the Madonie mountains to the sea, initially following a valley with hills on each side. Curious vertically inclined rocks jutted from the hillsides. For long distances the autostrada was carried above the countryside on concrete stilts. Back home I thought the road builders would have simply carved through fields and farms with little thought for the rural communities they were casually bisecting, here I suggested there was more consideration for the countryside. Julia smiled, 'Perhaps. Or perhaps it's just cheaper to plonk prefabricated chunks of motorway on prefabricated concrete supports.'

Colonel Castorini and the DG both woke up after Enna. Sleep had clearly put the Italian colonel in a philosophical mood.

'We say we are both seeking justice, Admiral, but there is a difference between you and me. You expect to find justice. I know Sicily, I do not expect to find justice here. The best I can hope for is to find the truth. For the sake of my own soul I seek truth. And I tell you something more, the only reason I still hope to find truth is because I am not a Sicilian. Truth and justice disappeared from this island centuries ago. Sicilians speak about their Greek and Arab ancestors but the reality is that they owe their character to more recent occupiers: the Spanish. In 1478 the Spanish brought the Inquisition to this island. They say

Sicily was the only place in Europe to experience a Counter-Reformation without first experiencing a Reformation. The Inquisition was not abolished until 1782. There is no tradition of justice here, only power. An Englishman once told me that all power corrupts but in Sicily it is the other way round, corruption brings power.'

He continued thoughtfully. 'I did not bring my cousin's son, Inspector Falzone, with us this afternoon because he would have had to tell his commissioner what we were planning. And if his commissioner knew that then he would tell his colleagues in Palermo. And if his colleagues in Palermo knew they would have told every gangster in the region and one of them would surely have warned Signor Bastamente. That is the Sicilian way.'

'But can't the *Carabinieri* do something about the corruption?' asked Julia. 'Doesn't the government care?'

The Colonel replied slowly, almost as if addressing a child. 'I am not a political man. I am certainly not a socialist or a Communist. Nor am I a fascist. In your country I would be perhaps a Conservative or Liberal. But in Italy what do we have? We have the Christian Democrats who are in reality neither Christians nor Democrats. They have been in power for over thirty years, since the Americans helped them win the elections in 1946. Sure there are other parties. In the north of Italy the Communists win millions of votes despite the Catholic Church preaching that it is a mortal sin to vote Communist and excommunicating Party members. But the Christian Democrats always come out on top.

'They say that the Christian Democrat Party has three legs: the Vatican, the Americans and the Mafia. Those who vote for the Christian Democrats are blessed by the Church, bribed by the Americans and delivered by the Mafia.

'The heartland of the Party is here in the south, the Mezzogiorno. And in Sicily the strongest of the three legs is the Mafia, just as across the water in Calabria it is the mobsters there, the 'Ndrangheta. The government does nothing about the Mafia because here the government and the Mafia are the same thing. Look at Salvo Lima, you know him? He is now a member of the Chamber of Deputies in Rome and before that he was a totally corrupt mayor of Palermo. They say he represents the Christian Democrat Party but in reality he has only one constituency, the Mafia. Or a name you must know, Michele Sindona.'

That was a name we certainly all knew, it had been plastered over the business pages across the whole world. Sindona had put together the biggest banking empire in Italy and then bought the Franklin National Bank in the US. When the whole edifice fell down it produced not only the near total collapse of Italy's banking system but one of the biggest bank failures in American history. The stories that started to hit the headlines seemed unbelievable but the Colonel confirmed they were far from exaggerated.

'Sindona started his rise by money laundering for the Mafia, he became the Mafia's banker but he was much more than that. He had known the present Pope in the past and became a financial advisor to the Vatican. He is close to Andreotti and the Christian Democrats. He was a friend of President Nixon's Treasury Secretary. And of course his banks handled transfers for the CIA. For example, what you call the Company used him ten years ago to channel funds to the Greek colonels to fund their coup. In the 1972 elections it is said more than ten million dollars of Company money went through Sindona's banks to friendly Christian Democrat politicians. Remember, the American taxpayer has provided funds for the Christian Democrats in every national election since 1946.'

The Colonel spoke with an air not of outrage but of resignation. 'One day one of the Party's three legs will crumble. Perhaps an American president will decide that fighting Communists is not worth destroying democracy. More likely the Americans will realise that the Mafia are as much a threat to them as they are to us. Or perhaps one day we will have a Pope who has higher concerns than Italian politics. But until then the third leg, the Mafia, is untouchable. Do not imagine that if Signor Bastamente is as well connected as I think he is that we will be able to hold him for long.'

We had turned north after Enna and eventually we reached the sea. From then on we followed the coast west towards Palermo, the autostrada strung between mountains and the Tyrrhenian Sea. Here and there the mountains pointed jutting fingers into the sea, creating a spectacular coastline and making the autostrada repeatedly tunnel its way through solid rock. The sea itself was a colour Julia described as turquoise. To me it was the palest of blues but Julia insisted she could see shades of green, something I put down to her sunglasses. She appealed to her uncle for support but the DG merely responded that in his years at sea he had seen every shade of blue and green not to mention grey and black.

The farmhouses here were quite different from the buildings we had seen, often abandoned, after we left Catania. Weathered grey stone walls had given way to terracotta roofs. Inspector Falzone would probably have said the Greek heritage was giving way to the Arab and he may well have been right. On the other hand, it might just have reflected the availability of building materials.

The Colonel apologised that unfortunately we did not have time to turn off to Caccamo to see what he claimed was the most perfect Norman castle in the world. A little later, near Trabia, a road sign pointed the way to more historical remains, this time a Norman tower. I wondered idly what remained of the character of the Viking Norsemen who, not satisfied with establishing themselves in Normandy, had invaded Sicily in 1061, five years before their more famous invasion of England.

'We will stop soon in Villabate for support from the local *Carabinieri*,' announced the Colonel. 'This is Mafia country. Villabate is the birthplace of Giuseppe Profaci.' I thought I detected a note of pride in his voice and guessed that Profaci was probably a local hero who had stood up to the Mafia. I could not have been more wrong. 'You know Profaci, he was one of the richest men in America. It is said that the Mafia boss in *The Godfather*, Vito Corleone, was based on Giuseppe Profaci.

'Villabate may look peaceful but do not be fooled. Let me tell you about someone else, Nino Cottone. He too was born in Villabate. He became one of Profaci's most trusted lieutenants in New York. But the American authorities caught up with him and he was deported back to Sicily. Back in Villabate he became one of the most powerful Mafiosi in the island, controlling the Palermo fruit markets. Then after the war the Americans took over. Men like Harry Bastamente. They may not have wanted Cottone in their own country but here he was useful. They made him mayor of Villabate and he became a power behind the Christian Democrats. So much for democracy.'

'Is he still the mayor?' asked Julia.

'Oh no. The fruit market was moved into another clan's territory and civil war broke out in the Mafia. Villabate was awash with blood. Nino Cottone came home one night and was machine-gunned on his doorstep. These things happen.'

We could see Palermo in the distance when the Colonel's driver pulled off the autostrada and headed away from the sea towards the mountains. We soon reached Villabate. The main street sloped upwards lined on each side by two- and three-storey buildings almost uniformly a light sienna colour. Shops, homes, bars and offices stood side by side with one on the left-hand side bearing a sign saying simply *Carabinieri*. As if to reinforce the message, a dark blue Alfa Romeo with the same inscription in large white letters on its side stood outside. We parked on the opposite side of the street and Colonel Castorini got out and marched across the road. He was away for about ten minutes, which gave the rest of us a chance to stretch our legs and our driver a chance to smoke. The few passers-by showed no sign of curiosity at the three strangers speaking English.

When Castorini returned he was accompanied by four *Carabinieri* who piled into the parked Alfa Romeo, one of them carrying a sub-machine gun. We stood by our Fiat for five or six minutes until another identical *Carabinieri* vehicle turned up. Three uniformed men sat in the car and one of them, a young *Carabinieri* officer, emerged and saluted the Colonel. He introduced himself as Tenente Romagnoli.

The Colonel rapidly rearranged us so that he sat with the DG in the back of his Fiat with one of the *Carabinieri* sitting alongside the driver and Julia and I moved to the back seat of the Alfa Romeo which had just arrived. Tenente Romagnoli joined us and proved to have passable English, albeit with a strong Milanese accent.

'The Colonel wants us to approach San Giuseppe Jato from Piana degli Albanesi. We will pass the Portella della Ginestra where the Mafia killed the Communists thirty years ago. He says you should see that. But there are more interesting places to see, even in Sicily.'

It rapidly became apparent that the lieutenant was not overjoyed by his posting. 'Sicily is not Italy,' he complained. 'They do not like Italians here. Especially they do not like the *Carabinieri*. When we appear they stop speaking Italian. It is a badge of honour in these mountains to shoot one of us. And the food! The sole of my boot is more tender than what they call *vitello*.'

His colleague, who seemed not to speak English, interrupted at the mention of veal and seemed to be pointing out that Sicilian wine was even worse than Sicilian meat. Having not had a bad meal since arriving in Sicily, I decided it was best not to respond and looked out of the window.

The countryside was very different to the landscape we had seen on the road from Catania. The barren rocky soil supported flocks of goats and the occasional olive trees. Grapevines straggling up hillsides could in no way be described as vineyards. The flat-topped hills near Syracuse had long ago given way to jagged mountains. Here and there shards of rock rose vertically upwards in what Julia informed me were 'folded sediments'. Layers of sediment laid down on an ancient seabed that had been thrust up into gigantic folds and then eroded away over millions of years. Geologically, Julia informed me, Syracuse is part of Africa. The Eurasian and African tectonic plates collide somewhere north of Syracuse and each year the African plate advances a few inches further towards Europe. The result today is the Mount Etna volcano I had seen when I first landed at Sigonella and the towering peaks we were now driving through.

An unusual bird of prey circled beside the road, its underside white rather than brown. I half expected Julia to tell me what it was but it seemed her ornithology was not as strong as her botany and geology.

We came to a village that Romagnoli called Santa Cristina Gela but which the only sign I noticed appeared to call Sëndahstinë. The non-Italian nature of this name was accentuated by the two little umlaut dots over each letter E.

Only then did Romagnoli show any enthusiasm, explaining that the name of the village was Albanian. The people here were the descendants of the followers of the fifteenth-century Albanian hero Skanderbeg. After Skanderbeg's death they had come to Italy to escape the Ottoman Turks, bringing their Orthodox Christianity with them. They still had their own bishop, said Romagnoli, and their own language.

People imagine that Albanians are Slavs, the lieutenant explained, like the other Balkan nations, but they are not. They are closer to Italians he insisted. They were part of the Roman Empire. The Venetians had built their cities. The King of Naples was once also King of Albania. But then Albania was occupied by the Moslems for 500 years until it was liberated during the First World War. Italy tried to help the Albanians, Romagnoli asserted, but their king was not interested in helping his own people so in 1939 Mussolini had removed him. It was an interesting version of history, but not one everyone would recognise.

'And that's why Piana degli Albanesi has its name,' he continued. 'It used to be called Piana dei Greci, the settlement of the Greeks, but when Mussolini occupied Albania he wanted to honour the Albanian community in Italy so he changed the name.' I had heard the name Piana dei Greci before but could not remember where, perhaps when Giuseppe Falzone had originally mentioned the Portella della Ginestra massacre.

As we approached Piana degli Albanesi itself we saw that it was perched on the side of a mountain, a jumble of houses sheltered below terracotta-tiled roofs. The main street sloped steeply upwards and, like Villabate, was lined with two- and three-storey buildings, their balconies jutting out as if designed to shade the pavements below. We passed a *Carabinieri* station, this one, unlike Villabate's, secure behind iron fencing. Also unlike Villabate's, there was a sign outside in Albanian, *Karabinerët*.

For no apparent reason our driver turned left on to a cobbled street and then right again out of the village. As we did so Romagnoli started to tell us about the Portella della Ginestra massacre. As Giuseppe and the Colonel had already recounted the story, my mind drifted off.

'You know,' Julia murmured to me, 'there is one person we have forgotten about: Robert Milan. The Colonel dropped him at the base, we know he went inside, but then what happened? How did he get out of Sigonella with nobody noticing? We know now that the Russians didn't help him, they didn't even know he existed. Somebody must have helped him. And where is he now? Castorini has been searching everywhere.'

'You think so? I'm not so sure. I don't know where he is now but it seems pretty clear who helped him leave the base. Do you remember what he was carrying when he left us at the hotel?'

"No I don't. Wasn't he just carrying the newspaper with my photo in it?'

'Precisely. He was carrying nothing when the dear Colonel picked him up.' I glanced at Romagnoli but he was so busy with his description of the perfidies of the Communists that he clearly had not realised he had lost our attention. 'Milan was empty-handed when he left us but when the Colonel dropped him off at Sigonella he was carrying an empty suitcase. Where had that come from? It could only have been provided by Castorini himself, who no doubt also arranged for Milan to leave the next day through the gate in the Italian area, a gate controlled by the *Carabinieri*.'

'But why would he do that? Surely not just to spite Di Benedetto?'

I shrugged. 'Who knows? Perhaps he felt sorry for Milan. Perhaps Castorini himself was once a misguided idealist.'

As the road twisted its way upwards Tenente Romagnoli had still paid no attention to our murmured conversation. The hillside disappeared away on our left and on the right steep cliffs loomed over us. After seemingly endless twists and turns a high, flat valley appeared and then became a huge natural platform with pointed crags on one side and a sheer rock face on the other. 'This is the Portella della Ginestra,' explained the lieutenant. It was easy to imagine a thousand people crammed on to the almost-flat ground between the towering rocks. 'Just ahead is the very spot where the Communist leader was speaking when the machine guns of Salvatore Giuliano's men opened fire.'

There was nothing to be seen. The sun was almost setting and long shadows were being cast across the landscape. A little away from the road a local peasant sat unmoving on a boulder, leaning forward on to his stick, and seeming to be part of a landscape that had not changed for centuries.

As we drew level Julia suddenly shouted 'Stop!' She reached over and tapped the driver on the shoulder urgently.

'That's him,' she said, turning to me, 'that's Robert Milan.'

XXIX

The driver looked confused but slowed down and Romagnoli instructed him in Italian to halt. Looking back I saw Castorini's car had drawn to a stop some way behind us. As we got out of our car a cowbell tinkled incongruously from the steep hillsides above. The man Julia thought was Milan put his stick aside and walked slowly over to the black Fiat. We walked back in the same direction and when we arrived the Colonel was making introductions as if the Director General of the Defence Intelligence Staff meeting a self-confessed spy on a Sicilian mountainside was the most normal occurrence in the world. 'And Gordon this is a man also seeking justice, a seeker after truth.'

The DG and Robert Milan shook hands, although neither with great enthusiasm.

'Signor Milan above all seeks to find himself, to understand who he is. When I encountered him, that evening after he had visited your niece at her hotel, we spent many hours talking. For me it was necessary to really understand our friend here, to enter his soul. Who was I dealing with? A Russian spy? A common thief looking for a way to make money? Or a man who knows not which star to follow to find his way home?'

'I'm home now, Colonel,' said the boyish-looking American, 'but I still seek the truth. Harry Bastamente is here. I saw him. His son drove through the village with an older man beside him in the car. That must have been his father. Then he drove off up this road, he must have passed right here where he killed my father in the massacre.'

'No Roberto,' said Castorini, placing his hand gently on Milan's shoulder. 'You must not think that. I promised you I would look at all the old files. I would find the truth. Your father was killed by the bandit Salvatore Giuliano and his gang. I have no doubt that there were more powerful figures behind him but not the Americans. Landowners, politicians yes. They thought like the Mafia thought. But this time the Americans were more subtle. They needed to stop the Communists winning elections, the last thing Harry Bastamente needed was to create Communist martyrs.'

'But he was here,' Milan insisted. 'My family saw him. Just a few days before the massacre. Right here in our village. He even attended mass. He had contacts here but now no one will talk about it. He was working with the Mafiosi.'

'Roberto, I have spoken to the magistrate who investigated the killings. He is an honest man. He is retired now and has nothing to lose. I trust him. He does not pretend to know the whole truth. Nobody does. But he knew Harry Bastamente. He knew what he was doing here in Italy. He knows Bastamente had business in Sicily. But he assures me that business was nothing to do with the massacre. The Mafia, the Christian Democrats, men who stood to lose if there were land reforms: they were all involved. But Bastamente, no.

'You are home now Roberto. You have followed your star. You have found your family and they have found you. Make peace with the past.'

Milan said nothing, just walked back to his rock, picked up his stick and sat back down. We left him there, the very last rays of the sun throwing a long shadow over him.

As we drove away the road immediately dropped precipitously with a deep valley on our left and just a few minutes later, as we were approaching San Giuseppe Jato, our driver swung sharply on to what seemed little more than a dirt track. The car bounced along, with the headlights and those of Castorini's Fiat dancing in front of us. One thing was certain: if the Bastamentes were at home they would see us coming. Away from our headlights the countryside was black and the long line of poles beside the track looked like a row of gallows illuminated by our passage. We had been going down into a valley but when the track divided in two our driver turned upwards and we seemed to be doubling back on ourselves. The driver was following the line of poles and I realised to my surprise that as well as an electricity cable the poles also carried a telephone cable, something I had not noticed anywhere else on our long drive from Syracuse.

Five minutes later we were approaching a building silhouetted against the hillside. The final stretch up to the house had been recently asphalted and we drew smoothly to a halt.

The house was much larger than I expected. It was also clear as we drew closer that it needed a lot of work doing on it. It was probably once the mansion of the local landowner but the solid stone edifice had seen better days. The plaster surface had fallen away from the wall on one side of the house and on that side one of the wooden shutters hung drunkenly from a single hinge and another had fallen off completely and lay rotting on the ground below. Clearly the Bastamentes' priorities were ensuring that the electricity and phone connections worked before worrying about external appearances. We drove past two tumbledown outbuildings and pulled up in front of the massive pillared entrance. A black Mercedes and a black Fiat 130 like Castorini's were already there along with a small runabout.

Lights blazed from the downstairs windows but the front door remained shut.

Castorini and the DG emerged from their car and I saw the Colonel take two of the new Beretta 92 semi-automatic pistols from the glovebox. He passed one to the DG, who looked surprised and declined the proffered weapon. 'I might be tempted to use it,' he said. Castorini offered the gun to me but before I could accept Julia took it and put it in her voluminous handbag.

As the Colonel and Romagnoli approached the front door the DG dropped back and spoke quietly to Julia and me. 'Better let the Colonel do the talking. He's a good man. Don't be surprised by what he says. I've just given him some information I was going to keep to myself. Something Janet has unearthed in New York.'

Before we could ask any questions the front door of the house opened and a woman stood looking down at us. Castorini had no chance to say anything. The woman started haranguing him, speaking so quickly that at first I couldn't determine whether she was speaking Italian or Sicilian. It didn't matter because the Colonel ignored everything she said. When she eventually stopped for breath, he replied in English. His words were designed to shock and to gain the initiative. They shocked me but they clearly shocked the woman in front of him far more. Her shoulders sagged and her defiance evaporated, her face a picture of blank incomprehension.

'Mrs Bastamente. I am here to arrest your son for the murder of your sister's husband, Giacomo Conti. We are coming in and my men will search the house.'

The Colonel and the lieutenant pushed past the startled woman. Julia followed but when I started to do the same the DG held me back.

'Stay here. I don't want anyone leaving the house.'

I wasn't sure how I would stop anyone who wanted to leave but I did as I was told. The Colonel's driver also stayed outside while the other *Carabinieri* followed everyone else inside. They were there for a long time.

I felt the final piece of the jigsaw had fallen into place. Janet had been asked to investigate Bastamente: could he have been born in Sicily with the name of Ramone? She had proved that hypothesis was impossible but then must have kept on looking and discovered something quite unexpected. Harry Bastamente had married an immigrant from Sicily named Daniela Ramone. What more natural then that when Bastamente wanted to create a fake identity for his secret bank account he should choose his wife's maiden name? Perhaps he had even used some of her documents when setting up the account; we would never know.

And suddenly I saw what should have been obvious long ago. There was no mysterious freelancer pretending to Behzad Sadeghi that he was named Ramone. Why would such an intermediary need a fake identity? No, the only name that had to be kept from Behzad was Harry Bastamente. If Sadeghi had any inkling that someone called Bastamente was connected in any way with the proposed meeting in Sicily he would have run a mile. The man we had glimpsed on that rainy night in Kefalonia was Harry Bastamente Junior, the son of the man who had been responsible for the murder of Davoud and Behzad Sadeghi's father. Bastamente Junior had needed a fake identity to hide the fact that he was his father's son so he used the one his father had already created in Canada; he too took on his mother's maiden name.

And now the whole Bastamente family, father, mother and son were gathered in the house in front of me. There was a large room to the left of the grand entrance and I could see people milling around, although I could hear nothing. Castorini and the DG were on their feet and Bastamente Junior prowled around the room. I couldn't see Julia but assumed she was seated by the door. On the other side of the room was a large armchair; whoever was sitting there was hidden from view but as much of the conversation was aimed in that direction it seemed likely that Bastamente Senior had placed himself in the most commanding position. He had not risen when the Colonel entered the room.

There was no sign of Mrs Bastamente but there was another figure in the room, darting around and gesticulating. It took me a few minutes to realise it was the SID man Di Benedetto.

Tenente Romagnoli was leading his men in a search of the house. Lights came on upstairs and I could see the *Carabinieri* moving around, accompanied by Mrs Bastamente who seemed to be recovering her composure. In one room I caught a glimpse of another figure, a woman standing by the window with Mrs Bastamente's arm around her. Instinctively I knew that this was Daniela Bastamente's sister, Chiara Conti, the woman Julia had seen in Marzamemi and who had been so reluctant to say anything about her husband's killer.

It was frustrating just standing outside the house watching. Di Benedetto and Castorini in the centre of the downstairs room were clearly arguing bitterly. Bastamente Junior was joining in until suddenly a hand appeared from the armchair and signalled for him to sit down. He looked startled but did as his father told him.

One of the *Carabinieri* entered at one point holding a pistol and five minutes later came back with another. At that point I distinctly heard someone, probably Bastamente Senior, shout 'You idiot.' It was impossible to say who he was shouting at.

Eventually Di Benedetto left the room and for a few minutes the conversation appeared to die down. Then Julia crossed the room to where Bastamente Senior was sitting. I had no idea what she said but suddenly Bastamente was on his feet and seemed to be responding angrily to her. He turned round and shouted something towards the doorway and his wife entered the room. The two of them exchanged words with Julia, who then returned to her seat. Daniela Bastamente left the room again.

After nearly ten minutes Di Benedetto returned and beckoned Colonel Castorini to join him in the hall. Five more minutes passed before the two men returned to join the others. Bastamente Junior started waving his arms around again and this time it was the DG who was becoming angry. Castorini put his hand on the DG's arm but the DG threw it off and came storming out of the house.

'They're getting away with everything. Bunny's murder. Romney's murder. Di Benedetto has been pulling strings. He called Rome. The Colonel's been overruled, told to keep out of security affairs.

'The *Carabinieri* found Junior's gun. I'm willing to bet we could prove it killed that fisherman and Jack Romney but apparently the Company don't want a fuss. Their team have just landed in Palermo. Bastamente has agreed to meet them there with Di Benedetto and tell them everything. Everything my arse! He'll keep on lying, blame everything on Romney. And Di Benedetto will lose that gun somewhere.'

With that Bastamente Senior appeared at the front door, fondly embracing his wife. Clearly for him the game was not up. His son followed him and they walked towards their car. Then they saw us and the older man changed course.

'You shouldn't have interfered,' he said, poking the DG in the chest with all his old arrogance. 'Tortellini would have been a brilliant operation. Stop the boat. Shoot Sadeghi. Stove in the hull and let all the evidence just sink to the bottom of the sea. Nobody's any the wiser. If that Sicilian idiot hadn't thought he could be clever and sink the *Mahsheed* without even leaving his own boat everything would have been fine. Or if he'd known the difference between a blast grenade and a fucking fragmentation grenade.'

The DG pushed him away. 'Everything would have been fine except my sister would have been dead!'

'There are casualties in every war.'

'But Bunny wasn't at war. None of us are at war. You killed her for money.'

At that Bastamente's head sprang up. 'No! The money was incidental. We put the Shah on his throne and we'll keep him there. That's our job, our duty. Sadeghi had to be taken out of the equation.'

'But he wasn't. My sister was taken out as you so crudely put it. You didn't expect that did you, you didn't know she was on board.'

'Of course I fucking knew. You think I'm an amateur? The spotter planes reported a man and a woman on board. Maybe it was Behzad Sadeghi and a girlfriend. Or maybe it was someone else. We knew he was expecting visitors, his brother from London. Either way if the boat sinks and Sadeghi goes with it we win and if it's somebody else he would sure get the message we meant business. The man's practically broke, he's desperate to keep his cushy life, apartment in Paris, Greek island, servants. He would have seen we held all the cards and weren't afraid to play them.'

Bastamente started to walk away. The DG looked as if he was going after him but Bastamente Junior appeared and stood in the way. 'Dad's right. If you hadn't interfered none of this mess would have happened. Jack Romney would still be alive, he wouldn't have talked to that stupid policeman and I wouldn't have needed to take him out. Just like my Aunt Chiara's blabbing husband.'

He spun round to join his father. Out of the corner of my eye I saw Julia materialise and reach into her handbag. But before she could pull out the Beretta another hand fell on to her wrist. Colonel Castorini looked into her eyes and slowly shook his head.

The DG marched away down the track and into the darkness, his anger seeming to hang in the air behind him.

Junior realised the *Carabinieri* had his car keys and angrily retrieved them before jumping into the Mercedes where his father was waiting for him. The Bastamentes pulled away from the house with Di Benedetto close behind them. We watched their headlights moving down the hill.

Suddenly there was a loud bang. The lights of the leading car swung crazily and then seemed to tumble head over heels into the valley below. The second car crashed to a halt with its headlights angled up at a rocky outcrop.

'That was a shotgun,' said Julia.

Colonel Castorini's driver already had his car in gear and as Julia and I piled in there was a huge flash from the valley below. The Mercedes had exploded.

We reached Di Benedetto's Fiat in a matter of seconds. The car was lying on its side with Di Benedetto himself trapped inside. We tried to push the vehicle back upright but couldn't move it until Tenente Romagnoli and the other *Carabinieri* arrived. Di Benedetto was barely conscious. As we laid him on the ground I realised Julia had disappeared.

Further down the track stood three shadowy figures. As I approached I recognised Julia and the DG, looking down at the still burning wreck in the valley below. Only when I reached them did I realise that the man who was standing next to them was Robert Milan. On the track next to them lay a shotgun.

Castorini joined us but said nothing. We stood in silence until the DG picked up the shotgun. 'There were two men,' he declared. 'I saw them running off down there. Mr Milan thinks they may have been poachers. They dropped their gun.'

He passed the gun to Milan. 'Give that to the Colonel.' Milan passed the weapon over.

Castorini looked the DG in the eyes. 'So two poachers mistook a Mercedes for a rabbit and then dropped their gun when they saw what they had done. I expect they wiped the gun clean first so that the only fingerprints I will find belong to the two of you, as I have just witnessed you both handling the gun. I suppose I should have Tenente Romagnoli put out an alert for two poachers too stupid to recognise a rabbit, too careless to look after their gun but too clever to leave any fingerprints.'

The DG nodded. 'That is one possibility. But as you yourself said only an hour or two ago, this is Mafia country. Who knows what has passed between the Bastamentes and the local bandits? They hired thugs from this area to sink the *Mahsheed*. Did they pay up when things went wrong?'

The Colonel was non-committal. 'That is a theory that will give the American investigators plenty to investigate.' With that he walked away.

Julia touched Milan on the shoulder. 'There is something you should know; it will probably come out now. Back there in the house I asked Bastamente about the massacre at Portella della Ginestra. He told me he was in Palermo that week, arranging funds for the Christian Democrats, but he swears he had nothing to do with the massacre. He was in San Giuseppe Jato because he had promised his wife to light a candle for the soul of her mother who is buried there. His wife confirmed that. He organised the murder of my aunt but not the killing of your father. Harry Bastamente, it seems, was a family man.'

Robert Milan said nothing.

From beside us came a high-pitched scream. Daniela Bastamente was looking down at the flames still licking the wrecked car below us, her sister Chiara trying unsuccessfully to comfort her. Neither woman comprehending what had happened to their families.

AFTERWORD

Historical events and characters have been depicted as accurately as possible in this novel. Some of these events continued to develop after July 1977, the period in which the novel is set.

In Iran the destruction of democracy by Operation Ajax and the increasing despotism of the Shah eventually led to the replacement of his regime by the equally murderous regime of Ayatollah Khomeini. Following the death of the red Islamist leader Ali Shariati in Southampton in June 1977, came the similarly unexpected death in October of Mostafa Khomeini, the son of the black Islamist leader. His death was widely blamed on the SAVAK secret police and this proved to be the spark that ignited widespread and increasingly violent protests. In January 1979 the Shah fled and, when Ayatollah Khomeini took over, the country descended into another bloodbath. Along with thousands of the Shah's supporters, democrats and other opponents of the theocratic regime were tortured and executed.

In 2000 the US finally came close to apologising for Operation Ajax. Secretary of State Madeleine Albright conceded that the CIA coup had clearly been 'a setback for Iran's political development'.

In Italy the investigations into the failed 1970 Borghese Coup meandered on, resulting in a series of trials over the next twenty years. Borghese himself died in Spain in circumstances still debated by conspiracy theorists. In 1978 some of the plotters were found guilty of conspiracy; Vito Miceli, former head of the SID, was acquitted. In the principal trial, all forty-six accused were acquitted, a decision confirmed by the Supreme Court in 1986. A further trial ended in 1991 when the accused successfully argued that after twenty-one years the charges were now time-barred. Owing to its suspected collaboration with the coup plotters, the SID secret service was broken up, with one of the successor organisations, SISDE, made responsible for protecting democracy at home. In 1992 the Deputy Director of SISDE, who had been the Chief of Police for Palermo at the time this novel is set, was arrested for collusion with the Mafia, including involvement in the infamous murders of leading anti-Mafia judges. After numerous appeals, his ten-year prison sentence was finally confirmed in 2007.

A concrete manifestation of the power of the Mafia is today demonstrated at the place where I imagined the final scene of the novel to be played out. As the tiny road descends towards San Giuseppe Jato, it suddenly lurches out into space and back again. The Viadotto San Antonio is a bizarre and completely unnecessary spiral viaduct that stands as a monument to the bravura of Italian design and the corruption of Sicilian life.

The Christian Democrats were the most powerful Party in Italy for nearly fifty years. Christian Democrat leader Giulio Andreotti was eventually tried for colluding with the Mafia and ordering the murder of a journalist. He was controversially acquitted on all charges, although the close relationship between the Christian Democrats and the Mafia in Sicily was acknowledged. In the so-called Maxi Trial of Mafia bosses running from 1986 to 1992, numerous accusations of collusion between politicians and the Mafia were made. When the trial concluded with convictions, the Mafia felt betrayed by Andreotti and his Sicilian associate Salvatore Lima; Lima was murdered two months later. Following a series of such scandals in 1994 the Christian Democrat Party disintegrated. With the end of the Cold War, support for the Party had become less of a US foreign policy priority.

In the US, Congressional investigations in the mid-1970s had revealed details of CIA operations which were unknown to most Americans, including the assassination of foreign leaders. In 1976 President Ford responded by signing Executive Order 11905 which instructed that 'No employee of the United States Government shall engage in, or conspire to engage in, political assassination.' Further restrictions on the Agency were instituted by President Carter in Executive Order 12036 two years later. Stansfield Turner, who had replaced future president George Bush as head of the CIA in March 1977, introduced sweeping changes that saw 800 CIA employees lose their jobs. Although the CIA became more open, many of its operations remained shrouded in secrecy. For example, not until 2016 was the CIA's part in the 1962 arrest of Nelson Mandela made public. The policy of regime change typified by Operation Ajax continued: three years after Turner's appointment the CIA lent its weight to a military coup that ended Turkey's experiment with democracy.

ACKNOWLEDGEMENTS

The research for this book was conducted on visits to Sicily with my wife Liz. Without her support, encouragement, grammar corrections and ability to act as an instant thesaurus this book would not have been possible.

On one visit to Ortygia we were fortunate to be accompanied by our friend Hélène Moore and her husband Tony Hunt. Tony is one of the world's leading structural engineers, the people who turn the impractical dreams of architects into buildings that stand up. In modern Britain engineers rarely receive the recognition they deserve and it occurs to me that much the same could be said about parts of publishing.

I cannot praise enough the inspired team at RedDoor – Clare Christian, Heather Boisseau, Anna Burtt and Lizzie Lewis – but I must also mention those freelancers who made the book stand up. Carol Anderson and Matilda Richards transformed my manuscript into a finished product, double-checking my research, ironing out internal inconsistencies and imposing a uniform style – although sadly insisting on replacing my archaic 'whilst'. Any remaining errors are of course my responsibility: I should apologise to Carol for preferring Chateau d'Or to Château d'Or, my memory insists the restaurant's signwriter missed the accent. I also want to thank Jason Anscomb who designed the striking covers for the Dylan Series.

Finally I must express my gratitude to all the friends who read the earlier drafts of *Families of Spies*. You know who you are. I am genuinely appreciative.

Brian Landers

Coincidence of Spies

MAY 1980

The street in Yaroslavl where the Turkish general, Samet Demirkan, was assassinated was wide but unremarkable.

There was an irony in the fact that the avenue had once been dedicated to Catherine the Great, the Russian empress who had devoted so much of her life to killing Turks. When the Bolsheviks came to power it had become Peasant Street. Today it bears the name of local hero Yuri Andropov who, for a mere fifteen months, was the country's leader, or to give him his correct title, General Secretary of the Central Committee of the Communist Party of the Soviet Union. That last name change had not yet taken place when Demirkan was murdered. Back in 1980, with Leonid Brezhnev still hanging on to the trappings of power, Yuri Andropov was chairman of the KGB.

I wondered how Andropov reacted when told that the Turkish military attaché had been shot dead on the streets of his own home town. Did he nod in quiet satisfaction at a job well done? Or did he scream at the three KGB minders who had been shepherding our group around without noticing the killer approach nor even noticing him depart? Would the three have dared to admit that they had been distracted by the tour guide's story about a train full of cats?

It was a story that appeared not to interest Demirkan, who was standing at the back of the group. I had looked around for my wife Julia and noticed him and the American, Ethan Jacobs, standing a little apart from the rest of us. Julia was standing in front of them.

Winter was officially over but the wind off the Volga was biting and the whole group were wrapped in their thickest clothes. The tour guide, who had introduced himself simply as Oleg and who was undoubtedly himself KGB, clearly did not enjoy showing a group of middle ranking members of the Moscow diplomatic corps around his city. He seemed determined to provoke an argument.

The French cultural attaché refused to rise to the bait when the guide smugly related the story of the Russian princess Anna, favourite daughter of Yaroslav the Wise, who was sent to marry the French King in 1051. After signing the marriage documents in both Cyrillic and Latin script she was amazed to discover, said the guide, how backward were the nations of Europe. Her new husband, Henry I, was completely illiterate and could not even write his own name.

Only Ethan Jacobs seemed as keen to argue as the guide. He had recently arrived in Moscow and had an innocuous diplomatic title I have long forgotten. He was in fact the new chief of the CIA's Moscow station and had all the fervour of a true Cold War warrior. Jacobs pushed his way through our little group as the guide started explaining how soviet education had banished superstition, as exemplified by turning the nearby Church of Elijah the Prophet into a museum of atheism.

'Why,' Jacobs demanded, 'don't you tell us about the magnificent old cathedral I'm told used to stand here in Yaroslavl, right where the Volga and Kotorosl rivers join? Why did the Communists blow it up?'

The guide trotted out the party line and then tried to deflect attention with a story about a train load of cats. It seemed that at the end of the Second World War the city of Leningrad was overrun with mice and rats. The inhabitants there had endured three years of siege during which they had been forced to eat all their cats. The patriotic citizens of Yaroslavl had therefore collected together all their own cats and sent them on a special train to Leningrad.

It was at that point, Julia recalled, that she heard a gentle cough behind her.

Turning around she looked directly into the eyes of Demirkan's killer but she only realised that later. The man was off before Julia had time to do more than register the peculiarities of his face. Demirkan was falling and Julia thought the stranger had accidentally collided with him. She reached for the General, trying to help him keep on his feet, but his legs were buckling. He was too heavy for her to do anything but cushion his fall.

The killer's gun had been pressed deeply into his victim's fur-lined coat and had in any case been fitted with a silencer. It was a moment or two before Julia realised how badly Demirkan was injured. Not until his wife pushed her aside did she look down and see his blood on her hands. It was then that the full realisation came: Demirkan had been shot and not only had she seen the face of the man who had pulled the trigger, she was almost certainly the only one in the group who had.

An image imprinted itself on her mind. Thin face, narrow nose, almond-shaped eyes, high forehead with short almost black hair. Most strikingly two deep, dark vertical crevices below the eyes. From more of a distance they would have looked like two identical birthmarks on the weather-beaten cheeks. It was a face she would never forget, although we were both sure Julia would never see it again.

In that we were wrong. Eighteen months later, when she had returned to her desk at the Defence Intelligence Staff in London, she would indeed see the face again. It was the face of a man the British police believed, quite wrongly as it turned out, was an IRA terrorist.

ABOUT THE AUTHOR

After giving up on an academic career, and deciding not to join the government spy agency GCHQ, Brian Landers helped a former Director General of Defence Intelligence and a motley collection of ex-spooks set up a political intelligence unit in the City of London. Out of that experience sprang the character of Thomas Dylan, a novice who over the years progresses through the labyrinthine world of British Intelligence.

Brian Landers has lived in various parts of North and South America and Europe. He has worked in every corner of the globe from Beirut to Bali, Cape Town to Warsaw and points in between, and in industries as varied as insurance, family planning, retailing, manufacturing and management consultancy. He saw the inside of more prisons than most during three years as a director of HM Prison Service. He has a Politics Degree from the University of Exeter and an MBA from London Business School. In his spare time he helped set up the Financial Ombudsman Service, served on the boards of Amnesty UK and the Royal Armouries, and was Chairman of Companies House.

Landers subsidised his university bar bills by writing a column for the local paper and since then has written articles for various journals, newspapers and websites. As a director of Waterstones and later Penguin his passion for writing was rekindled. His first book, *Empires Apart*, published in the UK, US and India, was a history of the Russian and American Empires. His next book was going to be *Trump, Putin and the Lessons of History* but the subject was so depressing that he turned to fiction.

In 2018 Brian Landers was awarded an OBE in the Queen's Birthday Honours.

brianlanders.co.uk

Find out more about RedDoor
Press and sign up to our
newsletter to hear about our
latest releases, author events,
exciting **competitions**
and more at

reddoorpress.co.uk

YOU CAN ALSO FOLLOW US:

  @RedDoorBooks

  Facebook.com/RedDoorPress

  @RedDoorBooks